THE

WAR QUELLERS

by

Mike George

The tameness of the English landscape and countryside, where the hills are small hills, the lakes small lakes, and at night the stars are small stars. The whole place appears a horrible and seedy compromise, like its smug society. I long for crueller climates, a more tempestuous people, and to shake the sand of this beastly place off my shoes.

Vita Sackville-West
1917

Heaven preserve me from littleness and pleasantness and smoothness. Give me great glaring vices, and great glaring virtues, but preserve me from the neat little neutral ambiguities. Be wicked, be brave, be drunk, be dissolute, be despotic, be an anarchist, be a suffragette, be anything you like, but for pity's sake be it to the top of your bent. Live fully, live passionately, live disastrously . . .

Violet Trefussis
1918

Two ladies with attitude ahead of their time

For Rae — and everyone

ONE

JENNY PRITCHARD lay stretched as sleek and supple as a cheetah on the hot talcum powder sand after lunch at the club house, closed her long-lashed hazel eyes and played with the scarlet motes that bounced in the black void behind her lids.

It was another humid Friday afternoon in the Gulf.

Jumma – the Muslim Sunday, when most of Ras-al-Am's European community of technicians and advisors were simmering on the beach in a relaxed torpor after the rigours of another harrowing week at the expatriate coal face.

This past week the Gulf had become like Piccadilly Circus with all the tankers that progressed up round the tip of Oman and through the volatile Strait of Hormuz taking advantage of a lull in maritime havoc to collect their precious cargo.

Even though Jenny's parents knew their gutsy 28-year-old daughter was able to look after herself, they were still concerned that she was living in the heart of the Middle East at such a tempestuous time, while waves of militant Islamic revivalism coursed through the whole region; the whole world for that matter. Although Ras-al-Am was a Big Boys' country with Big Boys' rules, those who lived there believed that it was far enough removed from mainstream Arab affairs to be touched by them other than peripherally.

Jenny and her army officer husband, Simon, had been in Ras-al-Am for nearly a year now and loved every minute of it. They grasped what the country had to offer and revelled in the adventure of it all. They had learned the rules fast and abided by them. Along with Bahrain, Dubai and Oman, 'spiritually' speaking Ras-al-Am was one of the more liberal of the Arab

7

countries, so there was no need to run the Saudi-style risk of imprisonment, flogging or expulsion for operating an illicit still in one's garage, or bringing back a Boots home-brew kit for low-key domestic wine and beer production. In any case, no amount of whingeing about the unreasonableness or illogicality of other aspects of Arab culture would make a blind bit of difference to the way things were done either.

Facts were facts.

Women were stoned to death for adultery.

Some of the more obscure bedu tribes still performed crude circumcision on their young women.

If you ran over a goat, you paid the owner blood money for it.

If you hit a camel, you paid more.

Hit two, and it was the owner's fault for letting them roam.

Run over a woman, you were in trouble.

Run over a man, you were in deep trouble - and would be advised to drive straight to the airport to catch the next plane home.

If a drunk (or even sober) Arab knocked *you* down, it was your fault, because if you hadn't been there it wouldn't have happened.

There was a certain logic, of sorts, but one that was difficult for most 'infidels' to come to terms with without carping.

Along with the diminishing sane minority at home, Jenny wished Britain's authorities would be as uncompromisingly cavalier with the millions of foreigners who so contemptuously used and abused her own country's facilities and loopholes, but the chances of that happening were less than teaching pigs to fly.

The European Beach Club was difficult to get to and cordoned off so as not to offend local susceptibilities, and if anyone could have offended them it would have been Jenny. Despite having borne two children her one-time model figure could still stop crowds.

The motes behind her eyelids were settling now and she was falling to sleep when a shadow fell across her body.

"Hi, Gorgeous; how're you doing?"

Jenny automatically shielded her eyes, expecting them to be seared by the sun as she opened them, but the giant body of Giles Carrington looming above her blocked its rays from her face.

Giles Carrington: Ras-al-Am's longest serving Brit-community expat was by all accounts a multi-millionaire.

Now fifty-three, he had been kicking about the Middle East since long before it had become fashionable to do so, like a resident continuum of Lawrence of Arabia and Wilfrid Thesiger combined, larded with lashings of lounge lizard. Strong as an ox, smoother than a purser's tread and ruggedly handsome to boot, he lived in a big house on a hill. Giles was the influential Director General of Ras-al-Am's Intelligence Directorate, the country's CIA equivalent, as well as being a personal friend and confidant of the Sultan Hamad bin Khaleel himself.

Jenny wanted to sleep off her curried chicken and white wine overload, and although Giles was the perfect gentleman she didn't feel like making small talk just now. Besides, she knew that behind his urbane façade he had always wanted her body.

"Hallo, Giles. What are you doing here?"

"Not much, m'dear; coupla beers with the boys at the bar, that's all. Where's your lot?"

"Jeremy and Susan are off swimming somewhere –" she scanned the water and waved to her nine-year-old twins splashing about on their blue lilo with the other kids in the shallows. "Simon's taken the boat for a spin. He and a couple of the chaps wanted to chug round that tanker out there. Giles –," she said, neatly changing the subject – "can't something be done about all these Ras-al-Amis infiltrating the place? It's awfully disquieting, you know. The last thing we want is the Religious Police closing us down."

"I know, darling. There's not a lot one can do about it, though. It is their country, after all. I know we more or less run it for them, but we're no longer the superior beings that once we were. Today we're the hired hands; barely suffered guests at best. Many of the young men you're talking about are the sons of influential ministers. They've been to western universities and like the taste of decadence, which is exactly what you represent lying there in that deliciously skimpy bit of kit with your leg crooked like that. There's nothing in town to occupy them, except Pepsi and Pizza, so it's natural they'll gravitate here to drink beer and ogle the girls. Take that one over there, for example . . ." Giles nodded towards a lightly moustached 21-year-old in his white dish-dasha and kumma cap, sitting on a whitewashed breeze-block wall swinging his legs and bouncing the heels of his sandals off the brickwork. "He's the Defence Minister's nephew."

A nubile young English girl, brown as a berry and undeniably voluptuous was sitting at the water's edge in a cutaway white one-piece, not quite knowing how to handle the banal chat-up line she was receiving from a 15-stone Ras-al-Ami youth paddling in the shallows beside her in his dish-dasha, knocking back a can of Heineken while being egged on by his friends sitting similarly attired on another nearby wall and working their way through several chilled six-packs of their own.

"If we complain, they'll have the club closed anyway," Giles said. "It's a delicate Catch-22. The best policy is to play each day as it comes; gingerly. Hallo – your young Susie's waving a bit frantically at you, Mother: I think son Jeremy might be in a spot of bother."

"Oh, shit," Jenny cursed, shooting to her feet and scanning the beach to find them. "What the hell's happened *now?"*

"MUMMY, MUMMY, MUMMY," she heard them screaming.

Sunbathers lowered sunglasses on their noses and stirred to take notice as the children's terrified pleas rose to a piercing crescendo above the hubbub of other beach sounds. Jenny's heart leapt into overdrive.

Clamping her hand over her mouth she moved forward down the beach on jellied legs before kicking-in and bursting into a sudden sprint.

Which of her twins was hurt?

What had happened, Chrissake? Oh – my *God,'* she

screamed.

It was her son, Jeremy.

The poor little chap was staggering up out of the water vainly attempting to break into a run towards her whilst frantically scraping ineffectually at a venomous yellow-bellied sea snake coiled round his leg, its fangs embedded deeply in his thigh.

The three men on board *Blaze Of Glory*, Simon Pritchard's flat-bottomed aluminium skiff, were glad that this Friday the Gulf was as flat as a black, glassy millpond. Usually the slightest wavelet slopping inboard sent a bone-juddering tremor clanging through the hull. With its hearty little outboard farting a healthy baked-beans and curry sound, the little craft skimmed across the torpid surface towards a large Panamanian-registered tanker parked with brooding solemnity three miles offshore.

Once these tankers entered the Gulf proper and neared the war zone further up the coast, their insurance premiums soared.

It was standard operating procedure to stand-off until the last minute before going in to load their oil.

Lieutenant-Colonel Simon Pritchard, Major Jack Hargreaves and Captain Tony Fanshawe, all regular British army officers on a two-year secondment to the Ras-al-Am forces, couldn't have looked less Horse Guards than they did this afternoon. All three sported one-day stubble and wore filthy shorts, flip-flops, maritime baseball caps and a sheen of sweat, whilst becoming increasingly pissed from the contents of *Glory's* galley, which consisted solely of a cool-box of Heinekens shoved beneath a tarpaulin.

"You're weaving something of an erratic course, my old son," Simon admonished Tony Fanshawe who was lolling indolently at the tiller. "Ease up a bit. We don't want to ram the bastard. It's bigger than we are."

"Bitch," said Jack.

"What?"

"You said bastard. A ship's a bitch. It's a she?"

11

"I stand corrected and beg her big-bottomed pardon." Simon belched and turned to toast the tanker with his upraised beer-can clasped in a styrofoam cooler. One of the tanker's crew leaning over the rail waved back at them.

The closer they drew to the tanker the more they realised how awesomely large she was. The 386,000 deadweight tons of steam turbine craft must have been 1,200ft long and 200ft wide. The reflection of her red-painted hull shimmered beneath the surface like some hovering Jules Verne ray ascending from the deep. Her 100ft sides soared above them like cathedral walls. The bridge-house and rusted white superstructure seemed evocative of a 1920s Brighton apartment block. A myriad tenders had scraped a random frieze of tyre marks round her hull. Her anchor had gouged out and bashed arcs in her bows where it had been unleashed a thousand times in swelling seas. An ugly spoiler-like proboscis protruded from her lower bow so that head-on she sat in the water glowering at them with all the seething malevolence of a Darth Vader visor.

"What the hell *is* that great lump stuck on the front?" Tony Fanshawe asked as *Blazing Glory* pop-popped slowly round the tanker's starboard bow.

"Suez Crisis," said Simon.

"Y'what?"

"Suez Crisis. Tankers then used to be much smaller. Because of the closure of Suez designers had to come up with a behemoth able to tackle the Cape of Good Hope. Fully laden this baby carries two-million barrels of oil, and to give you an idea how much that is, 3.4 million barrels is the daily production of the whole of Spain and UK combined. A tanker this size would burn 240-tons of fuel a day. That bulbous monstrosity on the bow breaks up the secondary bow wave, which gives 'em an extra half-knot of speed. They use it to shove in ballast."

"Close-to she looks as though she's seen better days," remarked Jack Hargreaves.

"Not so," said Tony. "More as if she's seen worse days and didn't enjoy them much."

Completing a full circle round this ultra large crude-carrying supertanker, like a water bug inspecting a river islet, *Blazing Glory's* boozy skipper and crew came upon a Ras-al-Am tender fussily conducting business at her stern. There was also an inquisitive police launch churning slowly by, setting a graceful undulation of waves sloshing against Glory's bottom. The tender pulled away and made-off to go round the headland back to port, leaving *Glory* gently bobbing on its settling swell.

"*Look there.*"

Jack Hargeaves stabbed a finger excitedly at a shadow darting just beneath the surface a metre away. "Barracuda."

"How's the tune go to *Up A Lazy River?*" Simon asked.

"Haven't got a clue, mate; but I reckon we should think about heading back for the beach fairly soon," said Jack.

"What the hell for?" Tony cried. "It's great out here."

"Not for much longer it won't be," replied Jack. "We've run out of beer."

"I don't believe it," said Simon. "Logistics support, Hargreaves? Nil. Give the throttle a twist, Tony old son, otherwise we're going to become three very smelly officers in a minute. That pillock up there's about to deluge us with slops."

Half-way up the hull towards the stern a galley-hand had opened a hatch to empty several bins and plastic bags of refuse down a chute. As the shipboard detritus splashed into the sea and began to disperse for marine predators to sniff and become tangled up in, Tony said 'Disgusting,' and promptly tossed his empty Heineken can over the side to float towards it.

"*You* should talk," Simon scolded him. "Hey – what the hell's that noise. Can't you hear it? Sounds like motorbikes."

"Some water-borne chapter of Hell's Angels, perhaps," quipped Jack.

Jack could have had no idea how close to the truth he was.

Blazing Glory was on the tanker's seaward side, out of sight from the beach.

Gerry Longhurst, the crewman who had waved down to them earlier, was still leaning over the port rail smoking a cheroot.

He, too, had heard the unusual noise and swung himself

agilely up onto the rail, clinging to a stanchion and leaning out precariously to see what it was. "Good God," he hissed to himself. "Perhaps I should tell the Old Man."

The tanker had been anchored where it was for two days.

Most of its 40-man crew were below in their bunks trying to sleep, despite the air-conditioning units being off.

Gerry was not On Watch.

He was off duty.

All the same . . . planing towards them out of the west, closing fast across the smooth surface of the sea, there came thirty or more Ras-al-Ami fishing huris, aluminium canoes with outboards. Each huri held around five men. Roughly 150 Arabs were coursing towards the tanker without invitation, their purpose and intention unclear.

Was it some kind of water festival – Gerry wondered?

Dare he wake the Old Man?

He was an irascible sod at the best of time; here in the Gulf with the AC off and a gutful of lunchtime booze . . .?

The flotilla of huris was closer now, sounding like a large swarm of mosquitoes, or Suzukis, their props frothing a maelstrom in their wake. Unless it was their intention to divide each side of her and continue on to some other destination, they were definitely heading for the tanker. They were going flat out, outboards screaming at maximum revs, the men squatting one behind the other in each craft like a Red Indian war party in souped-up armoured dories. Perhaps they were some hepped-up local environmentalists come to protest against pollution? Gerry didn't know what to do, except to stand there and take in the unfurling scene while awaiting developments.

"Hey, up there – any idea what this is all about?"

It was those three Brits hailing him as they came bumbling into view round the stern in their silly tin bucket.

Gerry opened both arms and shrugged helplessly down at them. "Haven't got a clue," he shouted. "You're local: is it ominous?"

"Shouldn't think so," Simon yelled back. "They're a pretty friendly bunch as a rule. Probably pissed, same as we are, and having a burn-up. Nothing to worry about."

The word *about* was the last that Simon ever uttered.

An echo boomed off the tanker's steel hull as a shot rang out.

A heavy lead ball smashed through the front of Simon's head and exited explosively from the back of his skull.

Tony Fanshawe and Jack Hargreaves froze with disbelief, both of them splashed with blood and their friend's brain matter.

"Jesus *CHRIST*," roared Jack, whipping round to face the approaching huris, all of which revved back to come alongside the tanker. A puff of expired cordite whipped away from one of the lead craft and Jack heard a crash as Tony's head, too, was blown away behind him. As a soldier he wondered for a second what the hell calibre they were using. Scrambling over the bodies of his two friends, Jack grabbed the tiller that was still warm and wet from Tony's grip. Opening wide the throttle he surged off back towards the beach. Hunched instinctively down he heard another crash and a lead ball whistled past, a hair's breadth from his right ear. This couldn't possibly be happening. He must be hallucinating. But a quick, horrified glance at Simon's sightless eyes staring back at him like a dead fish, and the bloody mash where young Tony's face had been, confirmed the reality of the situation.

From his vantage point high on the tanker's deck Gerry Longhurst saw the marksman bring his musket to the aim and fire, and couldn't believe what was happening. When the Arab fired a second time Gerry leapt to activate the ship's alarm. Riding at anchor in friendly waters, at that time of day, slumbering in their quarters after a liquid lunch the crew's reaction-time was fatally abysmal.

Most of them had their throats slit in their bunks.

Like Barbary pirates of old an advance group of Ras-al-Amis clambered up the lowered gangway to the stern where a stores crane had been left with its palletised net hanging over the side. Activating its electric winch they lowered the swinging net to their comrades clamouring below and hoisted twenty men at a time on board. Within minutes the motley rabble poured across the deck and down companionways slaughtering everyone they found, using knives, cudgels, cleavers, swords and guns of indeterminate origin. Gerry Longhurst died in the first wave, impaled to a bulkhead with a boathook through his neck and a surprised expression. The Skipper and Sparks were hacked down before either of them had time to initiate any communication with the outside world.

Their carnage complete, every crew member butchered, the deranged Ras-al-Ami fishermen hefted the bodies overboard to send them plunging into the sea. It took two men to unpin Gerry Longhurst and wiggle his body free of its boathook.

One by one the thirty or so craft reacquired their complements, revved-up and surged off back towards the west leaving the Panamanian-registered supertanker like the *Marie Celeste* – but in full sight of the beach.

Major (QM Retd) Bill Patterson, the Beach Club's resident steward stood by the window of his office staring intently through his binoculars.

Along with everyone else on the beach he had heard the distant firing, but had been preoccupied soothing Jenny Pritchard and trying to calm her young Jeremy while they waited for the ambulance to arrive. It had not been pleasant cutting the threshing serpent from the young boy's leg, but it had to be done. It was an extraordinary state of affairs. One of the snake's fangs had become lodged there. There hadn't been too many known adult fatalities from yellow and black Yellowbelly bites, but young Jem had been in a pretty bad state. His twin sister, Susan, was being cared for by friends, and the ambulance had arrived quickly to whisk Jenny and Jeremy away to the army hospital back at Masela Camp, where he hoped the boy would prove tough enough to pull through.

Now he was going to have to break the news to the little chap's father.

He could see Simon's bloody stupid tin skiff *Blazing Glory* weaving a homeward course now, about half-a-mile offshore.

What the hell *was* happening out there on that tanker, he

16

wondered?

Oh, well - : he replaced the glasses on the shelf behind his desk. Better go and tell old Simon the worst.

Damn shame, the poor little fellow getting bitten like that.

They were such a nice family, the Pritchards.

TWO

Roxanne Duprés clattered down the wide marble staircase of the Palace in her crimson heels, hurried across the mirrored foyer with its half-ton crystal chandelier suspended from the high-domed roof above, and brushed disdainfully past the two machine-gun toting military guards standing on the steps by the vast brass-inlaid bronze doors.

She squinted against the sudden glare of sunlight lasering into her green eyes. Loosening the sunglasses perched atop her black turban with its jingling diadem of miniature gold coins, she snappily inclined her head and jabbed their stems over her ears, dislodging a tendril of copper-coloured hair as she did so. A cluster of black pearls adorned the gold earring that pierced each of her lobes. The zip of her figure-hugging black jumpsuit had been loosened to reveal the swelling mounds of her voluptuous breasts.

Any red-blooded European male would have been excited by such exhibitionist deportment, but wrapped as she was in the security of the Sultan's patronage Roxanne was able to disregard the fact that it enraged many of the local Arabs.

Striding across the Palace forecourt she swung open one of the low-slung doors of her turbo-charged black Pontiac Firebird convertible parked beneath its barousti shade outside her grace and favour Palace apartment. Swinging herself into its red leather bucket-seat she switched on the ignition and gunned the big car to roaring life. Edging its squat tyres round the corner of the building she nosed its one-acre bonnet across the courtyard towards the Palace gates, drove contemptuously past the dutifully saluting sentries, switched on the car's sound-system and aimed the heavy piece of Detroit pressed-

18

steel and alloy down the palm-fringed Corniche which ran parallel to the warm jade waters of the Gulf. Roxanne Duprés, wealthy Arab's plaything from Walthamstow, was off on her regular afternoon's fun run.

She had been installed in Ras-al-Am three months.

For the past few weeks, since the weather had started to cool, she had been tarting herself up each afternoon and leaving the Palace at five-o-clock to drive the overpowered 7.5 litre car with its air-brushed gold acrylic eagle's wings spread across the bonnet the three kilometres down into Raman, the capital, to go cruising. It was inconceivable that she might find any sort of action there, but it made a change from being cooped up in the Palace all day at Himself's whimsical beck and call.

In common with most Arab countries Ras-al-Am tolerated an expatriate European community with its social strata, coffee mornings, beach parties and soirées, but Roxanne's unique position as Crown Prince Fahad's mistress precluded her attending any of these. The English men found her presence in the country mildly exciting, occasionally discussing or fantasising about how she came to be there while secretly preferring that she might have been German instead. The English women refrained from mentioning her at all; in their eyes she was no more or less than a courtesan, an Arab's doxy who by her calling had discarded all rights to respectability or social recognition.

Roxanne knew that Fahad adored her and was insanely possessive and jealous. None of his friends dared display even a covert interest in her for fear of spending what would be left of his life dangling by his thumbs somewhere behind the stone walls of their country's medieval fortress prison.

From Roxanne's standpoint their relationship was no more than a lucrative business arrangement, a short term contract that would sooner or later expire, hopefully to her considerable advantage. She had grown reasonably fond of the 23-year-old prince, but she would not be unnecessarily fazed by a premature return to England. She sensed that there was a political undercurrent swelling beneath the surface of life in

Ras-al-Am. Until his father, the Sultan, had flown to Britain on a state visit last week, Fahad had been involved in important meetings with him and the country's ministers almost daily. This had prevented him spending more than a few hours with her, and she had got used to spending her days 'amusing' herself.

With a surge of power she pulled the car out to overtake a gaily bedecked Toyota truck and a sand coloured army Land Rover speeding down the open road ahead of her. With the Land Rover becoming a diminishing speck in her rear-view mirror she entered the suburbs of Raman where she had to reduce the car's speed to a gurgling crawl.

The centre of the capital was a modern, high rise little Arab metropolis, but here on the outskirts its environs were redolent of that earlier Arabia. Wild-haired Ras-al-Ami tribesmen down from the hills who looked as though they had been living off honey and locusts for forty days in the wilderness wandered the dusty streets in leather sandals and colourful ankle-length wazars with ammunition bandoliers buckled about their sinewy bodies. Others moved from bank to video store, their silver-mounted .303 virility symbols slung nonchalantly across their shoulders, Lee-Enfield rifles retrieved almost a century before from the battlefields of Mesopotamia and lever action Martini-Henry carbines that had 'drifted' there from Rorke's Drift, purchased from gunsmiths who worked with tools long outmoded in Europe.

The wives of these fine-featured, dark-skinned warrior swayed gracefully along behind them, their gold nose rings flashing reflected sunlight and drawing men's glances to deep, dark eyes. Occasionally one of them would clasp her laha veil with her teeth and draw it partially across her face to grant some braver admirer a coquettish glance before averting her gaze and gliding warily on by.

Nudging the V8-Firebird through this indigenous throng Roxanne recalled the day Fahad had first taken her for a flight in his helicopter, for a bird's eye view of the capital and its surroundings. He had told her that only four miles offshore the seabed dropped to one thousand fathoms, and that the pressure at those depths was two thousand pounds per square inch, which nature bred big fish to inhabit. Pilots in the Sultan's air force had seen shapes moving beneath the surface larger than the shadow cast by their own aircraft. Surveying the unspoilt beaches from the helicopter Roxanne had seen shoals of sharks hoovering indolently about the shallows for sardines, where the tide lapped knee-deep along the foreshore. She had seen 20ft manta rays flap past, and giant sailfish leaping out of the warm sea like Polaris missiles. In their flimsy outboard huris local fishermen rode the broiling wake of whales surging and plunging beneath their prows like submarines receiving erratic counter-orders to surface and dive. Poisonous four-foot orange and green sea snakes, moray eels and deadly stone fish abounded in this marine Elysium, which although scarcely conducive to dinghy sailing or bathing could, with a shift of religious and social thinking and a little tasteful exploitation become transformed into an Arabian Riviera.

A muezzin's voice crackled electronically into the air from the speakers on the minaret of a nearby mosque, calling the faithful to prayer. *Allah-u-Akbar* . . . wailed the resident DJ from Allah's Disco, forever top-of-the-pops in Islam.

Roxanne drew up at the first set of traffic lights. With her music drowning the muezzin and the car's chrome exhausts burbling with anticipation, she drummed a counterpoint rhythm on the steering wheel with her long red fingernails. The lights were taking longer than usual to change. A phalanx of colourfully fringed Toyota pick-ups and rickety buses lumbered in front of her across the intersection. Blast it – she thought, and swivelled in her red leather bucket-seat to see if she could reverse into a side street to turn. Her foot slipped on the clutch and then her green eyes shot wide with shocked presentiment.

The entire street had gone quiet. It was as though she had suffered an attack of complete deafness.

Everyone seemed to have turned and was watching her. A group of Arabs standing at the roadside began to move menacingly towards her, the lower halves of their swarthy faces covered by their chequered shemaghs. They darted their eyes up and down the street and then of one accord dashed forward.

The lights were still red. She was blocked in by traffic.

In desperation she slammed the car instinctively into reverse, crumpling her boot and tail lights against the lorry bumper behind in a frantic attempt to escape.

What was happening?

Was she about to be accosted?

Abducted?

Raped?

She drew her long legs up out of the well in an attempt to leap from the car and flee. This lifted her straight into the outstretched arms of the men leaning over the car grabbing at her with their strong brown hands. She was heaved into the air by her armpits and felt a hand clamped firmly over her mouth. Her sunglasses flew off to be crushed underfoot. Her wildly threshing legs kicked off both high-heeled Jimmy Choo sandals which landed amongst the dust and detritus in the gutter. The black turban was knocked from her head in the struggle, her hair exploding into a swirling copper fan about her shoulders.

The traffic lights turned to green.

One of the Arabs leapt into the Firebird to drive it off across the intersection and away.

Roxanne was powerless to struggle against the superior strength of the large Arab who had her firmly clasped around her waist, her arms tightly pinioned to her sides. He ran down a narrow alley with her bouncing painfully against his hip. Roxanne had bitten her lip and could feel the metallic taste of blood in her mouth. The zip of her jumpsuit had come undone to her waist and the suit slipped from her shoulders. Its tautened sleeves pinioned her arms even tighter. Her large creamy breasts were fully exposed, thrust proud by her contorted position. She cursed for not having worn a bra.

Suddenly her captor slipped and lurched, releasing his hold on her as he fell. Roxanne slithered painfully across the filthy gravel of the alley grazing her breasts, her outstretched wrists and bare feet. Despite the pain and indignity she scrambled to her feet and raced ahead of them down the alley. A shard of glass sliced through the sole of one foot, but she ran on unheedingly, struggling to re-zip the front of her jumpsuit to contain her leaping breasts. Perspiration splashed from her brow and coursed down her spine. Tendrils of wet hair lashed her face. Her heart and lungs hammered against her chest wall. She gasped for air between sobs of anguish.

Who were these people? Didn't they know who she was? Perhaps they did, and that's what this was all about. What did they want with her? What was she supposed to have done?

What was happening?

She could hear their sandals slapping against the gravel close behind but dared not glance back across her shoulder. Thirty yards ahead she could see the alley opened onto a main thoroughfare and thank GOD . . . there were some Europeans standing there, two men and a young blonde woman. They were watching what was taking place, pointing but apparently reticent to become involved.

"HELP me; oh, please – for God's sake *help* me," Roxanne screamed, then she stumbled and fell.

While the group of Europeans turned away and moved off, the pursuing Arabs picked her roughly up and bore her struggling back down the alley . . .

Crown Prince Fahad was angry.

He had undergone a ministerial harangue that afternoon defending the Finance Minister's proposals for increased funding to complete the installation of one of Raman's badly needed new desalination plants. Now he craved one of Roxanne's relaxing massages, but she was not in her apartment. She was always in her apartment waiting for him at this time every evening, freshly bathed, perfumed and seemingly eager to please. But today one of the servants told him that she had not returned home from her afternoon's drive. The American car he had bought her was not parked beneath its barousti shelter.

She had left no message.

Fahad was a superior male; a future Sultan. It was

inexcusable that a woman should flaunt her privileged position in this manner, showing a flagrant disregard for his position and needs. She would have to be chastised, but then even he smiled when he thought how futile such a course would be. She would merely blow in his ear, suggestively wiggle one of her hips at him and flick the hem of her skirt and he would have to throw her back squealing onto the silken bed cover and leap on top of her. His anger dissipated, turning to concern.

He liked her driving around Raman each evening, being seen abroad looking sexy, enhancing his image. Was it possible that on this occasion her car had broken down somewhere – or had she been involved in an accident?

Out of the question. With its distinctive and instantly recognisable Palace registration plate the Police would have notified the Palace Office instantly.

It was worrying though. Where could she be?

Any further thought was startlingly shattered by someone activating the Palace alarm system.

Fahad had heard the piercing siren tested on numerous occasions, but never this late before. Could it possibly be . . .?

The noise of feet clattering along corridors, doors banging, and shouting in the courtyard led Fahad quickly outside to where a crowd of guards and Palace retainers was gathering at a small side entrance to the Palace wall.

One glance revealed what had happened. A sentry lay crumpled in a pool of his own blood beside the open iron gate, mown down by an incisive burst from a machine pistol.

To what purpose? It was madness. No one was going to 'rob' the Palace. The dead sentry was more than likely the victim of some tribal vendetta. Because of his Sandhurst training Fahad had long ago recognised that although they were armed to the teeth with all the latest weaponry, his father's Palace Guard amounted to no more than a ceremonial deterrent.

Palace security would have to be reviewed and tightened.

As soon as the Police had arrived Fahad walked pensively back across the courtyard, readdressing his mind to Roxanne's whereabouts. She might be homesick or be in some sort of reflective mood.

It was a warm, clear night. Fahad glanced up to see a plummeting shooting star burn out overhead. He turned off the marble-chip pathway to cut through the mimosa trees onto the immaculate lawns, daily watered and tended by a team of Asian gardeners. The lawn was awash with moonlight that bathed the tinkling marble fountain in an eerie glow.

Fahad moved towards it, subconsciously wondering whether the pump might be faulty, because the fountain did not usually tinkle: it splashed.

It was then that he saw Roxanne.

Her naked and ravaged body had been dumped amongst the disturbed goldfish, lilies and koi carp. Her long legs dangled over the fountain's lip like someone fallen backwards into a bath.

The whites of her eyes started sightlessly up at the moon. Her throat was black from bruising. She had been garrotted. Her breasts had been mutilated. Both nipples had been removed. With the stiletto-sharp point of a knife someone had cut across her chest the crudely incised Arabic word for WHORE.

Fahad gagged, retched, vomited and shook uncontrollably while the impact of the horror engulfed him. Then he threw back his head and rent the night air with a single howl of anguish and desolation. He subsided to the grass and fell forward onto his knees, burying his face in his arms and rocking to-and-fro with grief. Palace staff began to appear; some of the more daring filtered hesitantly across the lawn towards him.

Who? Why? For what earthly purpose had this heinous, despicable act been perpetrated?

Fahad knew it would be only a matter of time before he found out. When he did – people would die horribly.

THREE

Masela Camp lay nestled in the foothills like one of Andalucia's whitewashed pueblo villages, although the Sierra Nevada mountains would have appeared to be about as tame as the South Downs compared to the unyielding peaks and jagged fissures of the inhospitable jebel that backed onto Masela Camp's southernmost aspect, deterring any potential assault from that flank.

Masela Camp was Ras-al-Am's Aldershot. It housed the headquarters of the Sultan's Armed Forces and the country's Ministry of Defence.

The camp was home to Ras-al-Ami, Indian, Baluch, Pakistani, Sri Lankan and British personnel, totalling about 10,000 souls in all, give or take a colour or two and the occasional extra creed who had slipped in unobserved as a supernumerary inmate eking out his deprived private life undetected in some empty and disused store shed by the perimeter wire.

Additionally there were cohorts of camp followers – tailors, barbers, cobblers, quacks and dhobi-wallahs. Less itinerant than their Kiplingesque forebears, today they secured their fragile appointments by tender and contract.

A three kilometer arterial road ran through the centre of the camp from its imposing main gate which was manned 24/7 by soldiers – known as jundees - of its Baluch Guard Company.

Numerous tributary roads ran off this highway, often at random, giving access to the camp's remotest store shed and paint shop. When the camp was first built these roads had been dusty tracks, but over the years they had become black-topped, white-lined and lit, bordered by rows of young trees and shrubs nurtured daily by cruising water bowsers.

The camp covered twenty square kilometres of military real estate contained within a 10ft high wire fence. Its principal buildings, its offices, messes, quarters and sub-units were located in the central hub of the complex. A safe distance from this main conurbation was the ammunition depot, a separately fenced camp within the camp in Masela's otherwise empty south-western corner. Six brick-built watch towers surrounded the ammunition depot, with searchlights manned by armed guards with rifles and machine guns.

Masela Camp was dramatically undermanned at the moment.

There were two reasons.

Firstly – it was Jumma: Friday: Holy Day: the Muslim Sunday.

Secondly, the bulk of the army was away.

The artillery, the tanks, and the warrior battalions of infantry usually stationed at camps in the hills around the country had gone with the headquarters element from Masela Camp into the desert heartland of Ras-al-Am on manoeuvres.

Masela Camp had been on skeleton manning for a week.

Jenny Pritchard sat in a private room in the Force Base Hospital, now terrified while she kept caressing her son Jeremy's little hand and praying beside his bed because an inconsiderate Indian doctor had decided to explain to her in graphic clinical terminology exactly what *might* happen.

Jenny stared at him in absolute horror as he turned and left the room, unaware of the effect his prognosis had had on her. She was well grounded woman, but she was also a young mother now distraught at what she had been told. She shuddered and put her head in her hands. She could do with a shot of something herself; preferably brandy.

Through the half-open door the white-uniformed British nurse in her cubicle across the corridor was speaking on the telephone. Sensing Jenny's distress she finished the call, hung up and came in. "How's the little fellow doing?" she enquired in a whisper.

27

"About the same, I suppose." Jenny sighed, giving the nurse a wan smile. "I'm just a bit shocked by that doctor's suggestion that we could lose him."

"Not a bit of it." The nurse patted her shoulder. "This time tomorrow he'll be bouncing about again right as a trivet, you mark my words. Cup of tea?"

"Please; love one; thanks," Jenny smiled appreciatively.

When she returned a few moments later with tea and some biscuits, she asked: "Like to hear some scandal?"

"What's that?"

"One of my friends has just telephoned from the Police Hospital," the nurse said. "You're never going to believe this, but – Roxanne Duprés has been found murdered."

"The Crown Prince's mistress? Good Lord – I don't believe it. Wow; that's going to cause some fuss, isn't it!"

"I'll say," the nurse agreed. Across the corridor the telephone rang on her desk. "'Scuse me," she said, going off to answer it.

Jeremy was now sound asleep. Jenny smoothed his brow and caressed the back of his hand. Sensing the nurse's return, she turned and gave a start to see that it was Jack Hargreaves standing there.

"Jack," she gasped, pleased to see him, and then "You're looking worried – what's the matter? Simon must have heard by now – I've been expecting him here for ages. Where on earth is he . . .?"

Jack shuffled uncomfortably, hardly knowing where to begin.

"Jenny – I'm afraid there is something rather dreadful that I have to tell you. It's about Simon. He's . . ."

He got no further.

With a crash like a thousand dinner services the plate glass window beside them imploded in a myriad lethal shards.

Jack fell to his knees, a fragment of glass protruding from his jugular like a stalactite.

Jenny was blown screaming across her son's bed with a shower of splinters embedded in her back like arrows.

Masela Camp's ammunition depot had exploded.

FOUR

Lieutenant-General Wally Stubbs twitched his scarred upper lip and snorted. The gruff and rugged General, 5ft 7in, 170lbs, was a squat, strong man who resembled a cross between Humphrey Bogart and a janitor in a working men's club.

Swiping one hand briskly across his stubbled face he cleared an obstruction from his throat and with the agility of a man half his age – which would have been twenty-five – unzipped his sleeping bag and rose, fully dressed apart from his boots, to greet another rose-pink Arabian dawn.

It was 0530 on a Saturday morning, in the first week of the Ras-al-Am army's autumn exercise.

"Chai, Masood," the General barked, alternately massaging his buttocks and jowl, grimacing an isometric face exercise as his orderly came careering with obsequious devotion across the lunar landscape of that part of Ras-al-Am bearing a steaming mug of tea as though it were some holy chalice.

The Commander of Ras-al-Am's Land Forces farted, then reached into one of the large patch pockets of his Indian-made Denison smock hanging from the branch of a frankincense tree, groped for his Silk Cut cigarettes and with a flick of his Zippo lit one. Exhaling an acrid flume of smoke into the early morning air he took Masood's proffered mug of condensed milk thickened with tea, and stonked off with it to perform the same early morning function as lesser men.

Later he emerged from behind his rock, adjusted his dress and stood sipping his off-white, cardamom-flavoured brew while harking to the dawn chorus of coughing and spitting that went on all around him. Bearded, dark-skinned Ras-al-Ami

29

jundees gave themselves perfunctory licks and a spit from their water bottles. Others squatted in huddles beneath a rocky overhang discussing politics like a pack of kennelled Alsatians, despite the earliness of the hour.

The sound of a pestle ricocheted round the clearing as one of the Baluch cooks pounded herbs for the curry and dhal which would soon be served up for breakfast on communal fuddle trays the size of dustbin lids.

The General strolled across to watch another grinning Baluch mercenary mixing dough into buns which he flung from forearm to forearm, turning them into flat raw chappatis which he jabbed twice with a prodder before lobbing them onto a crude hot-plate, an iron slab mounted ten inches off the ground on empty ammunition boxes, with a calor gas burner roaring beneath it.

When the meal was ready the General sat cross-legged on the ground with the rest of them, scooping up his dhal with pieces torn from a chappati and then pouring water over his hands to rinse the herbs' pervasive yellow dye from his fingernails.

Afterwards the cooking pots and tin trays were cleaned with gravel and wet sand and the ladles and sieves strung out on bushes to dry.

The General glanced up.

Two black-shrouded bedu tribeswomen and a young boy were hurrying across the rocks towards the encampment. They had come to seek medical treatment for the boy's suppurating eyes. When it was explained that none was available the women shrugged philosophically, muttered *"Allah Kharim"* and accepted mugs of tea, turning away to raise their beak-like burqua masks from their faces to drink unobserved.

General Stubbs had no inkling at this stage what a bitch of a day it was going to turn out to be.

General Wally, as he was affectionately known, was a latter day Glubb Pasha who had first fetched up in the country a decade earlier as a British army lieutenant-colonel on secondment to Ras-al-Am's newly formed Ministry Of

Defence, which in those days had been housed in a series of huts alongside an old whitewashed fort in the heart of Raman.

The heat, the desert, the expanding local army and lack of red tape – all this appealed so much to the gung-ho bachelor colonel that he had opted to stay. He resigned from the British army and became a contract officer for the then younger Sultan Hamad.

Quelling local skirmishes, arranging ceremonial parades, sourcing and buying new tanks and guns free of restrictive financial constraints, Colonel Stubbs – as he then was – had forgotten more matters military than the Arabs would ever learn and was so dedicated in successfully completing his tasks that he was regularly promoted until finally he ended up commanding the whole shooting works - a 50-year-old lieutenant-general pulling in a tax-free £150,000 a year, plus perks. The perks included a chauffeur-driven air-conditioned Mercedes parked in the triple garage of a sumptuous grace-and-favour mansion, with servants, on a hillside, with a pool, above Masela Camp. Additionally a generous annual bonus was paid into his Swiss bank account by the Sultan.

His name apart, Wally Stubbs hardly fitted the usual perception of what a General would look like. He could never be mistaken for an elegant cavalryman or suave Guards officer with monocle, cigarette holder and gold-plated spurs, expounding a well-enunciated view on things whilst leaning against an ante-room fireplace dinkily nursing a small sherry. He was a heavy smoker who also drank too much, but nevertheless – with a faded pair of hard-won SAS wings on his shoulder – he was still one very tough hombré who preferred being out in the field with his pack and a rifle to manning an overflowing desk back at headquarters.

"Sayid, Sayid -," General Wally spun round to see his orderly, Masood, hot-footing it towards him again across the rocks. The jundee skidded breathlessly to a stop in a rush of shale and jabbed a piece of paper at him.

"Message from Signal's tent, *Sayid,"* he gasped.

General Wally squinted as he skimmed the brief message. He cursed beneath his breath. Ramming the slip of paper into a pocket he hurried over to the camouflaged command tent to dig out the army's deputy commander, Brigadier Mustapha Said, drinking coffee and telling beefed-up war stories to a group of junior Ras-al-Ami officers. Beckoning the 32-year-old brigadier to join him, the General stepped back outside the tent.

"We're going to have to sort out communications better than this, Mustapha," he said angrily as soon as they emerged through the tent flap. "Last night the ammunition depot at Masala was blown up, and I've only just been informed about it. It may have been an accident, or not. We don't know yet. I shall have to fly back there immediately. It will take me an hour by helicopter. You know the form here. Keep things rolling until I return."

FIVE

Hamad bin Khaleel, the 45-year-old Sultan of Ras-al-Am, placed his silver Georgian soup spoon delicately onto the Wedgewood plate decorated with his country's gold scimitar motif (the Ras-al-Am embassy in Montpelier Square had delivered a 150-setting china and cutlery service to the venue - Claridges - the previous day), dabbed his lips with a crisp lawn napkin embroidered with the same motif, and turned to address Her Majesty Queen Elizabeth, who as principal guest was seated at his right hand.

It is not known what Sultan Hamad said to the Queen, probably no more than a passing pleasantry to do with the consommé, to which the Queen would respond with her consummate ease. Monarchs and statesmen did not restrict their conversation solely to affairs of moment and high import.

Seated on the Sultan's left, soup also finished, elbows on the table and his chin resting atop both hands in his usual relaxed manner, Prince Philip conversed in subdued tones with Sayyid Khamis bin Tariq about – who knows what - harems and hashish?

His Highness Sayyid Khamis bin Tariq, the Sultan's bearded, astute, Oxford-educated and wealthy Deputy Prime Minister for Defence and Security picked one fingernail at a gleaming gold tooth and sagely agreed with whatever Prince Philip was saying.

Invitations had read 12.30 pm for 1.15 pm. It was now 1.40 pm. The soup plates had been cleared and the fish course served. After that they went on to exotically prepared lamb and trimmings, some puddings, Ras-al-Ami sweetmeats and a

33

choice of Brazilian or Kenyan coffee.

At 2.15 pm the Sultan summoned the wealth of majesty that was his to command and rose to address his assembled guests.

Hamad wore a heavily gold-embellished cream woollen bisht, the formal cloak which resembled a lady's peignoir, with a red sash at the waist of his tasselled white cotton thobe, and three distinctive orders on his left breast. His head was turbaned in the coveted emerald-green, red and gold Imama-al-Hamida, worn only by elite members of the Ras-al-Ami Royal Family. Unusually, he wore no ceremonial khunjar, although many of these ornate silver daggers could be seen gleaming at the waists of his fellow Ras-al-Amis seated as hosts at the other tables.

Just as Hamad was adjusting the microphone to speak, a liveried footman bearing a message on a silver salver emerged through the curtains behind him and proffered it discreetly in a white gloved hand to His Highness Sayyid Khamis. The Deputy Prime Minister for Defence and Security took the message and dismissed its bearer. He broke open the envelope's seal with a butter knife and removed the single folded sheet of paper just as the Sultan began to speak in a halting, rich baritone voice . . .

"Your Majesty; your Royal Highnesses; my Lords, Ladies and Gentlemen. On this, the penultimate day of my most enjoyable state visit to Great Britain, I feel it is an appropriate occasion for me to . . ."

Beside him Sayyid Khamis emitted a strangled gasp. The Sultan paused in his speech and turned to regard him. Sayyid Khamis was slumped in his plush high-back chair with a glazed, shocked expression. Despite the training instilled by years of diplomatic wheeler-dealing, his face had turned ashen beneath his swarthy skin, indicating a heart attack or stroke. Prince Philip gazed on solicitously, while the Queen peered concernedly round the Sultan to see what was amiss. The Sultan spoke quickly to Khamis in Arabic. Sayyid Khamis responded with a wan smile and limply lifted a podgy hand to indicate that the speech should continue. It was a tribute to Hamad that his seven-minute address was delivered without fluster. He concluded:

" . . . and so it is with confidence that we look forward to enjoying even closer ties between our two countries than those which have already been forged . . ."

Hamad resumed his seat to polite and prolonged applause. Clasping both hands beneath the broad sleeves of his bisht he turned to acknowledge Queen Elizabeth. She appeared to be complimenting him afresh on his perfect command of English whilst laughingly confessing to her own inadequacy in Arabic, but now she suggested that perhaps they should try to find out what had been wrong with Sayyid Khamis, who had regained his composure and was saying: 'Excuse me,' to Prince Philip while leaning forward to pass the communiqué he had received from their embassy along to the Sultan. Hamad quickly read the message before politely handing it to the principal guest to read as well. She smiled and pointed out that she wasn't too hot on written Arabic either. Briefly the Sultan explained to the Queen and her consort that in the past forty-eight hours Ras-al-Am had suffered three incidents of civil unrest: an attack on an oil tanker, a Palace murder and the army's largest ammunition depot exploding. The Queen and her husband recorded their sympathy and concern and a few minutes later they all arose.

Sultan Hamad escorted his royal guests to their carriage awaiting them at the doors.

His state visit to Britain over, tomorrow he would be back at his palace in Raman, where only Allah knew what catastrophic dramas lay in wait.

SIX

General Wally Stubbs sat attentively on the edge of a long sofa in the Sultan's office while Hamad and his son Fahad, both coolly attired in gleaming white thobes and sandals, sat opposite him in regal red leather armchairs.

"General Stubbs," said the Sultan, steepling his fingers. "For many years you have been a loyal servant of my country. You have contributed greatly to our development over the past decade, helping us to emerge from a medieval backwater to a wealthy oil state. We are a beneficent and progressive monarchy ruled by a non-political government of ministers. In such a rapid development as ours however, there are bound to be rival factions simmering in the wings. Our Intelligence Directorate and Police Force have suppressed those few dissident elements which have appeared from time to time, but these latest outbreaks -," Hamad enumerated them on his fingers: "the attack on the oil tanker, the heinous murder of Miss Duprés – " Crown Prince Fahad uncrossed and recrossed his legs – "and the blowing up of the ammunition depot – for these events to have occurred almost concurrently indicates that dangerous dissidents are at work. The tanker incident has caused enormous embarrassment. A full enquiry has already been initiated, but international observers will have concluded that we have become aligned with Iran, or something. Teheran, too, will want to know what it was all about. Miss Duprés' murder and mutilation? The Police seem unable to produce a single idea or lead. Our London agents have confirmed that before Fahad brought her out here as his plaything she was an international call-girl; hooker, hostess -? I don't know what you call them these days. There is some consolation in that she was acknowledged as high-class, so I suppose Fahad should be commended upon her appearance, if not her credentials . . ." at this remark Crown Prince Fahad wiggled one of his big toes in its sandal, regarding it sheepishly. "But so far as can be ascertained at this stage," the Sultan continued, "she had no family or dependants and the British Ambassador has agreed that we should probably bury her as soon as possible, in our small Christian cemetery here. So much for our immediate concerns."

The Sultan leaned forward to retrieve his coffee cup and take a sip of some of its thick content before continuing:

"Ras-al-Am today lies between two cultures. While being on the one hand part and parcel of the twentieth century's western ideals, in the remoter reaches of our country there are still some bedu who have not yet seen a motor car."

General Wally wished the Sultan would get to the point. Hamad had always had an especially soft spot for his blunt, Yorkshire-bred army commander, but had never granted him dispensation to smoke in his presence. Dying to light up a Silk Cut, he contented himself with settling back in the sofa and recrossing his legs.

"Perhaps," the Sultan went on "we have neglected our internal affairs of late because of the greater external events raging around us. First we had the Iraq/Iran confrontation on our doorstep and now the Soviet occupation of Afghanistan, to say nothing of Palestine and Israel bubbling away the whole time. It is worrying that with our limited resources we are situated so close to the crucial Strait of Hormuz. The Gulf of Oman is mined, and there are foreign warships galore patrolling up and down out there. Russia and America never know whether they want to fight each other – and now China is starting to impress everyone with how powerful she is. Stuck, as we are, in the middle of all this, life is potentially somewhat volatile, wouldn't you say?"

General Wally folded his arms and grunted agreement. Prince Fahad persisted in jiggling his sandaled foot.

"Now," said the Sultan, "when we least need them, we've

got domestic troubles brewing as well. I want to find out what they're all about and why. Who's behind them, and what we need to do about the situation. Can you make that your priority please, General?"

General Wally found himself caught by surprise. His immediate reaction was *What sir? Me, sir? No, sir; Why, sir?* This was a task for the country's Intelligence Directorate and Police Force, not the Army. The Sultan knew that. Why, then, was Wally being asked to overstep his professional purlieus like this?

"Of course, sir," he said, uncrossing his legs and sitting forward on the sofa with clasped hands. "I would suggest that the Army's intervention might ruffle Giles Carrington's feathers a bit though, and those of the Inspector General of Police – so may I enquire Your Majesty's reasoning?"

The Sultan smiled.

"A new broom, General," he said. "Word will get out if I instruct the Intelligence Service and Police to step-up their activities. You have jundees and officers living in the hills. Their homes and families are there. They will be aware of any shifting groundswell and will be able to inform you discreetly. What is the extent of damage to the Masela ammunition depot?"

"Miraculously, sir, not total. It would seem that a person or persons as yet unknown got in there, with or without inside help, laid a charge with a time detonator in one of the bunkers and assumed that when it went up the whole lot would blow, in a chain reaction. In fact the explosion was contained. Its blast damaged one wing of the hospital where I'm afraid Major Hargreaves, one of my loan service officers, and the lovely young wife of the late Colonel Pritchard were killed. Major Hargreaves was with Colonel Pritchard and Captain Fanshawe when they were killed in the tanker attack. They were in a private boat nearby and were the rebels' first fatalities before they stormed the ship. Mrs Pritchard's sister and her husband will shortly arrive from England to take charge of the children. Twins - Jeremy and Susan. Little Jeremy's in hospital at the moment recovering from a snake bite."

"A warring horde of Ras-al-Ami fishermen. Pointless. Mindless." Sultan Hamad tugged at his beard. "What was their purpose? Nobody saw them. No one knows who they were or where they went. Fahad, speak to the Finance Minister after this meeting. Make sure that Mrs Pritchard's sister receives appropriate compensation from us. Discuss something similar with him for the other two officers' families as well, will you please? Was this the same faction who murdered Miss Duprés, I wonder? It seems reasonable to suppose it is. What does it all mean, General?"

"A warning, sir. Whoever they are they can't stop now. They're hell-bent, and I feel there is going to be more of the same and worse to come."

"I fear you're right. That's why it must be addressed and stopped. Quickly."

"It might already be too late for that, sir. I suspect this may be the tip of an uprising. A full-scale revolution even." General Wally stroked his chin for a second, and then asked: "May I have Your Majesty's permission to recall the Army from the field?"

Sultan Hamad arose from his chair and walked across the carpet to gaze out of the window at the Palace gardens.

"Why?" he asked the General, uncertainly.

"While they are still in the field sir, their barracks remain unmanned and ripe for sabotage or take-over if there is a rebel force at-large out there. If they are in barracks communications and subsequent redeployment would be much easier."

"Are you suggesting, General . . ." the Sultan smiled knowingly, "that my Army's communications in the field are not quite faultless?"

"In the panic of a fire-fight situation some of the signallers do tend to become a bit excited, sir. They forget their English radio procedure and revert to Arabic. This is quite understandable, but the Brits can't decipher the babble, you see." The General grinned. "With what appears to be brewing I believe we would be best advised to have them back home, on-call in their barracks."

"Very well, you'd better recall them."

"Thank you, sir. And there is something else for which I would request Your Majesty's authority as well."

"And that is?"

"There is an organisation in London sir, which specialises in work of this nature. Their operatives are first class men. I know them well and have worked with them before. Their experience and contribution would be invaluable to us. May I have Your Majesty's permission to call in one of their teams?"

"By all means, Wally. I imagine you are referring to that undercover agency, the Zeta Group?" The Sultan nodded, a twinkle in his eye. "You look surprised. You shouldn't be. Most heads of state know of their existence. It is an excellent suggestion. They'd obviously be the best men for the job. Do you know how to contact them?"

"As a matter of fact I do, sir."

"Of course you do. After all, you were their founding father, weren't you."

Lieut-General Wally Stubbs shook his head perplexedly as he descended the wide marble staircase of the Palace.

He acknowledged the cracking salutes of the two Royal Guard jundees guarding the entrance and climbed into his black Mercedes with its scarlet and gold bonnet-pennon and three gold stars mounted above its registration plates. His driver, Abdullah, sensed the General's introspection as they drove out of the Palace gates and back along the Corniche towards Masela Camp, twenty miles to the north.

Half an hour later they drove past the saluting Baluch guards at the camp gates and Abdullah swung the Mercedes up the tree-lined slope to the General's house at the top of the hill. The General climbed out, walked up the steps and went inside.

He removed his pistol belt and shemagh headdress and dropped them onto a chair. Normally he would have worn formal attire for an audience with the Sultan, but on this occasion he had been called in from the field.

He went into his private study, locking the door behind him. Opening his safe he took out a file which he carried across to his desk. He opened the file and then picked up the receiver of the red phone, with its direct link to London.

A Zeta team could only be summoned if the situation met certain criteria. The situation in Ras-al-Am met every one of them.

General Wally knew exactly who should comprise this particular Zeta team, a team which should arrive in Ras-al-Am as soon as possible if it was going to avert one of the bloodiest revolutions the country had seen in its long history.

SEVEN

LONDON

It was 8.55 am.

Lt-Col (Rtd) Chris Morton, late 3-Para, alighted from his taxi, strode along the bustling thoroughfare for fifty metres and then turned down a grimy Dickensian alley. Grey-sided warehouse walls soared claustrophobically above him like vertical tectonic plates. Refuse-packed black plastic bin liners were stacked on the cobbles outside the rear entrance to an Italian delicatessen.

"Morning Solly," Chris cried in his usual jovial manner to the morose little Jewish tailor wrestling with the shutters of his one-man sweat-shop, founded by his Polish great-great-grandfather in 1860. "Rain today?"

"More than likely. Usually does." Solly blew fag ash over his moth-eaten maroon sweater and shuffled back inside his dingy workplace to crank up his sewing machine for another day's worth of alterations.

Chris Morton strode on a further 20 metres stepping over discarded banana skins and other detritus until he reached a door with a faded bronze plaque proclaiming head office of the improbable sounding United Fruit Packing Company. Unsuspecting members of the public who happened to enter this alley with no interest in getting their fruit packed would have hurried by without a glance. More observant aficionados of the espionage genre might experience a momentary frisson, but the United Fruit Packing Company usually managed to conduct its business undisturbed by any but those bona fide enquirers who sought their services and knew where to find them.

Chris opened the door and went in.

He was faced by a narrow linoleum-covered passage with a bike propped against one wall. At the end was a winding staircase. He went up to the identically lino-covered landing at the top and opened one of the doors. The walls of the original three rooms on this floor had been removed to create a spacious area crammed with desks, maps, computers and other clutter. This was the office which since his retirement from the army six months ago Chris shared with his director, Reuben Dumperley.

He removed and hung up his coat, pulled out the worn but comfortable green leather-buttoned captain's chair from his desk and sat down, wondering what lay in store for him this day. No sooner had he leaned forward to reach for his desk diary than the red telephone beside him started to *purrrrp*. Quick off the mark this morning, he thought – glancing at his watch: specially for a Saturday.

It was 9.05 am.

Reuben Dumperley was just arriving; he could hear the sound of the older man's substantial frame ascending the staircase outside.

"United Fruit Packers – Morton speaking," he told the mouthpiece. "Yes – of course; one moment please, he's just coming in."

Reuben Dumperley barged through the door like a grampus, grunted surlily, unbuttoned and hung up his Aquascutum, took off and hung up his suit jacket and waddled over to his desk. Chris Morton winced. Today the director was wearing a straining blue and white striped shirt, red braces and a yellow bow tie. No one would ever take him for a retired vice-admiral. He whipped a canary yellow snuff rag from his pocket, trumpeted into it loudly and briefly inspected the deposit before stuffing it away again. That done he looked across at Chris still holding the telephone, and raised one eyebrow.

"Good morning. Yes – it's for you. General Wally Stubbs from Ras-al-Am."

Reuben Dumperley grunted again, furrowed his brow and

picked up his own phone. "Wally, dear boy; how very good to hear you. How the devil are you? What can we do for you?"

Their conversation lasted seven minutes. At the end of it Reuben said, "Right, Wally: message received and understood. We'll activate immediately," and replaced the receiver. "Always makes me chuckle - that," he said, tapping the tips of his podgy fingers together.

"What does?"

"Saying Right Wally to a general. You've not met him, have you! He's a venerable old war horse. You've never seen anyone less like a General in your life. You'd think he was a Pioneer Corps colour-sergeant. But he is good. Damned good. It was he who started this whole shebang, you know."

"Yes, I do, but tell me about it again," said Chris with amused resignation.

Vice-Admiral (Rtd) Reuben Dumperley snorted some more sinus and pipe clinker into his long suffering snuff rag. Folding it all away and tucking it back into his pocket again he sat back with his hands behind his neck. "Wally was SAS, as you know," he said. "A half-colonel then, staging through Baghdad engaged in some quasi-nefarious misdemeanour or other. Well . . . job done, one night he was supping an ale in a sleazy Arab gin-bin called the Zeta Farani Club. This establishment's hole-in-the ground slash-pit was overflowing with unpleasantness, so Wally took himself out to the alley at the back to relieve himself. There he stumbled across a fellow European, face biting the dust, clawing at a length of cheese wire cutting into his larynx while some hefty Iraqi felon was yanking its wooden handle with a knee in his back for purchase. Wally didn't think this could be quite right, so being an ex-Harlequin full-back he drew back his right leg and let fly a drop-kick at the Iraqi's left ear. It was a successful conversion and the miscreant lunged with a thud amongst the overflowing dustbins. The white man was relieved and grateful. He struggled to his feet, rubbed his savaged throat, spat out some blood, dusted himself down and introduced himself as one Don Ferguson, a tough and normally self- sufficient traveller who happened to be an ex Royal Marine commando. Just what he was up to that night, getting himself garrotted in a Baghdad alleyway is still a mystery, but the two men re-entered the Zeta Ferani Club together – mainly because Wally hadn't finished his beer. Apparently a meaningful discussion then took place between them which resulted in the birth of the Zeta Group. That was ten years ago. There are now thirty good guys on our books, mostly ex SAS or SBS with one or two other funnies thrown in as well, all keen for excitement and the chance to earn big bucks by hiring out their skills. It's a pity you got your leg shot up, Chris. With your background we could have used you on field work, but your Deputy Comptroller's job is just as vital. Anyway – cutting to the chase it's Ferguson who Wally wants out in Ras-al-Am. Currently he's finishing up that Thailand job with his Kraut sidekick, Hans Ehrlich. We've also got to call in Chuck Henderson from Surinam, our new American guy. Righty-ho Christopher, my boy. We've got a full morning's work ahead of us rounding up this trio of misfits, so let's get started."

A flurry of rain splattered against the office's grimy windowpanes and a gust of wind dislodged a grey Edwardian slate, sending it slithering off the roof to dash itself to smithereens in the alley below.

Reuben Dumperley unscrewed the cap of his Mont Blanc fountain-pen and drawing a pad towards him, started drafting signals.

EIGHT

SOUTH AMERICA

Surinam is a slab of Amazonian jungle and coastal swamp on the northeast shoulder of South America. She gained her independence from Holland in 1975. The 500,000-strong Surinamese only managed to enjoy five years of this new-found 'freedom' before a military coup overthrew their government over issues concerning control of the trade in cocaine. The war had serious consequences for the Maroons – the Surinamese slave-descendant Bush Negroes, known as the 'Damned of the Earth'. Their villages were demolished, and roads, water pipelines and power lines, schools, public buildings, clinics and businesses destroyed.

In 1986 a guerilla commando group was formed to fight for equal rights for the country's minority Maroon population. A Dutch organisation operated by a Surinamese running a coffee bar in a part of Amsterdam's red light district, set about recruiting mercenaries to support this Jungle Commando. Hearing this on the grapevine, an ex Green Beret, Chuck Henderson, fetched up there and got temporary work as the bar's manager/bouncer. Three weeks of that almost drove him crazy, but he achieved his aim and acquired the telephone number he needed. He called it at ten-o'clock next morning, when it was suggested that he should report later that evening to an address on the outskirts of the city. The people he met were impressed with his military credentials, and eagerly accepted his services. Four days later he flew by Air Maroc from Amsterdam to Casablanca, and from there down to Rio de Janeiro. From Rio a Brazilian airline flew him to Kouru, in French Guiana, where he signed his contract to serve as one of the Jungle Commando mercenaries. That was three months ago. Now he was hunkered down in the gunwales of a pirogue, one of the motorised canoes the guerilleros used to navigate the network of streams through Surinam's dense tropical rain forest; but Chuck and the five men with him were not in a stream: they had cut their motor and silently drifted along hugging the foliage that overhung the west bank of the Maroni River, the 800 metre stretch of water forming the border between Surinam and French Guiana.

At times like this, swatting mosquitoes and swiping sweat from his neck and brow, with a wry grin Chuck Henderson always asked himself what the hell he thought he was doing.

If he'd had more brain instead of brawn and worked harder at school he might have a proper job by now, a wife, home and kids back in Nebraska, instead of living out of a maggot infested hold-all on a diet of rice, alcohol and anti-malaria pills.

Chuck's mission today had been to blow a bridge at Albina, a village garrisoned with 400 pro-government troops. He and his boys went in, laid their charges and retreated back to their pirogue concealed by the river bank – but then they were spotted.

A Dutch DAF YP408 eight-wheeled 1200 kilo armoured personnel carrier and three Brazilian EE9 Cascavel armoured recce cars came bursting out of the foliage onto the Morengo-Albina Road. It was a detachment of the enemy's Echo Company Commando closing fast, clattering along the road on the far side of the bridge to find and kill Chuck and his group.

They should have started the motor of the pirogue and been speeding away back up-river by now, but they were trapped. Not only did they have these rapidly approaching armoured vehicles to contend with, but now a government patrol boat had put out from Albina and positioned itself in the middle of the river, scrutinising the bank where they were hiding. If Chuck's party broke cover they'd be blasted out of the water – if not by the patrol boat, then by the machine-guns on the

APCs and recce cars.

Thankfully the vehicles had momentarily stopped on the far side of the bridge. Chuck saw a sun-flash dart from the lens of their commanders' binos as he scoured the river bank.

"Blow, you bastard – BLOW," Chuck swore, willing the bridge to go up. The second-hand on his watch flicked agonisingly by.

Another 60 seconds. Had he got it right? Was this damn thing going to blow or not?

Would they get away alright? Or would their bullet-ridden carcasses soon be slithering into the disgusting Maroni River, unmourned and remembered only by a few demi-monde waterfront bar hops? Chuck reckoned he burned more adrenalin a day here than a Formula One did oil.

Wildlife squawked and chirruped around them.

They were dripping with sweat and discomfort in the tropical heat. The tension was unbearable, but they had to wait, huddled in the pirogue until either the bridge blew or something else happened.

The five guerrillas were whispering anxiously in their local Taki-Taki dialect. Jabbing out his arm one of them pointed excitedly at the far side of the river. He had seen a high speed French Guianan patrol craft come creaming across the water to draw alongside and challenge the Surinamese government vessel.

It was a heaven-sent diversion.

"ROW, you bastards – Row," Chuck ordered them, clutching a paddle himself and nosing their pirogue out from the bank.

Two of his boys grasped the remaining paddles and jabbed them into the water. The pirogue began moving faster, edging silently away up river.

Suddenly the water around them erupted into a seething, lead-zipped cauldron, accompanied by the staccato crackle of machine-gun fire. The armoured vehicles' commander had seen them alright.

The fighting convoy surged forward over the bridge towards them, incessantly firing as they came. 7.62 and 12.7

mm bullets *thwacked* into the pirogue.

One of those paddling suddenly jack-knifed forward with a bullet in the back of his skull.

"START THE ENGINE," Chuck roared: "LET'S GET THE HELL OUT OF HERE . . .".

The engine coughed twice but then sprang richly to life. The small craft shot forward and away.

Despite having the French Guianan patrol vessel alongside, the Surinamese boat still opened fire on them. The water hissed and plopped about them like a bubbling casserole of death.

"HOLY SHIT," bellowed Chuck. "I need this like a hole in the head," then grimaced when he glanced down at the youngster in the blood-drenched gunwales with half his head blown away . . .

. . . then their ears were split by a massive *WHOOSH* and a *CRUUUMP*.

"Hallelujah Jehova*SAT*," Chuck whooped. "The bitch has *BLOWN*, boys – the goddamn bridge has BLOWN."

He slapped his thigh gleefully as buckled sheets of armour plating, chunks of crank-case, human entrails and baulks of bridge stanchions arced into the broiling water of the River Maroni.

The bridge had blown just as the lead government vehicle was crossing the middle of it.

It had been one HELL of an explosion.

Chuck chuckled, realising he'd used too much plastique, but what the hell! He wasn't an accountable mining engineer. He was a hired killer, doing the job he was paid to do. The goddam bridge had blown. That's all that mattered.

Behind them the two patrol boats rocked and collided against each other in the wake of the explosion. The Surinamese vessel had finally ceased firing. When they reached a bend in the river, the two vessels slipped from their view at last.

Chuck glanced back over his shoulder and saw his boys grinning happily at him. They liked big bangs. He may never get his name in lights over Broadway, but amongst mercenary society he knew he was building something of a reputation for himself.

After an uneventful but gruelling journey up-river, Chuck's party reached Langatabbejte Island, the hard-construction village with a dispensary and small airport which was the rebels' exclusive stronghold.

As soon as they had clambered ashore the guerrillero with the hole punched in his skull was manhandled into a wheelbarrow and in an ignominious hurry trundled across to their makeshift field hospital. A French Aide Medicale Internationale doctor poked about and dug out the bullet with a screwdriver.

"You're thick-skinned," he grinned at Chuck, "but these Bush Negroes are thick-skulled as well. You'd be dead now if you had this thing inside you." He held aloft the crumpled 7.62 sleeping pill between his thumb and index finger. "Whereas this chap will only have a sore head for a while, then he'll forget about it."

Chuck left the hospital and scuffed back across the clearing to retrieve his battered hold-all from where he'd dumped it on the ground.

As he walked he peeled off his filthy green vest, using the sodden ball to mop sweat from his armpits.

Short of being a coal miner or shovelling shit, he reckoned mercenaries in action had one of the filthiest jobs in the world. Usually in extremes of heat and discomfort too. He felt like John Wayne come in off a trail drive.

Unstrapping the machete from his waist he shoved it inside his canvas grip. Christ – he thought: a Laundromat would be nice. A cold beer, shower and change of clothes too, for that matter.

Good meal. Good woman.

What the hell was he doing, daily putting his life on the line like this, living like some dispossessed rat?

He knew the answer. He was getting kicks while earning a living the only way he knew how, and hopefully being paid well for it along the way.

Funds were meant to have been transferred to his Wells Fargo branch in Lincoln, Nebraska, but last time he'd had a chance to check, nothing had been deposited there yet.

Several other mercs had reported the same shortfall in their Agreement also. They all knew from experience that sometimes it took months for the stuff to arrive. Appealing as it might appear on the surface to some, mercenary-dom was a dicier profession than even show-business, it seemed.

Chuck had been out here three months and was now tired of the place. Whenever it was too much for his explosive nature to handle, usually when the guerrilla diet and activity had freed him of 10 kilos he could ill afford to lose, he would slip across the border into French Guiana for rest, recuperation and some naughties. He would like to have gone over there tonight, but it was too much hassle. Besides, he was tired.

Tonight what he wanted was to catch up on sleep.

Purloining a rolled-up canvas camp bed from a pile strewn on the ground outside a ramshackle shed, he made his way across to a small clearing between the trees. Dumping his grip and leaning his FN rifle against a nearby tree he swiftly assembled the bed, lay the rifle down alongside it and stretched out with his hands behind his neck.

Cursing, he sat up again to loosen his bootlaces.

Transistorised music, wood smoke and mist drifted across the twilit clearing. Exotic birds cawed from the treetops. Small items of wild life scurried busily through the rustling undergrowth. Large juicy green lizards basked openly on warm, flat rocks, the flickers of their lidless eyes and quivers along their underbellies the only indication that they were living creatures.

Chuck was soon asleep.

It was a deep, well earned sleep.

He dreamt of the long-legged French lovely he'd met on a beach at St Tropez the previous summer. Topless and high-stepping like a spirited filly she came through his dream up the sand towards him from out of the sea, holding her head to one side squeezing water from her long blonde hair, silhouetted against the sun like an ad for Polaroids, Martini, or Lamborghini.

Chuck had to squint to focus on her luscious body as she drew closer to him, a miniscule thong and black postage stamp patch stretched tautly across her crotch.

Infuriatingly, this image then began to fade and Chuck felt himself drawn begrudgingly back to the reality of his exhausted body in its jungle setting. He half awoke, wondering what had disturbed him. It was now dark, the camp stilled.

He became conscious of a tingling sensation in his left arm which he thought must be pins and needles.

Although the treetops encircling their camp were awash with tropical moonlight, the area around Chuck's canvas bed was pitch black.

He shifted his body, flexing and tensing his numbed forearm for several seconds before realising that he had not been sleeping on it at all. He clenched his fist again.

His arm felt as though it was encapsulated in some sort of heavy wet plaster cast. Then as his night vision slowly adjusted he became aware that there was a large, dark shape huddled alongside him on the ground.

At first he thought someone must have dumped a pile of canvas there, but then his heart rate increased and his anxiety heightened when he saw the unmistakeable glint of two implacable yellow eyes flickering next to his own.

Then with horrified disbelief he understood. His whole arm was disappearing into the gaping maw of a giant Green Anaconda.

The largest snake in the world.

Chuck knew that Central and South American water boas, anacondas, wrap their coils swiftly round their victim's bodies, pause for the panic-stricken inhalation, sense the terrified exhalation and then crush to prevent further inhalation. The head of an anaconda is often large enough to form a 24 inch by 20 inch triangle. The creature's jaw span is awesome. It is able to ingest and then digest its victims whole . . . not unusually victims the size of donkeys.

Anacondas can weigh 100 kgs and take ten people to lift

them. Being aquatic creatures, their mouths are teeming with bacteria, their breath pestilent.

How this particular specimen came to be swallowing Chuck's arm without first crushing and asphyxiating him was a puzzle. His first wild yell was loud enough to cause other exhausted rebels to stir in their sleep. His second anguished bellow drew their attention to there being something wrong, and then momentarily he blacked out.

Charlie Bowater, a British merc who had been flogging round the Surinamese rain forests since forever, was enjoying the relief of an early a.m. bladder relief. Quickly he switched on the beam of his heavy-duty MAG flashlight and with mounting horror saw what was happening.

Leaping back across the clearing to his equipment he stooped and in one deft movement drew his razor-edged machete with a rasp from its scabbard.

Giant anacondas can grow up to 35ft in length, weigh 40st and have a girth the size of a man. This one consuming Chuck's arm was an average 30ft, but still no mean adversary.

Charlie Bowater was a big man with broad shoulders and massive arms. Straddling the serpent he raised his machete to bring it arcing forcefully down with a dull *thwack* 3ft behind its head, trying not to sever Chuck's arm in the process.

He shouted to summon help. Others of the guerrilleros had blundered to their feet and were gathering with bleary-eyed stupefaction round this man v beast tussle, quickly developing into a scene of nocturnal butchery.

Charlie again raised his machete to hack bloodily at the great writhing snake whose wildly threshing coils caught two of the men and swiped their legs out from under them, making the others scurry back out of harm's way.

Sweat glistened from Charlie's brow before with a final mighty *thunk* he succeeded in cutting the snake's body in two. Gushing gobs of blood the heavy 30ft detached length of anaconda sprang backwards to act out its death throes in the flattened grass. The erratic peristalsis of its head section continued sucking at Chuck's arm.

Each of the reptile's muscular contractions revealed his

gory fingers and glistening fraternity ring protruding from the raw cut of meat.

Charlie Bowater grasped what was left of the snake in both fists and tried to pull it off Chuck's arm, but despite his massive strength it was too slippery and heavy for him to gain sufficient purchase.

"Corporal Velasquez: meat hooks: in the cook tent: get them – NOW," he barked in Taki-Taki."

The NCO quickly responded and reappeared with two dully glinting steel hooks. With a vicious jab Charlie embedded each of these deeply into the anaconda's scaly integument. Bracing himself, he again started to heave.

Chuck was dragged gurgling across the rough ground.

Like a tailor ripping a sleeve from a part-built bespoke jacket and a sound like a galosh being sucked out of mud the last of the snake was finally drawn from his arm.

With Chuck now free, Charlie hurled the green residue disgustedly behind him, its fearful eyes and jaw muscles still flickering as it wrestled with its own death.

The guerrilleros now switched their attention fully to the damaged American mercenary. Even in the moonlight Chuck's face was ashen. His left shoulder was swollen and misshapen. But apart from its coating of blood and slime his arm appeared to be alright. Only the shoulder was dislocated.

With one boot in his armpit, an adroit tug and a *scrunch*, Charlie quickly reset it for him.

Next morning those with cameras involuntarily shuddered while they photographed the snake's remains. They kept it to marvel over until lunch time, but the ants, flies and smell told them it was time to douse both sections with kerosene and burn them.

Chuck had some difficulty performing push ups that day and his bruises were the colour of the ochrous River Tiber in full and thunderous spate.

Two days later, when Chuck was practising with his crossbow, embedding a series of bolts into a possumwood tree 50 metres away, whose sap the Caribs used as arrow poison – Chuck was endeavouring to split each preceding bolt with the successive one - Charlie Bowater slapped down his earphones with a shriek from receiving that day's transmission, scribbled hastily on a pad and ran across the clearing towards him.

"Have you or have you not just shot your last bolt for the SNLA"? Charlie grinned at him. "American mercenary – him have friends in high places. God alone knows how they found you, or how they got through to us here in Disneyland. This just came in over the air. Mean something to you?" he enquired, thrusting the scrap of paper excitedly at Chuck, on which he'd scrawled the message **For Henderson SNLA stop London immediate 'Z' stop.**

It took a second or two for the fog in Chuck's brain to grasp its meaning, then he whooped, threw himself back in the grass, slapped his palm against his brow, and hissed *"Yesssss."*

"So what is it?" Charlie asked anxiously. "Good – or bad?"

Chuck did a rapid succession of jubilant sit-ups before leaping to his feet and performing a mock war dance round the grinning Charlie Bowater.

"What it means, ol' buddy, is that I've earned a reprieve," he laughed, and abruptly stopped frolicking about. "It's from an organisation I belong to in London," he said, becoming serious. "I haven't heard from them for over a year. I'm on their books for any occasional 'funny job' that comes up. What this means is they want me to haul ass over to London for a proper contract and a full, clearly defined briefing about the mission, whatever it may be. This is the A1, chateau-bottled, gold-plated, ocean-going real McCoy, Charlie m'boy. When y'gotta go, y'gotta go: And I gotta go."

"What about your contract with *these* people?"

"It's just been broken." Chuck grinned. "They haven't paid me yet, and by my reckoning it doesn't look as though they're going to. I can't hang around any longer waiting to get my head blown off for no pay. I'm on my way, buddy-boy."

"Where do you reckon this job might be?"

"Who knows? Timbuctoo, perhaps? Great Wall of China? Who cares? It's outta here, that's all that matters. Hey, Charlie – thanks again for what you did the other night. I owe you –

okay?"

"Sure. Forget it, right? Send me a post card from China."

As they talked both men hurried back across the clearing past guerrilleros lolling idly about smoking, chatting and volubly arguing in Taki-Taki with each other.

Chuck stooped to retrieve the grip holding all his worldly possessions, none of which amounted to much except his precious passport and papers in their waterproof pouch in one of the grip's zipped side pockets.

"How are you going to get there?" Charlie asked.

"Dunno," said Chuck. "Work it out as I go along. Guess I'll 'borrow' one of the pirogues and go down-river to French Guiana. I left some emergency money there for safe keeping, with a woman in Cayenne. I'll clean up there, buy some gear, arrange to fly from there to Miami and then on up to London."

By now they had reached the river bank and Chuck hefted his grip into the gunwales of one of the moored pirogues. Satisfying himself that it had a full tank he turned and handed his crossbow to Charlie. "Hang on to this for me, will you? I guess I'd probably not get it through your Customs at Heathrow, would I!"

"Tell 'em it's a souvenir."

"Of what?" Chuck cast a disparaging glance back round their campsite. "Keep it. Make like you're Robin Hood. Shoot some trees. See you at the reunion sometime."

"When and where's that going to be, then?"

"Pretty soon – in hell: I guess."

Chuck started the motor and edged the little craft out towards mid-river.

"Be seeing you, pal," he yelled back to Charlie, left standing forlornly on the bank, giving a hurried farewell wave. Fully opening the pirogue's throttle Chuck surged off on his escape route down to the coast, on the next adventure in his life.

General Wally Stubbs's Zeta Team was assembling.

NINE

THAILAND

It was a hazy, overcast morning in the high 80s on the Gulf of Siam.

At Pattaya's famed Jomtien Beach the chairs and tables in front of the Cobra Windsurfing Club awaited the arrival of that day's occupants like serried troops paraded for the arrival of dignitaries.

Soon the haze would burn off.

It was going to be another scorcher of a day. Already the beach was beginning to fill with people who trickled in on motorbikes and mopeds, or filtered down from the holiday chalets laid back in the trees.

The skimpiest of lightweight clothes were slipped off to reveal even skimpier-clad skin beneath, some of it bikini'd, some tanga'd or thonged, most of it topless and in one or two daring cases, completely naked.

A big, ruggedly handsome European scuffed his way across the sand towards one of the vacant sun beds. Onto it he dumped a substantial cowhide shoulder-bag which looked as if it might have been purloined at some time from a felled Pony Express rider. The bag contained his several passports, wallet, various denominations and amounts of currency, his camera, pen, notebook, a half-full pack of Marlboros and a disposable plastic lighter, along with other assorted junk which until recently most men had carried in bulging jacket pockets.

Peeling off his logo-free T-shirt he tossed it on top of his bag.

Don Ferguson, 45, was 6ft tall and despite the cigarettes

was still able to gallop up hills toting a machine-gun and to use it effectively when he got there.

Knowing how to keep his head down and butt clenched while nasty pieces of hot shot and shell came slicing through the foliage towards him had kept him alive and clean-trousered for quite a few years.

A Royal Marine Commando at 19 and CSM at 32 he had become disillusioned with the aftermath of subsequent defence cuts. He was also the victim of an unsuccessful and now long defunct marriage to a Pompey barmaid called Gloria, who by all accounts was still dispensing her favours with voracious liberalism to anyone she fancied. This meant almost anyone who asked, which included most of the Fleet. It was the combination of all these facts that had made Ferguson turn freelance on his 34th birthday.

Over the years he accumulated £180,000 in the Jersey branch of Grindlays, acquired chipped teeth and fingernails, a perma-bronze, an unwelcome varicose vein down the back of his left leg, some stereo equipment, a Canon camera and various memories of steamy workouts with Thai teenagers, that army of lithe brown jungle-bunnies who flocked down from the northern paddy fields to improve their lot in the fleshpots of the south. He owned a chestful of colourful medal ribbons he could seldom wear and a small flat in Plymouth he was disinclined to return to.

"Hail, ol' buddy. Wie gehts?"

Ferguson had seen the tattooed blond Bavarian body-builder, Hans Ehrlich, come jogging towards him along the beach like a small mastodon in overdrive, with the first of that day's consumption of wooden toothpicks protruding from his teeth. Hans chewed those wretched toothpicks like cud. It had nothing to do with keeping his teeth clean, more to do with some obscure aspect of the macho sub-culture, an affectation which puzzled and amused Ferguson.

Only the previous day one of the coterie of little girls hanging aound at the beach bar they used, had ingenuously enquired of Hans why he did it, only to be told "'Cos logs is too big."

"Iss another great day," Hans remarked, breathing normally despite his three-mile jog to get there. He tongued the toothpick across to the east side of his face and hunkered down beside Ferguson on bulging thighs.

Hans could have been a doughty sidekick in an Arnold Schwarzenegger movie, but Ferguson doubted he would remember his lines. He read comics for one thing, and not many men of 35 lived on such a pulp diet, but whatever Hans's shortcomings and lack of social grace, he had a superbly useful physique.

Hans had been a brutal and fearsome sergeant in the French Foreign Legion's 1er Etranger de Parachutistes when Ferguson first met him, sprawled in a Central African gutter one evening. He retrieved and carried the German's vomit and blood-caked body to the nearby house of a doctor friend who owed Ferguson a favour, which he repaid by slicing away the big German's clothing, hosing down his reeking body outside in the yard and then reassembling and riveting together his shaved skull, where an hour before someone had slapped a mule-stunning crack into it with a piece of lead pipe.

Hans's constitution was such that it only took two days for him to recall his own name, shake himself down and decide that thereafter there might be more fun to be had if he took up with Ferguson for a while, instead of returning to the Legion.

The two of them had just returned from three weeks in the hill country up on the Laotian-Burmese border where they had undertaken 'negotiations' with a cartel of drug barons on behalf of a grateful Thai government department. Now they were enjoying a deserved rest in this den of entrepreneurial iniquity – Pattaya.

"It was a very good party last night; *Ja*"? Hans remarked, sifting a shovelful of beach through his salami-like fingers. "But I see you are alone. Oyl is not with you today?"

"Gone visiting."

Ferguson's Thai girlfriend had the unlikely name Oyl.

It amused him to introduce her to his friends as "My goil Earl," although she didn't seem to find it quite as funny as he did.

59

Hans appeared puzzled that his normally gregarious friend did not seem disposed to converse with him this morning, so he stood up and brushed the sand from his palms, bade Ferguson a perfunctory auf wiedersehn and removed his bulk further down the beach to find more girls to impress.

Ferguson smiled at the retreating back of the Teutonic leviathan and not for the first time thought all Hans lacked was a plumed helmet and leather crossbelt, studded kneepads, a broadsword and a young eagle perched on his shoulder affectionately nibbling chunks from his ear.

He felt a tap on his own shoulder and turned to see not an ear-pecking bird of prey but a coolie-hatted masseuse standing beside him offering to smooth away his ills and turn him into a new man.

These strolling baggy-trousered beach masseuses were not into the tits and soapsuds frivolity practised in the perfumed parlours in town.

These were for real. They would nearly break you in half, given half a chance. Ferguson declined with a smile and the little old lady shuffled off down the beach in pursuit of the Incredible Hulk, who was now nowhere to be seen.

It seemed the tide was so high it was almost coming into the drawing room, so with three loping strides Ferguson hurled himself into the water and surfaced to do a fast crawl seaward for fifty strokes before swimming back with a forceful breast stroke towards the beach, where he threw himself back on his sun bed and went to sleep.

When he awoke later with a start and glanced at his Rolex he realised he had been stretched out in the sun for over an hour. The UVs were pulsing their relentless rays across his scarred and battered body which if it had not already been a deep mahogany would be burned to a frazzle by now.

He had been awakened by a stiff breeze suddenly whipping up across the Gulf of Siam. Empty deck chair canvases were snapping furiously. Sand was stinging his face.

Out on the water ecstatic windsurfers were doing it standing up, scudding across the choppy surface of the waves, snapping into cleverly executed turns and back again. All around him people were packing up. Ferguson decided he would call it a day as well.

He stood up and brushed himself down, shook out and folded his towel, slipped his khaki T-shirt back on, shorts and trainers, picked up his cowhide bag and left.

Fifteen minutes later he was standing beneath the powerful shower jets in his room at the Royal Garden Hotel.

Several pairs of Oyl's shoes lay strewn about the floor, her toilet articles were in disarray across the dressing table, her crumpled jeans, skirts, shirts and a tiny black thong lay dejectedly cast in one of the cane chairs.

Ferguson knew that letting a lone male loose in Thailand was like releasing a drunken diabetic in a chocolate factory. Even an iron will could not resist an investigative exploratory indulgence or two.

His latest girl, Oyl, was 28. The smooth shapeliness of her body and tautness of her unblemished skin, that of a 19-year-old, would drive a European woman of the same age into a hair-tearing frenzy of envy.

"Do you think I would jeopardise my livelihood by letting it become the bearer of disease," Oyl had assured him during their pillow talk together one night. "There is no room in my body for sickness. It cannot exist there. I would not let it enter. And besides . . ." she'd whispered wetly into his ear, snuggling up closely under his chin and sticking the inside of one lissom thigh tackily across his abdomen, "besides – I only go with lovely clean mens like you."

Ferguson had imagined promenading Oyl down Plymouth High Street one Saturday morning, or parading her at the Golf Club wearing gold slippers and a cling-fit gold lamé sheath slit up each thigh, flashing her shapely brown legs at cocktail hour.

She came from the Laotian border and was taller with more aquiline features than a pure-bred Thai. Her low, husky voice and confident demeanour created the perfect meld of youth and experience. She had a bottom like a firm peach, a ridge of muscle in her otherwise plank-flat belly, and breasts like small melons. Her arms were slender and she could have modelled jewellery on the red-nailed fingers of her exquisitely shaped hands.

For the last two days she had been away visiting her mother, but would be back again tomorrow.

Showered and shaved, Ferguson strolled along peaceably enjoying a detached view of life on the Strip only to be overtaken by two European gays scurrying along like agitated housewives with folded arms off to sort out some luckless headmaster. One was a good-looking, rangy-thighed blond in bleached sawn-off jeans, thick leather belt and cutaway mauve vest, rippling past in the full bloom of muscular youth.

His companion was a stoop shouldered little queen hurrying to keep up. He should have rolled over and dropped off years ago, but perhaps he had once been famous and those sort were never prepared to let go. Like birds changing mid-flight formation the pair veered off down a side street heading to join others of their persuasion for early evening drinks at the infamous Cockpit Bar.

Lights were coming on in all the bars now and Ferguson had a mental flash of those rustic families he had seen at dusk in 'Nam, squatting round a single hurricane lamp, washing, preparing their frugal evening meals, tending their babies or hammering out sheets of bent metal in preparation for some enterprising venture the next day.

Dusk seemed to be an especial part of South East Asia's kaleidoscopic life.

He smiled when he noticed many of the bar girls shucking off their day time flip-flops to dunk their little feet in bowls of turbid water, like pot plants drawing up nocturnal freshness by osmosis. They huddled together, jabbering in small intimate groups, squinting into plastic-backed pocket mirrors while titivating themselves for the night's endeavours, applying mascara with spit, eye shadow, rouge and lipstick, and finally brushing and combing out their lustrous blue-black hair.

The closer he drew to the Strip, Ferguson realised a substantial part of the US Navy was in town.

This usually meant all manner of shenanigans.

There were always enough whores in Pattaya to meet the heaviest demand on their services, and at a day's notice reinforcements could be bussed down from the Bangkok and Chiangmai motherlodes in the north, a few of them pouting catamites in drag. The more professional of this 'specialist group' had undergone the full kit and caboodle body conversion and become paid up members of the trans-sexual frorority. Some of these went on to join the globally touring groups of beautiful Bangkok Lady Boys who had become popular showbiz acts in recent years, their spangled 'stars' belting out Shirley Bassey numbers like there was no tomorrow.

Ferguson saw there were plenty of all sorts in town tonight. A commotion on the pavement opposite drew his attention to two men staggering along supporting a third lurching between them clutching a face masked with blood.

Ferguson knew what must have happened. Whenever the Fleet was in it was not only Thai girls who made a killing, but anyone with an ounce of acumen usually managed to get in on the act. When a ship's crew had a run ashore several of them ended up being carried back on board bruised, blackened, bloodied, broken, angry and wiser men, having had seven kinds of shit kicked out of them by Thai boxers.

Through first hand experience Ferguson, ships' doctors and others had acquired a healthy respect for the expertise of these pint-sized pugilists. When they hastily set up a ring in some Pattaya bar, donned baggy silk shorts and enormous gloves and bound their feet ready for the fray, it was as though they were preparing to ambush the latest batch of gullible white boys, who they knew had never encountered their breed before. A few beers at the bar with the unusual attraction of a couple of Thai fellows sparring in the adjoining ring? It always seemed like an inviting challenge.

Ferguson crossed the road to have a look at this newest boxing emporium the blooded combatant had just evacuated. It was redolent of what some similar establishment must have been like at Pearl Harbour in 1940. An enormous utilitarian bar awash with slops was dispensing beer to several hundred Tshirted American sailors, with an equal number of bare-legged jungle-bunnies crawling over the men's ears, hair, shirts, pants and pockets as a prelude to selling them a jump in the hay, but the main attraction was the boxing ring in the middle.

"Hey, 'Johnny' - you wanna turn too?"

One of the two boxers prancing playfully about up on the canvas was happily grinning, offering the loan of his gloves to another American boy to step up and tap his friend, the other flea-weight Thai boxer round the ring a bit. Even the other Thai was smiling inanely and nodding in support of this suggestion. Funny little death-wish fellows, folk might have thought: after all 'Johnny' was almost 6ft tall and weighed about 180lbs, whereas Ping-Pong and his mate were only about 5ft 3ins and 110lbs.

"Nah,'s alright," Johnny declined affably, taking another quick swig of his beer.

"G'arn, John-Boy," his mates encouraged him with back-slapping bonhomie, until Johnny gave in and climbed into the ring.

A barker/referee appeared in the ring behind him and signalled for silence, to cry: "Any you gen'l'mens wanna place bet, mebbe? Hunnert baht each on yow fwend to win. Whaddyow say? Easy money. More fun yeh"?

A guy in a frayed sarong, vest and flip-flops started rushing round with a greasy hat to gather up the hastily proffered bets. Only a few of Johnny's friends were artful enough to harbour misgivings about how the money might be reapportioned afterwards.

The preliminaries completed, a bell sounded and the scene started to become a whole lot nastier.

Nice young Johnny didn't quite know what hit him as 5ft 3ins of professionally trained Thai fighting fury erased its grin and unleashed a whir of flailing arms, legs, fists and feet, all pummelling impacts about Johnny's previously unsuspecting person, which left him reeling.

Johnny and his friends soon got the message.

To cries of: "C'mon, John-Boy, give him what for," soon followed by: "Come *on*, Johnny; for chrissakes, man – _kill_ the little bastard," Johnny discarded any thought of Queensbury rules and went hell-for-leather to knock one infuriating little Thai bundle into kingdom-come.

His efforts were as fruitless as swatting a fly in the dark.

After the third round Johnny's boot-faced companions retrieved him from the ring in a state of near insensibility, while the vicious adversary splashed about the blood-spattered canvas in a travesty of a victory hop before disappearing through the ropes and out the back for a tea break, and to avoid any vengeful recriminations.

"Go on, Jensen: *you* get in there and sort him out," someone yelled.

"You wanna 'venge yo fwend?" the Thai entrepreneur responded. "Jolly good show. Bets now two-hunnert baht," and up into the ring shambled Big Jenson McKlusky from Idaho and the engine room. All he intended to do was knock the next little chap's block off with one blow and call it quits, but three minutes later he had his right ear kicked off and staggered out of the ring nursing two broken ribs.

"Shit, this is ri*dic*ulous, man," snarled one of the irate Americans standing beside Ferguson. "Surely there's *some*one here to redress the balance and beat some shit out of that cheeky little bastard?"

"I tried to once, when I was younger," Ferguson told him, shouting to be heard above the hubbub. "Got a busted kneecap and broken nose for my trouble. Only way's to shoot 'em."

"Here's a guy looks like he intends doing something about it," the American grinned, indicating the ring with his beer can and finger. Ferguson glanced towards the ring, and groaned.

A hulk of a man was making his way slowly through the enthusiastic crowd.

Hans Ehrlich.

The previous three weeks of Spartan activity up on their border mission, combined with the past week's swimming and daily training along the beach had honed Hans's awesome musculature to a perfect peak. His pec slabs rippled like dustbin lids. His trapezius resembled a hanger for a suit of armour. The deltoids looked like moulded clay and his ridged abs like a tank track. The sweat-sheen from the battery of overhead lights accentuated Hans's peaks and troughs. His eyes glinted.

Ferguson was relieved. It was not the glint of battle he saw in the pale blue eyes, a glint which he knew so well, but the sparkle of amusement.

The big German was only playing. He extended his left arm and – the first Thai now having returned - beckoned both boxers with his fingers to come and take him.

The first little Thai appeared hesitant at first, then erupted across the canvas, sprang into mid-air, twisted his body into a half turn and lashed out with his left leg, aiming a vicious kick at Hans's chest.

Hans had sensed his small opponent's exact move. Instead of the usual backwards feint, he took a giant pace forward and thrust his chest out, reducing the distance between them to meet the attack full on.

This deft counteractive ploy threw the Thai's timing awry. His foot met Hans's chest sooner than he'd meant to, with the result that he was prevented from snapping his still straightening leg to its full extension.

At the moment of impact Hans took one enormous inhalation and expanded his chest to its full girth.

His pectorals acted as an unexpected springboard.

The surprised Thai was hurled back through the air, flailing his arms in a struggle to regain his balance, but with a panic-stricken expression he soared out over the ropes to land in a crumpled heap of limbs and silk shorts right in the laps of the wildly cheering crewmen in the third row.

Hans had laid not so much as a finger on him.

The furious Thai was spitting tacks as he scrambled to his feet, juddering with indignation amongst the discarded beer cans and cigarette butts. With a banshee oriental howl he leaped back towards the ring, more determined than ever to kick Hans's eyes back into their sockets, but a well-placed American foot tripped him up and sent him slithering down the wet lino to fetch up with a *clang* wrapped around one of the fire buckets by the steps.

Hell-bent on destruction the second Thai took off from his corner like a brainless kamikaze and he too let fly a vicious kick aimed at removing Hans's head.

Like King Kong plucking aircraft from the sky, Hans merely caught a hold of the Thai's ankle, then reached out and retrieved his other threshing foot. Holding the wriggling Thai upside-down by his ankles he walked across to the rope and deposited the little man head first into the same fire bucket his stunned friend was still embracing with his teeth.

The audience went wild. This was western supremacy at its best. One in the eye for the Pacific Basin.

Hans picked his silk shirt off the corner post and slipped it back on again, tucking it into his pants and readjusting his belt. He stepped between the ropes and out of the ring, declining the forest of beer cans thrust at him as he passed. Ignoring the accompanying rain of hefty back slaps he made his way over to Ferguson.

"It's pointless expecting you to maintain a low profile, isn't it," Ferguson rebuked him light-heartedly.

"Sorry." Hans grinned. "Just a quick burst on my banjo, that's all. I only ran five miles today so had some excess energy to dispose of. What brings you here, anyway?"

"Just out for a stroll. Few beers. Laughs – that sort of thing."

Later, when Ferguson got back to his hotel he found the briefest of notes pinned to the door of his room:
SPEAK IMMEDIATE H
Crumpling the note in his fist he went and hammered on Hans's door.

It was unlocked, and opened to his blow.

Although almost midnight Hans was showered, dressed and completing the finishing touches to packing.

"Going somewhere?"

"*Ja.* So are you," Hans told him curtly, buckling the strap on one suitcase. "There's a taxi waiting downstairs."

"I'm not sleeping in a taxi, I'm going to bed," Ferguson retorted stifling a yawn.

"You're going to Bangkok. This was waiting for you at Reception while you were doing walk-about."

He handed a fax across from the dressing table.

"Our plane leaves at 0400 and there's a two-hour drive ahead of us. We should shift."

"Hang about," said Ferguson. "All this says is **CONTACT LONDON IMMEDIATE Z**. Well – let's contact London."

"I already have," Hans snapped testily. "Thank God we've finished this Thai stint. There've been a string of incidents in a Middle East oil state, place called Ras-al-Am," he paused – "you know it, don't you? Didn't you say you'd been there once?"

"Certainly," Ferguson affirmed. "Know it well. I was a contract officer in their army a few years back. It's General Wally Stubbs's parish. What's been happening?"

"According to Reuben Dumperley when I contacted him, the Crown Prince's English mistress has been murdered."

Ferguson spluttered.

"His *what*? His *English* mistress? Crown Prince Fahad's a grown man. He speaks English fluently."

Hans made a silent gesture of despair.

"Well whaddya know? Young Fahad with a girlfriend,eh! Randy little git. What else?"

"A horde of local fishermen went banzai and stormed a Panamanian tanker, killing all the crew and tossing them overboard for the sharks. In addition to that, part of the army's principal ammunition depot's been blown up, and then this morning some saboteurs tried bringing down a Ras-al-Am Air Force jet. All this in the last three days – looks like the blue touch paper is fizzing on some sort of area of mounting discontent, wouldn't you say?"

"I'd say," Ferguson agreed. "Well – it looks as though it's next stop Raman, doesn't it. I suppose we'd better go."

This chapter of General Wally Stubbs's Zeta team was now almost complete.

TEN

The Middle East
Ras-al-Am

Squadron Leader Peter Irwin stood on the shimmering tarmac apron outside 1 Squadron's Ops Building adjacent to Raman's International Airport, grinned to himself and thought what a nice day it was.

The temperature this morning was 115 degrees Fahrenheit.

Airwork personnel in short-sleeved blue shirts, shorts, rolled down socks and suede desert boots, scurried about diligently and dirtily, servicing the squadron's Augusta Bell helicopters. The 205s and 215s with their 5,000lbs payload capacity were the Air Force's short range workhorses for ferrying stores, supplies, personnel and visitors up to the Army's remote jebel outposts, and were critical, too, in their casualty evacuation role. There were seldom enough of them, they were in constant demand and needed to be meticulously maintained. The Airwork employees were a rough-hewn team who responded well to their demanding job.

One of 1 Squadron's Rhodesian pilots came out of the Ops Building's flyscreen door, letting it bang behind him and strolled across to a waiting machine broiling beneath the merciless sun. Bas McLoughlin carried his flying helmet and gloves and wore the Air Force's regulation lightweight green zippered flying suit with a heavy black-handled knife strapped to his calf, a pair of suede desert boots, web belt and a 9mm Browning with a spare magazine of 10 rounds clipped to its canvas holster.

"Morning, Peter," he called, waving to Peter Irwin and some American officers who had just arrived in two Toyota Crown staff cars and were loosely grouped adjusting their shades and trouser belts.

69

"Hallo, Bas. Daily milk run?" Peter enquired.

"Not today, mate. Off to pick up a Special Forces chap stuck up in the hills somewhere with a bullet in his leg. See you in the bar lunchtime, 'kay?"

"See you, Bas – That's Bas McLoughlin," he explained, turning to face his American charges. "One of our best heli pilots . . . and no mean feat as a ladies' man, either, although as you'll have noticed there aren't too many of them for him to perform on out here. They're so rare that if ever one's in the offing the squadron rearranges its daily flight plan round Bas's social life. Anyway, gentlemen – you've read the outline brief on 1 Squadron and have been brought up to speed with its current role in support of the Army's Raman Brigade. Is there anything you'd like to ask me?"

Peter awaited their response, relaxed and confident, a 43-year-old British expatriate who knew what he knew. One thing he knew was that a succession of US Presidents were itching to gain a foothold in Ras-al-Am, a foothold which Sultan Hamad had consistently denied them. Yet despite his enlightened policies and his anglophilia, Hamad sometimes regretted the necessity for the highly visible British presence in his sultanate. They had sown seeds of permissiveness. What would it be like with Americans?

Individually Americans were charming, and usually tried and managed to tread warily, but a brigade of US Marines traipsing ashore at Raman, knowing they were to be denied women and bars but still expecting a good time off duty, would reduce the capital area's populace to a bemused frenzy.

What of any longer term prospects? Americans usually moved in for the duration. If they secured a presence in such a strategic Middle East foothold as Ras-al-Am it was unlikely they would relinquish it. The shock to the nation's culture would be complete – especially when 'the good times' inevitably followed. On hot nights Raman's harbour-front Corniche and waving palms would become the Saigon of the Gulf. The Sultan knew there was an inevitability about the twentieth-first century's approaching encroachment over his land, and that he would be unable to remain the ultimate arbiter of its selectivity forever, but he had vowed to keep such incursions at bay for as long as possible.

The US, though, persistently reminded him that however much of his nation's budget he channelled to defence, there would still be limitations to the deterrent his British-run forces could provide to counter any serious aggression against Ras-al-Am and his sovereignty. Why not divert his budget to more profitable areas of development, and let America take care of his country's defence realistically? Because of her Middle East strategic importance, any threat to Ras-al-Am would be a threat to America, the west and to world peace as well. America, then, would be obliged to assist Ras-al-Am. Why not let her start doing so now . . .? And so the argument continued.

Sultan Hamad's sole concession to the US overtures had been to invite observers to view certain aspects of the autumn military manoeuvres.

Today Peter Irwin had been deputed to host this small party of US Air Force officers round the airbase to assess aircraft landing capabilities. Tame stuff – but it ate into Peter's workload and meant he would have to cancel his squash game that afternoon in order to catch up in the office. Time was when as a thrusting and career conscious young RAF officer he would have welcomed such an opportunity to reveal his zeal. Now he preferred playing squash in the afternoons.

"Tell me, Raa'id," asked the portly bemedalled American colonel from beneath a scrambled-egg peak and mirrored shades, using Peter's Arabic form of rank. "How do you assess your pilots?"

"Ras-al-Ami pilots, Colonel – or British?"

"Both, I guess."

"We do have more than two, of course." This attempt at humour failed on the American waveband, so he quickly continued: "We assess them annually. Their superiors write confidential reports on them, much the same as I'm sure you in the US forces do."

"Yeah, Raa'id, sure," the American colonel persisted testily. He was hot and would have liked a cold beer and he wasn't quite sure whether this super-cool limey guy was deliberately being obtuse to rile him, or was just plain dumb. "But how do you reckon them?"

"Jolly nice chaps on the whole, I think, most of 'em."

"Hell, Raa'id, can they *fly*, goddammit?"

Peter Irwin looked at each of the Americans in turn.

There were six in the colonel's party. Mainly they wore stony expressions, portraying either detachment or embarrassment, but a couple of them were trying not to smile at their senior officer's bluntness.

"Yes, Colonel," Peter replied. "As a matter of fact they can fly quite well. I rather believe that is why most of them are here."

"I mean, I know this is a chopper squadron you got here and Skyvans and Defenders, but say, f'r instance, some of those Jaguars you got, I mean, if your mission is to scout the desert floor, how low could those babies go, huh?"

"Pretty much as low we'd like them to. I guess."

"No shit? You gonna try to tell me you got pilots in this little desert air force o' yourn can fly at fifty-feet?"

"They do it going up, Colonel, so I see no reason why they shouldn't be able to do it coming down."

"Bullshit, boy. I don't believe you. I flew in 'Nam and I was good. Damn good, you better believe that – and I never got lower'n fifty-feet."

"Perhaps there were trees in the way?"

"Trees, *sheeeit*. Hell no, there weren't no trees. We'd got rid o'all the trees. Now – how low can your boys fly?"

Peter thought he'd better show him.

In slowly measured tones, feeling like Michael Caine with a dangerous glint in his eye, he growled: "Colonel, in less than three minutes I can have six Jaguars flying in so low they'll take the shine off your shoes, and . . ." he lowered his gaze to take in the colonel's chest . . ."and off some of your medal ribbons too, sir."

"You hear that?" The colonel wheeled round to his embarrassed aides. "Our crap-shootin' limey friend here reckons he gonna show us how to *flyyy*. Why, I reckon . . ." He swung round to readdress Peter, but found he was already strolling away from them, speaking into the pocket size SABE transmitter he was carrying. "Just what the hell . . .?" bellowed the irate colonel . . .

Like most people Peter had suffered slights over the years for which he had thought of retorts in the bath afterwards, but each of those experiences had been worth it for the opportunity fate had now offered him on a silver platter to enjoy.

Sultan Hamad's air force had modelled itself almost exclusively along RAF lines. Neither Biggles, Rockfist Rogan nor the real aces of World Wars One and Two had survived by behaving like aerial cowboys. Pilots who beat up airfields for no reason other than bravura, usually suffered severe censure. Today though, as luck would have it, the Station Commander was away.

Peter Irwin weighed up his chances.

Both honour and the Air Force's professional expertise had been challenged in a most unsavoury fashion.

Peter knew that 15 miles to the north six Jaguar aircraft were at that moment climbing 5,000ft into the air prior to descending to do a wadi bash, a routine low-level patrol along valley floors searching out suspicious activity and advertising their presence, while also lending verisimilitude to the Army's current manoeuvres that were underway.

If his ploy went wrong Peter could have several dead pilots on his hands, a large bill and a court martial, yet despite such daunting deterrence the opportunity was too good to miss.

He had already raised the Jaguar flight leader over the air.

"Romeo Leader, this is Boxer. Come in. Over."

The smartly packaged, transistorised electronic circuitry crackled in Peter's palm.

"Romeo Flight Leader. Reading you. Send. Over."

"Roger, it's Peter. I'm in the process of selling the Air Force to some doubtful Americans down here who question our ability to fly. If you're not doing anything specific at the moment and felt inclined to disabuse them of such a notion, I'd be most grateful. Over."

His airborne friend's affirmatory chuckle was music to Peter's ears.

"Romeo Leader. I read you. You're on. Where are you? Over."

"Bang on the pan outside 1 Squadron office. Over."

"Romeo Leader. Flight peeling off to reform now. Be with you in figures two minutes. This'll cost you a bottle of sherbert, Peter. Keep your head down. See you in a jiffy. Out."

"Champagne's on ice, waiting for you, Roger. Give, 'em stick for England. Out."

"*Christ*, you British are casual, the Colonel snarled. "There I was in the middle of speaking to you and you just upped and turned your back on me and walked away. I thought you British officers were meant to be gentlemen. Why, if I . . ."

"Colonel, for the most part we are gentlemen – when the occasion allows. You asked to see a low level fly-past," interjected Peter firmly.

"Mebbe I did, but that sure as hell doesn't excuse bad manners. Why, if I . . ."

" . . . If I might suggest, Colonel, I think it would be advisable if you and your officers were to adopt a low profile. Our planes will be here quite soon."

"Low profile? What you talkin' 'bout, boy?"

"Colonel, I would appreciate it if you would refrain from calling me 'Boy'. Apparently you have been more successful in your career than I have in mine, perhaps they do things differently in America, but I imagine we are both of a similar age. My rank is Squadron Leader, or as you seem to prefer, Raa'id. And my name is Peter Irwin. You are quite at liberty to call me Peter, and when I say I suggest you adopt a low profile it means I think you should get your goddam ass on the floor, Buster, because the planes are coming into view over that scarp, *now . . .*"

Peter dropped onto one knee, and all the Americans' heads whipped round to follow his gaze. Six green dots appeared over the western horizon, approaching them rapidly.

The Americans smiled at Peter kneeling, and dismissively stood their ground, wishing they had defied the security ban and brought cameras with them.

The oncoming Jaguars swept silently in, low and lethal,

towards the airstrip. Quickly they loomed larger in the cobalt sky, and then one after another peeled smoothly out of formation, turned from their approaching arc, fell sideways out of the sky and levelled with the runway. Flying in close line astern they sped along at 50ft above ground level, rapidly reducing to 40ft; 30ft; 20ft; . . . and then for 800 metres tore past with a decibel-shattering roar at a speed of 550 knots and no more than 10ft above ground zero.

In the face of this awesome display of aerial bravura each of the Americans had hurled himself face down onto the tarmac.

As if the planes hadn't been enough to do the trick, Peter's heart started to thud even faster in his chest, and he froze with horror at what he then saw. "Oh, *sheeeit*," he mouthed, not wanting to shout out in front of the Americans.

As the sixth Jaguar flashed past in front of them at virtually ground zero, he saw an airport Land Rover had come accelerating out from some buildings and was bucketing across the airstrip directly into the plane's path.

Was its driver *blind?* Had his *brain* snapped? What the hell had happened?

It was all over in seconds.

The Jaguar's alert pilot flicked-in his plane's re-heat, there was a deafening rush of flame as its afterburners ignited the raw fuel injected into the tubes, and instantaneously the plane banked almost perpendicularly to surge with phenomenal impetus into the sky, just nudging the top of the Land Rover's superstructure as it roared past.

As the Jaguar thundered away to reform with the other five planes and resume their more legitimate business beyond the hills, the Land Rover went careening and breaking up across the tarmac as though landing off a cliff. Already a crash vehicle was screaming out towards it, its crew jumping off alongside before either vehicle had completely come to rest.

Peter's throat flickered with presentiment as he returned quickly to the Ops Room, leaving the Americans clambering to their feet and trying to regain their composure.

One of the less career-conscious of them hurried eagerly after him.

"I gotta admit it, those sure are one hell of a rip-shit bunch of flyers you got there, sir," he enthused, dusting his knees as he spoke.

"I'm glad you think so," Peter retorted. "We can fly quite low at times. When need arises."

"As for that finale with the Jeep, I gotta tell you, that was something else. What *timing*. What split second orchestration. I mean, *Sheeeit* – I ain't *never* seen anything quite like that before."

"No? As a matter of fact nor have I," Peter admitted drily. It was still nice occasionally to be able to be infuriatingly British, he thought, leaving the American staring open-mouthed at him as he mounted the steps to the Ops Room in anticipation of the bollocking of his life. The fly screen door banged shut behind him.

ELEVEN

"JEEZus CHRIST -," wailed Lt-Col David Marks, the 42-year-old Commanding Officer of the Sultan's Armoured Regiment as the G-forces exerted by the Jaguar's climb pulled his mouth into a rictus that set cathedral bells ringing in his brain.

Flexibility was the hallmark of most army officers, and David Marks was trained and well used to adapting to the host of different situations he encountered in his daily round, but looping-the-loop in a fighter jet had left him foundering a bit, he had to admit.

He clenched his fists, hung in his straps and went where Allah, aerial dynamics and the will of Flt-Lt Roger Laycock, the pilot, took him.

It had all started in the mess bar the previous evening when he and the Air Force agreed it might be a good idea for him to get a bird's eye view, other than by the usual helicopter, of his regiment's exercise positions on the plain.

Everything had been quite exhilarating until Roger, the flight leader, received that call from his idiot compadre down on the ground; then it was like taking off in a rocket to Mars. David was slammed back against his seat so forcibly that he felt the snot sucked back up his nostrils in one long slither. *Ugh.* He had no doubt that from the ground their performance cut a dash in most people's eyes, but he was now extremely pleased that when at the age of 18 he was trying to decide between pale blue and khaki, he had failed his aircrew selection test at RAF Hornchurch and remained a ground-borne pongo for the rest of his service.

Roger Laycock was now pulling out of his searing climb to level off at 5,000ft to circle and approach the wadi to pursue their original patrol.

The view was breathtaking. It was like flying over a school atlas.

Blue sky with eagles in it; blue Arabian sea with shark and barracuda gliding about; on the ground jagged, barren and inhospitable jebel with camel thorn, snakes, scorpions and furnace-like temperatures.

What on earth was he doing? What had possessed this normally rational man of 42 with a good education, a lovely wife and two promising teenaged sons, to be playing silly buggers in a jet plane over Arabia at 11.10 hours on a Monday morning?

He should have been in a blue pinstripe at an office in London, or striding out across the South Downs in a Barbour and tweeds with his dogs.

When was he going to stop playing soldiers, grow up and settle down?

Even though he was a cavalry officer, to remain fit and on top of the climatic environment David made a point of gambolling up razor-sharp mountain sides with a rifle and large pack occasionally, able to beat a company of fit 20-year-old Baluch and Ras-al-Ami jundees to the top. Not many UK men of his age could do that.

Plus he had a healthy bank balance.

These were just two of the reasons why this normally sane and rational man of 42 was in a jet plane over Arabia at 11.10 hours this Monday morning.

"Masara Point ahead." Roger Laycock's voice crackled through the earphones, interrupting David's thoughts.

The six planes were weaving along the wadi floor as though flying through a computer game's simulated high street: Marks and Sparks on the right, Debenhams on the left . . . Cave mouths, shelves, ledges and rock formations flashed past, resembling some troglodytic society's shop fronts.

David recognised his regiment's laagers immediately, their emplacements and dry stone sangars erected against the dun-coloured hillsides. He was satisfied that they were well camouflaged. Knowing the location of each position David knew what to look for and where, but an enemy pilot would have problems locating them.

It was fun playing jet pilot for a day, he thought as Roger Laycock pulled the Jaguar into another steep climb and together they and the other five planes swept up out of the wadi and away back to base.

After they'd landed, his bowels still in an uproar David tottered down the Ops Room steps to find his driver waiting agitatedly on the forecourt.

"I'm glad you're back, sir," the Baluch corporal threw up a salute. "The General wants to see you immediately."

It was no more than a 10 minute drive from the airport to Masela Camp. General Wally's house overlooked the camp from a commanding position on the plateau of a rocky sienna bluff in the foothills of the surrounding jebel. The house resembled the low-slung whitewashed hacienda of a Spanish grandee, its walls and slopes draped with pink flowers and greenery, affording it privacy and an air of opulence.

General Wally was standing in the drive wearing a green T-shirt, a baggy pair of hockey shorts and beaten-up trainers.

"Glad you made it so soon." He beckoned David to join him and stroll across to sit on a nearby stone wall, just out of reach of the sprinkler playing on the sloping lawn. "Enjoy your swan?"

"Yes, sir. Very useful – thanks."

"News travels fast, Davey. I gather one of the pilots in your flight totalled a Land Rover that was trying to knock him off course while he was doing a close-up inspection trip of the airstrip?"

"I believe so, yes sir. I did catch some fairly strong language coming over the air, but only learned afterwards what had happened. His evasive action must have been pretty impressive, though."

"Bit worrying, David, on top of everything else. Apparently it was a driverless vehicle."

"How do you mean, sir?"

"No one driving. It had been set on course with the throttle jammed."

"Shit; that's a bit ominous, isn't it, sir?"

"Exactly. Some bugger in a work hangar was quick off the mark there alright. Obviously the incident's connected with all this other brouhaha that's brewing up around us. The Air Force will have a board of enquiry of course, but I doubt they'll ever find who was responsible, although I guess their Peter Irwin's going to find himself up for a bit of a roasting. This isn't what I called you in for though, David. I'm pulling the Army in from the field."

"You mean . . . cancelling the manoeuvres, sir?"

"Yes, I want everyone back in their camps, on call, until we know what this whole shebang is about and it's going to escalate. Signal's already gone. They're breaking camp now. Your second-in-command's fully capable of bringing your regiment's tanks in, isn't he?"

"Absolutely, sir: but I guess we'll find out for sure, won't we."

"Good, because there's something else I'd like you to do for me. Three gentlemen – I use the term advisedly, will be arriving here some time during the next three days . . . I don't know where from or which flights they'll be on. One of them is an American, name of Chuck Henderson. There will also be a big blond Bavarian number, name of Hans Ehrlich – and a Brit - Don Ferguson. Check incoming flight manifests, meet them personally, and book them in to the Tasa Hotel. Soon as they've cleaned up and rested, bring them to me. You're role is Link Man. And, David - ."

"Sir?"

"Keep quiet about it."

TWELVE

White, modern and imperious the Tasa Hotel sat atop a hill at Merrin Heights, the swishest residential development in the whole of Raman.

The people who lived in the well-appointed Arab mansions, were mostly high-ranking Ras-al-Ami government officials, commercial executives and their wives and families, assorted consuls and pro-consuls, and one old Etonian gun-runner – Giles Carrington.

Semi-naked and bronzed, Giles sat sprawled in a cane chair on the top veranda of his sumptuous home, sipping ice-cool lime juice and inwardly seething.

He could feel the sun topping-up the colour on the leathery skin of his well-defined physique. It was a body which despite the ravages of time and the abuse that had been heaped upon it, still tapered to a narrow waist and slim hips.

But gun runners got themselves zapped occasionally.

Giles Carrington had been in the top league of his profession, and his body bore ample evidence of the price he'd paid to be there. Livid cicatrices laced his skin in testimony to the sharp and heavy metal he'd encountered. As well as a savage khunjar scar in his groin, a jagged red contour snaked from his left armpit to his navel where he had once come to grips with some vicious razor wire.

Another angry scar indicated that either a butcher with a blunt cleaver had removed his appendix, or he'd twisted himself off someone's bayonet. His broad pectoral slabs had at some time withstood grenade shrapnel bouncing off them, and it was evident that various calibres of bullets had ploughed in and out of his back, as though he were a bomber stitched with

81

flak.

At age 53 and 6ft 4in Giles had been stabbed, shot at, blown up and trampled on more times than he could remember.

He no longer ran guns or accepted Sultans' contracts on their enemies, nor did he go adventuring up the Araby coast very often, but was now a respected elder citizen, as well as being the titular head of the Ras-al-Am Intelligence Ministry.

At his time of life he should now have been able to sit back and enjoy the fruits of his labours and prestigious infamy, but there were two great regrets in his life.

Giles Carrington had no son. He was sterile.

It had happened near the mouth of the Red Sea, off the Gulf of Aden near the island of Socotra, in 1957. Giles had been smuggling a cargo of ammunition from Mombasa to Oman's Masirah Island on a lateen-rigged dhow, when one of the hastily recruited waterfront scum he'd been obliged to employ suddenly decided that he didn't like this particular English very much and stabbed him deeply in the groin with a rusty khunjar, the curved and ornately gilded dagger Arabs wore tucked in their waist belts.

The consequence of Giles's wrath at this personal affront was that the ill-advised Arab was terminally wasted later that night. Giles slipped his dismembered pieces over the dhow's side by moonlight. Russian submarines might still see his skull grinning up at them from the sandy seabed off Socotra, grinning from the small fish darting in and out of his nostrils and eye sockets, but grinning also from the fact that his dagger thrust had robbed the reviled English of the children he yearned to father.

"Count your blessings, old son," the British Army medical officer in Aden told him, once the potentially gangrenous wound had healed. "You'll still be able to get it up, but without the fear of impregnating anyone."

Leaning forward, Giles placed the knife with which he had been shaping a piece of wood back on the table, poured himself another fresh lime juice from the jug, popped an olive into his mouth and stood up to walk over to the brass telescope, set on its tripod by the veranda's balcony.

Peering down over the balustrade he could see Ngabile, Sekelaga and Lwiza, his trio of gorgeous young 'supplementary' Zanzibari wives (the 'senior' ones were in the house), swimming naked in the pool below. Nature had given the three of them all-over tans at birth, and they only ever swam nude for convenience and its delicious sensation. Giles stifled a smile when he thought of the consternation that would have ensued if he hadn't had a 15ft wall built around his property. He was also virtually inviolate through the Sultan's patronage.

Sultan Hamad had been Giles's friend and mentor for almost 30 years. The length of his domicility in the country had gifted him Ras-al-Ami nationality. He had developed a powerful voice in the forging of national policies and had long been on the Palace 'A' List for receptions, dinners, functions and parades.

The Sultan's dynasty had ruled this country for over 200 years, having usurped the previous ruling clan through a bloody confrontation in the mid-eighteenth century, a clan whose descendants, living in England, harboured a deep resentment towards their usurpers.

Despite Ras-al-Am's leap forward into the twentieth-century, the current fall in oil prices had left the country's coffers clanking with small change. Long-term projects had been abandoned or shelved. There had been a dramatic cutback in the expatriate European and Asian labour forces that effectively ran the country. The economy had to be shored up with massive international loans that mortgaged Ras-al-Am's future well into the next century.

However, none of this was the reason for Giles's second great abiding regret.

Mohammed al-Ajmi was the reason for this. He was also the reason why Giles was inwardly seething – firstly because he was late for their appointment, and secondly because of the chain of events that had led up to the appointment being made.

Glancing up from admiring the three glistening beauties splashing about and giggling like Alma-Tadema models in his pool, Giles saw two large black Mercedes turn into his drive and scrunch slowly up to the house.

Mohammed al-Ajmi and his entourage had at last deigned to arrive. Late, as usual – fully in keeping with Arab practice.

After living amongst them for 30 years Giles was thoroughly attuned to the Arab psyche, and could understand why they were not a universally popular race. They used their fingers like bradawls to dig out their nostrils, hoiked and spat all over the place and held their male friends' hands in public, then made an enormous fuss when heathen westerners pointed the soles of their feet at them if they'd been obliged to sit cross-legged on the floor. Moreover – when awarded the arguable delicacy of a sheep's eye, a delicacy you had earnestly tried to avoid, and you carelessly picked it up in your left hand, the one Allah had decreed should be used to wipe their bottoms, they got indignant about that too.

Why didn't they learn to use knives and forks, instead of fingers?

If Jesus on a donkey appeared down one of Ras-al-Am's back streets, so long as his papers were in order he would scarcely attract a second glance . . . while Jaguar strike aircraft furrowed contrails in the azure heights above, and computer operated artillery boomed in the surrounding hills. Funny old world, thought Giles, this half Bethlehem, half Star Wars.

The curtain was drawn back and Mohammed al-Ajmi came out onto the veranda. The Sultan's 27-year-old nephew was a small man with hawk-like features. Oxford and Sandhurst educated he was an urbane intellectual, but a fanatical light gleamed in his piercing gaze.

Avoiding the protracted ritual of Arabic greeting he shook Giles's proffered hand and arranged himself in one of the veranda's cane chairs.

"What's the problem?" he demanded, uncharacteristically coming straight to the point.

"Perhaps I should ask you that, Mohammed?" Giles retorted, offering his guest a lime juice which he sipped gently.

"I think we should review our strategy," continued Giles. "The activities over the past few days have jeopardised our entire master plan. Your cousin's mistress has been murdered.

84

An oil tanker has been over-run and all its crew killed within Ras-al-Ami waters. Your people were responsible for trying to destroy the Army's main ammunition depot – and then only this morning some fool tried to bring down one of the Air Force's fighter planes with a Land Rover. What the hell is going on, Mohammed? Why not put an advertisement in the paper announcing our intention, informing them we're just having a few practise runs first so that they can get used to the idea?"

"Giles, I agree," the Arab conceded, taking another sip of lime juice. "Things have got out of control. You and I are the overall strategists. The al-Bakri brothers are our field commanders and tacticians. Over the past months they have raised a considerable rebel army and engendered unswerving support for our cause. Unfortunately, the al-Bakri bothers are at odds with each other over the implementation of our policy. Suleman, the older brother, supports our strategy. Hilal, the younger one, is a hot-head. He has been agitating for a long time to get on with it. Fifty per cent of the rebels support his view. It is they who sprang the leash and perpetrated the atrocities of the past few days. The force is now divided. Those who are loyal to Suleman and are still waiting to carry out our plan, and those who support Hilal whose actions, as you so rightly say, have trumpeted our existence and agenda to the authorities. This means that now there are only two courses of action we can take."

"And they are?"

"Either we abort, and skulk off like foxes, or we must bring everything forward and activate the master strategy now."

"We are now too far involved to escape detection," said Giles, "nor do I think such a course would attract much clemency at our reckoning, do you? We have no option. We must activate immediately."

"I agree." Mohammed nodded. "The Army is still on manoeuvres in the field, but I understand it has been recalled to barracks. They will need a few days to re-establish themselves so we must strike before then, while Masela Camp is still on skeleton manning. In the meantime, tell me – where

85

is your man, Mr Horne? Will he be beside you in this venture?"

"We can count on him. I pay him enough to go through hell and high water for me – besides which he enjoys the nature of the work I give him. He's doing a job in the hills at the moment, but he's due back later today or tomorrow."

"Very well," Mohammed said, getting up. "I will gather together the Grand Council of Brothers tonight and let them know of our decision."

With a swish of his gleaming robes he strode from the veranda, leaving the curtain through which he passed flicking its hem with the disturbance.

Giles opened a box of cheroots and tucked one between his teeth. Snapping shut his gold lighter he leaned over the balustrade once more to watch his wives still at play in the pool down below.

It was a bold step he and Mohammed were about to take, but in his opinion a necessary one. Great moments seldom came lightly. One was now afoot.

History was in the making and he, Giles Carrington, had been cast as its principal architect.

Out in the wild blue yonder, as General Wally was fond of calling Ras-al-Am's furnace-like interior: out in the bundu, the boondocks, the ulu, Brigadier Mustapha Said, the Army's Deputy Commander, was ill at ease.

Instead of allowing him to continue lolling comfortably about enjoying his rank and privileges and impressing junior officers with his trumped-up 'war stories' before turning in for the night, the wheel of fate had capriciously chosen to stop for once with its arrow pointing in his accountable direction.

With barely suppressed glee one of the Baluch sergeants in the Signal Regiment had burst into Brigadier Mustapha's tent and thrust an OP IMMEDIATE signal at him. The Brigadier had been enjoying his third demi-tasse of after-dinner coffee with a cross-legged huddle of sycophants, and although the signal imbued him with enhanced importance he resented its intrusion into his socialising.

He read:

CANCEL MANOEUVRES STOP WITHDRAW ARMY IMMEDIATE TO STATIC PEACETIME LOCATIONS MESSAGE ENDS

Mustapha's crown-and-three-pips combination were propped up solely by his family's influence at Court, and much wind and bluster. Then again, he *was* the Army's Deputy Commander, and despite his shortcomings his rank and position gave him considerable influence.

He could do it. There was no war on. All he had to do was utter the right cries, press a few buttons and the Army would collapse its tents, break camp and rumble into its own withdrawal.

His subordinates would see to it. Some of them were quite good. The blame for any foul-ups would devolve upon them, of course.

In any case he didn't feel there was much that could be done tonight. Was there?

Better to let everyone get a good night's sleep and then move out after first light, after a bit of breakfast.

He waved a dismissive hand at the half-dozen or so junior officers who constituted tonight's coterie, and they stood up and withdrew back to their own tents.

When they had gone Mustapha's brow furrowed as he addressed his problem.

He twitched and fidgeted about how best to handle the situation. Months of planning had gone into this manoeuvre. Had the Sultan had another of his whims, or was something ominous arising in the Gulf? Or in Raman itself, even?

It was puzzling.

There was only one cure for puzzlement he decided. Reaching out for his valise he relieved it of its bottle of David Walker Black Label.

THIRTEEN

The distinctive green-white-and-burgundy Gulf Air Golden Falcon Lockheed TriStar Flight GF 126 stood cooling on the shimmering apron at Bahrain's Muharraq Airport, having completed its long-haul during the night from Heathrow via Schiphol and offloaded half its passengers.

Its doors were open. Most of its seats were vacant. The NO SMOKING signs were on.

The cabin crew had nothing to do during the remainder of this hour's stopover but relax and exchange gossip with each other.

It was 7.00 a.m. Those passengers going on to the Sultanate of Ras-al-Am sat dozing, reading or staring into space.

Among them was Julie Adams, an attractive 23-year-old brunette sitting in an aisle seat halfway down the cabin. Julie was a nurse, dedicated to her profession, but no longer able to live comfortably on a UK salary.

The prospect of glamour and financial reward in the Middle East appealed to her, and she had signed a two-year contract in London to join the expatriate nursing sorority at the Ras-al-Am Armed Forces Base Hospital at Masela Camp, near Raman. It would be her first real grown-up adventure and she was both full of trepidation and excited.

Less than 24-hours ago one of the doctors at her old hospital, St Thomas's, had pumped what had felt like a pint-and-a-half of immunoglobulin into her buttock to ward off hepatitis.

Her tired, cramped body was also in the process of immunising itself against cholera and yellow fever, tetanus, polio and malaria.

Their Bahrain stopover now complete, the cabin crew roused themselves to smooth their beige slacks and readjust their Arab-style headgear to start stowing the hand baggage of the fresh passengers filing on to the plane for the last leg of the journey down to Ras-al-Am.

Julie knew nothing about ethnic groupings in the Middle East, and she was finding it difficult to pigeon-hole her fellow passengers. Pakistanis and Baluch in light baggy pyjama suits jostled with turbaned Sikhs and home-going Ras-al-Amis in their dish-dashas and embroidered kumma caps.

Two blowsy Englishwomen in limp dresses and flip-flops seated themselves in front of Julie and started to discuss the availability of products in the Gulf compared with any high street at home.

A biblical-looking bearded hill tribesman, white-swathed and dignified took the aisle seat next to her and sat staring hypnotically at the back of the seat in front of him. It was wonderful.

All the new passengers were on board now and the two seats beside Julie were still empty. What a relief. She would be able to stretch out to sleep. Then she glanced up and her heart sank. Oh, no – .

Advancing down the aisle towards her came a gargantuan individual toting a canvas bag that looked as though it contained 100 bricks.

Behind this blond, toothpick-chomping giant was an almost equally large man hefting a battered leather shoulder bag that might once have contained the Dead Sea Scrolls. How had they been allowed to bring them on board as cabin baggage?

Each of them was wearing a well-worn bush jacket with the sleeves rolled up, tough sand-coloured whipcord slacks and suede desert boots. They were brown mahogany, rugged as hell, devastatingly attractive, and Julie somehow knew their allotted seats were the two vacant ones beside her.

While the blond behemoth crammed his canvas hold-all into the overhead locker, his swarthier companion looked down and flashed Julie a dazzling smile.

"I'm so sorry we've come to descend on you like this," he

apologised. "Would you prefer to have the window seat?"

"Well, er – yes; thank you, I think I will," Julie replied, unaccountably flustered. "You're going to have enough trouble squeezing in as it is."

She unbuckled her seat belt and wriggled over. The darker man chuckled as he eased himself in beside her, leaving the aisle seat free for his companion.

Julie gazed out of the window, trying to pretend they weren't there. It was hopeless. The two men suffused the entire cabin with their presence.

It was like sitting next to Clint Eastwood and Arnold Schwarzenegger. Julie couldn't stop her heart thumping or her knees from shaking. *Damn* sexuality – she thought, struggling to suppress her feelings. They were probably no more than a couple of oil roustabouts, or out-of-work cowboys of some sort.

The TriStar's crew had boarded and gone forward to the flight deck. Soon the engines were whining, the air conditioning came back on and the captain taxied the plane out onto the main runway, increased to maximum revs, let off the brakes and they zoomed down the tarmac to lift off on their journey to Ras-al-Am.

They flew south-east over Qatar and on across the other Emirates before turning south over blistering jebel and the shimmering haze of the Gulf where the world's oil tankers could be seen queuing to await their call forward through the perilous Strait of Hormuz.

"Do you work in Raman, or are you just visiting?"

Julie was startled by the deep voice rumbling in her ear beside her. She turned to acknowledge the question, only to find herself mesmerised by a pair of sparkling blue eyes framed in laughter lines.

"I'm going to work in the military hospital there," she replied. "I'm a nurse. And you?"

"Just passing through for a while," said the man. "We're photo-journalists."

"I'd wondered what you were toting in those enormous bags of yours." Julie laughed. "I suppose you're covering something to do with the war?"

He smiled non-commitally. "Have you been this way before?" .

"No, never. I'm a bit worried about it, because one of the first things I've got to do when I arrive is go up-country to collect a car."

"Why's that? Plenty of rental agencies in Raman."

"It's a silly story. Until last month my sister was a hospital nurse at a place called Basira Oasis, but she refused to perform a personal service for an influential Arab gentleman, so now she's a nurse in Bournemouth. She was given only twenty-four hours to leave the country, so she had to leave her car behind. I bought it from her and now I've got to go and collect it."

"Shouldn't be a problem," he reassured her. "There's a good road from Raman to Basira. Takes about three hours each way, mind."

"How will I get there?"

"Grab a lift in a military vehicle. They're going up and down the whole time. Er – excuse me a moment," he said, turning to acknowledge a nudge from his companion. Julie followed their gaze and saw that another hulking brute was bearing down the aisle towards them, a man she remembered seeing board the plane at Schiphol. He was beaming from ear to ear.

"What the hell are *you* two guys doing here?" he boomed, "as if I didn't know . . ."

The three men rained affectionate slaps and punches on each other and pumped each other's hands.

"*Chuck*: Chuck bloody *Henderson*. Where the hell'd they get *you* from? Prison?"

"Could say that, Ferguson. From a hell-hole called Surinam, as a matter of fact. Four days ago I was stuck up the Maroni River and couldn't be more happy than I was to get a signal from the Man. Same as you, I guess. Where have you and Hans been hiding?"

"Thailand. We left Don Muang this morning."

"Ma'am, excuse all this noise," the American acknowledged Julie. "These guys and I go back a long way together. We haven't seen each other in a few years. I couldn't believe it when I saw them get on the plane just now. I had to come across and renew our acquaintance, you understand."

"Of course." Julie smiled. "Are you a photo-journalist too?"

The American paused for an instant. "Er – not exactly, no Ma'am. I collect butterflies."

The hell you do – Julie thought, excitement coursing to the tips of her toes.

"Ladies and gentlemen, we shall shortly be landing in Raman. Will you please return to your seats now, fasten your seat belts, put your seats in the upright position and extinguish all cigarettes. On behalf of Captain Withington and his crew we hope you have enjoyed your journey."

The TriStar descended to land with a rushing squeal and a squirt of rubber smoke from its scorched tyres as it surged up the runway, decreasing speed every second.

Sister Julie Adams and General Wally Stubbs's Zeta Team had arrived in Ras-al-Am.

It was 8.30 a.m. local time.

Feeling like an anchovy wedged between two doorstop-sized slices of bread Julie edged along the aisle between Ferguson and Hans, the passengers shuffling ahead of them.

Julie pushed her sunglasses into her hair as she stepped out into the white hot glare on the platform at the head of the aircraft steps: Jesus Christ.

Sunshine.

Oh, *Wow! Shit* – it was hot. Oven door stuff. Julie gazed and squinted excitedly about at her first landfall in the Middle East. It was difficult for her to maintain her carefully cultivated façade of ice cool sophistication and aloof detachment.

This wasn't Knightsbridge. Out here she *hadn't* seen and done it all before and did not feel like assuming an expression of bored indifference. This was real earth stuff: a political earthquake zone surrounded by Israel, Iran and Iraq.

As they walked across the tarmac to the airport building the American caught up with Julie's new 'friends'. The three men stood head and shoulders above the rest of the passengers. They stood back to allow Julie to enter the cool of the airport ahead of them. As her handbag and small hold-all glided through the X-Ray machine operated by Ras-al-Ami airport police, she noticed that Ferguson, Hans and Chuck Henderson had been ushered through without having their bags checked. They were met by a rugged-looking sun-bronzed Englishman in a green army uniform emblazoned with Arabic insignia; he led them through passport control desk and customs without stopping. Julie wondered whether she would ever see any of them again.

Half-an-hour later, when a visa had been stamped in her passport and an obnoxious Arab policeman had rifled through her cases, Julie was free to depart the airport main doors where she was greeted by two friends of her sister who had come to meet her.

"You're Julie?" one of them asked. "Good; I'm Samantha. Welcome to your sunny new life. How's Tess? We want to hear all about her. The car's over here. Your flat's all ready at Masela Camp. It's only five minutes up the road. The Army's away on manoeuvres so you couldn't have arrived at a better time. There's nothing to do."

The girls laughed.

"Matron hasn't even got your name on the roster till next week," said Jenny, "so you'll have plenty of time to settle in. We're going swimming this afternoon. Want to come?"

"Well, yes – of course. I'd love to," Julie replied breathlessly as Samantha banged the boot lid shut and they all piled in to her white Toyota Starlet. "This is all too much. I'm overwhelmed. All this . . . *and* they pay us £1,500 a month. Tax free," Julie cried.

"Not quite," Jenny corrected her, as Samantha slammed the car into reverse, straightened up and roared out of the car park. "The exchange rate's a bit on the blink at the moment. All you'll get this month is £1,475."

"Oh, rats. In that case I shall just have to go back to Britain," Julie laughed.

She had only been in the country five minutes, and was loving it already.

FOURTEEN

Drongo Horne ignored the stares he was attracting as he sat sipping his third cold beer at the tinted panoramic window of the Tasa Hotel's cocktail bar.

In the early evening this window popularly became a vantage point to watch the sun go down and see the promenaders starting to appear.

During the day it overlooked off-duty air stewardesses posturing with Pimms and gins in their bikinis round the pool. It also overlooked the tennis courts and the beach, the Gulf of Ras-al-Am and the mauve haze of the inhospitable jebel from which Drongo had just returned.

A dozen or so sophisticated, nicely-dressed guests sat in the air-conditioned comfort. Three of these were in national dress, the remainder Dutch, German or British.

Heide Ritter from Düsseldorf had been in Raman for three days with her husband Dieter, on a sales trip for Magirus Deutz's heavy truck division. She was bored already. She had spent the morning at the poolside and slipped a wrap over her bikini to join Dieter for his lunchtime drinks meeting with the company's Ras-al-Am agent. Heide knew her husband would have preferred her to have dressed more formally, but she didn't give a damn. The weather in Germany had been so atrocious that she wasn't going to waste a second of this sunshine trip.

She toyed with her Martini, impatiently rocking her crossed leg and high-heeled sandal while Dieter droned on with Mustapha about their business problems. Heide thought that in his traditional dish-dasha Mustapha looked about as glamorous as the Ghost of Jacob Marley.

All Ras-al-Ami men looked the same to her, attired in tasselled white bed-sheets down to their ankles. Why didn't they wear soft kid boots or something more romantic, instead of sticking their bare feet into clompy sandals that accentuated their big toes? Where was some Wolf of Kabul, or Red Shadow?

Just then her gaze fell on the interesting-looking man with a black eye-patch, sitting at the bar.

Drongo Horne invariably fetched up at the Tasa for a long slow wet when he came down from the jebel, and over the years had come to treat the place as his local. It allowed him to relax and readjust to normal living before reporting back to Mr Carrington. It never occurred to him that his brigand appearance might cause consternation to the more civilised guests. He parked his Toyota Land Cruiser outside, brusquely acknowledged the boys at the door in near faultless Arabic or Urdu, strolled through to the bar, propped his Kalashnikov against the rail and sat quietly drinking his keenly anticipated line-up of beers.

Drongo's origins were obscure.

It was popularly believed that he was part British, Belgian and/or Polish, but no one – not even himself, apparently – knew for sure.

His clothes were black with sweat, thick with dust, sand and dried blood. His hair and scalp were matted and filthy. His backside had stopped itching but was still as rich as a curry pot, so he always ditched his pants when cleaning up after a field trip, condemning them as beyond redemption.

The green web combat belt round his waist was heavily slung with water-bottle pouches, a holstered 9mm Browning, a first aid kit, a Puma hunting knife and a bayonet. Suspended from a thick gold chain around his neck was an ampoule of morphine. His hands were black, chipped and broken nails thick with dirt.

Mesmerised by his appearance, Heide watched his every move and now endured a frisson when he placed his tankard on the bar and slipped a hand round his hip to draw the bayonet from its scabbard. She shuddered to think that he might suddenly have seen someone's reflection in the bar's mirror and was about to turn and hurl the blade at them, but all he did was start to dig some of the dirt from under his nails.

Breaking off his conversation with Mustapha, Dieter leaned over to touch his wife's knee. Preoccupied fantasising about the man at the bar, she failed to notice her husband had finished his discussion.

"Will you join us for lunch, Liebling?" he asked, unaware of her distraction.

"Oh." Heide clutched her throat, and turned. "I'm sorry. I was distracted watching that interesting man up at the bar. It's not often you see someone so colourful, is it?" She laughed.

"He looks a bit drab and dirty to me," Dieter remarked dismissively. Mustapha looked over his shoulder to see who they were talking about.

"That is a very bad man," he told them quietly. "His name is Drongo Horne. The Police have been trying to have him deported from Ras-al-Am for a long time. He is the chief lieutenant of Giles Carrington, a very influential Englishman and friend of the Sultan. The Carrington person is the head of our Intelligence Ministry, but he is reputed to have done very bad things as well."

"How interesting," said Heide. "Yes – he does look as though he might be capable." Her pulses racing with presentiment, Heide dragged her gaze away from Drongo Horne and jabbed out her cigarette. "No, I won't have lunch, thank you. I think I'll go for another swim instead. Perhaps you'd like to collect me from the pool when you've finished?"

The three of them stood up. As they walked past the bar Heide caught Drongo Horne's single eye in the mirror, lowered her gaze, and then caught his glance again before moving on. Silly girl, she thought excitedly as she went outside to the pool. What the hell am I getting myself into now?

Drongo couldn't fail to interpret the message he'd received, nor could he work out what the scene was. Presumably that was the woman's husband and they were staying here at the

Tasa? It was unlikely that any shenanigans could ensue with a set-up like that. Nevertheless, glimpsing Heide through the bar window as she removed her wrap while walking towards the pool - fully aware that the unveiling of her body was being observed - nevertheless, delay was the worst form of denial, Drongo reminded himself, placing 4-rials on the counter for his beers, retrieving his Kalashnikov and tucking it under his left arm as he swung round on his rubber-soled boots and left the bar.

"How about *that?*" Chuck remarked, drawing the others' attention to the glamorous blonde teetering across the poolside's astroturf towards them, disrobing as she came.

"Not half bad," agreed Hans, leaning on one elbow to pay attention. "Hey, get a load of this," he said, nudging Ferguson who lay on a lounger with his eyes closed, a frosted beer atop his chest.

After Colonel David Marks had whisked them through the airport and ensconced them here at the Tasa, he'd told them: "General Wally's compliments, gentlemen – you're to relax, get a good night's sleep and I shall collect you at 0800 tomorrow to take you to Masela Camp for your briefing."

The three of them slept for a couple of hours, showered, ate a light brunch, and now dozed in the sun at the poolside.

"What are we being paid for this?" Chuck asked.

"The usual Zeta rates, I suppose," Ferguson replied, opening one eye as Heide Ritter sauntered past them. "Between ten and twenty thou., depending on what the job entails."

"I've earned most of that already," Chuck groaned, "holding myself in check when *she* walked past like that."

"Mebbe you should get a medal as well," Hans suggested. He got up and dived into the pool.

"Hallo –what's this?" Chuck glanced across the pool to the entrance. "Ferguson?"

"Wassamatta?"

"I sense trouble approaching."

"Relax; it's only a guy come to look at the pool."

"Dressed like Rambo? I don't think so. This one's a pro. Look at him. He's here for something."

"Sure – and she's lying over there under that tree, gyrating her hips for him."

"You reckon? Yeah – maybe you're right. "No accounting for taste." He grinned as they watched the man in the eye-patch saunter round the poolside towards the stunning blonde.

The man laid his Kalashnikov down on the astroturf and hunkered beside the woman who stretched languidly along a lounger. They saw her smile and respond to his advance.

Ferguson closed his eyes and Chuck picked up the lurid paperback he was reading while Hans swam successive lengths of the pool. Somewhere not too far away they heard the voice of a muezzin calling the faithful to prayer.

Hans heaved himself out of the pool and came back to drip and clean out his ears beside Ferguson. They heard a yelp.

"What's that?" Ferguson opened one eye again.

Chuck folded down the corner of his page and closed his book. "Our blonde number's decided she doesn't like that big boy scout after all. He tried squeezing her thigh just now, but she slapped his wrist away. She had to do it again when he tried it on a second time, so presumably she's seriously not interested. Now he's started licking her."

"Her what? asked Ferguson.

"I told you already. Her leg."

"What a player." Chuck chuckled. "Man after my own heart."

"Hardly," scoffed Ferguson. "He's got *some* style."

"Not a lot – look at that," Hans interjected, dropping his towel and moving off round the pool towards the couple, who were now struggling. The man seemed unperturbed that he was in public view. The woman had slipped from her lounger and was trying to regain her feet while the man laughed and kept nudging her with his boot. She began to scream. Everyone at the pool was watching, transfixed by the unfurling drama, but apart from Hans no one moved to intervene. Unaware that he was being approached from behind, the man darted out his hand and ripped off Heidi's bikini top. She cried out in horror, flashing her arms across to cover her breasts.

"ENOUGH," Hans roared and hurled himself at the startled aggressor. The two of them crashed to the turf with a thud. The man writhed free, leapt to his feet and swept his Kalashnikov from the ground by its barrel. Swinging it once he fetched Hans a *CRUUMP* with the butt on the side of his head, sending him reeling backwards.

"Holy shit," Ferguson yelped, bounding to his feet. "Come on Chuck. Move."

Both men sprinted round the edge of the pool to where Hans lay groaning on the ground, blood welling from this latest head wound. The terrified Heide cowered beside him. As Chuck and Ferguson drew closer to the man he swung to face them both, aiming the Kalashnikov at Ferguson's chest and slickly cocking it.

"Christ," hissed Chuck. "This guy's a lunatic."

"You've only got to look at his good eye to see that," Ferguson retorted. "What now?"

"*Far* enough," snarled the man. "That's far *enough.* One more step and you're dead. Back away, now. Go back where you came from. None of this is your business."

"Oh yes it is," snapped Ferguson. "You've just cracked our buddy's head open. I'd say that makes it our business."

"Tough shit. He shouldn't have interfered in my affairs. Now back *away*, like I told you."

"Who the hell *are* you, buster?" It was Chuck. "You shouldn't be allowed out of your cage without a keeper, you know that? You sick in the head? You know what I'm going to do? Christ – I'm going to kick your grimy ass."

He stepped forcefully towards the man.

There was a *craaaash,* a whiff of cordite and an empty case flew out of the rifle's breach to clang against a chair leg. An instant furrow appeared in the turf between Chuck's feet. Then everything happened at once.

Everyone at the poolside leapt to their feet, screamed and dashed for cover. Heide Ritter leapt up, raised her arm and determinedly smashed the heel of her sandal into the back of her aggressor's neck.

Ferguson hurled himself forward and drove the sole of his foot into the man's solar plexus, dislodging the black patch from his sightless eye.

The Kalashnikov flew into the air. Chuck grabbed it and promptly tossed it into the pool.

Clutching his midriff the man darted away backwards from them.

"Okay, you guys – you'll be seeing me again," he snarled, jabbing his fingers at them. "The name's Horne. Drongo Horne. And don't you ever forget it. You're going to regret having been here today, I promise you that." He glanced down at his gesticulating hand and then stabbed his middle finger at them in a gesture packed with loathing and obscenity. He whirled round and moved quickly off, scattering chairs and tables as he made his enraged way to the exit.

"Nice chap," said Ferguson.

"We sure do meet 'em, don't we. Been a friend of yours long, Ma'am?" he asked Heide facetiously.

"Of *course* not. He's an *animal*. An absolute *animal*," she spat vehemently.

"I'd say that's a fair approximation of the truth," Chuck agreed, grinning. "May I help you on with your bikini, Ma'am?"

The woman started, then swept her arms up to cover her naked breasts again. Chuck retrieved the small halter top from the ground and handed it to her.

"How are you, old son?" Ferguson asked, kneeling concernedly beside Hans, relieved to find he had regained consciousness, the blood already coagulating round the wound on his temple.

"Woozy," mumbled Hans, trying to climb to his feet. "I seem to have met my match there, alright. Who the hell *was* that comic-book villain, chrissake? He took me completely by surprise. I don't like him very much at all."

"I don't think he likes us very much, either. His name's Drongo Horne, apparently, and we've been instructed not to forget it. We shall all be meeting up again fairly soon, he said, for a further reckoning."

"I hope so." Hans grunted, rubbing his head gingerly. "I shall look forward to that."

FIFTEEN

The Ras-al-Am Army was collectively puzzled. Why this sudden withdrawal . . .?

The Brigadier's signal had arrived at all units' locations just after first light that morning.

A decade ago the Army had consisted of a few Palace Guards wearing wazirs and chaplis, carrying outmoded rifles; then in re-appraising his country's needs Sultan Hamad had begun to give in to the overtures made by the world's military hardware salesmen.

His new Army was only about 15,000 strong, comprised of five Ras-al-Ami warrior battalions and three regiments of Baluch mercenaries, plus an artillery regiment and David Marks's tanks and armoured cars – but it was an army equipped with an array of state-of-the-art weaponry. Some of its officers had been to Sandhurst, and ex-British army officers were contracted as mentors to each regiment.

Adopting a warlike posture to defend a country cannot be done from a huddle behind a copse. Defence has to be established right across the enemy's axis of advance.

The Ras-al-Am Army, now deployed over a 50 mile radius, had been ordered out of the field back to camp.

For some self-aggrandising purpose, however, Brigadier Mustapha Said decided that he was going to recall each regiment to a central location first. This was logistically ludicrous. Did he intend to indulge himself with delusions of grandeur, standing atop a jebel crag taking the salute? The British officers were outraged by its lunacy. Many Ras-al-Am officers also raised their eyebrows and were indignant at the order.

An army on the move is an awesome sight.

The modern, motorised Ras-al-Am Army with its armour, artillery and associated arms and accoutrements span up one hell of a dust-cloud that morning, when it came churning in from its various desert locations to form up in the middle of an uncharted gravel plain.

It took four hours to become fully assembled.

Phalanx upon phalanx paraded hot, dusty and tired beneath the blazing rays of the noon day sun.

Beside them their vehicle engines pinged as they cooled after their dash to this unnecessary rendezvous.

Without having been shelled, bombed or machine-gunned, without the steel shards and smoky holocaust of real war slicing them into medical cases, this morning the Ras-al-Ami Army had at least acquired some indication of what one aspect of war *could* be like.

Flanked by his aides, the megalomaniac Brigadier stood silhouetted on a high bluff overlooking the plain, switching his calf with a fly-whisk. He was enjoying himself, beaming nervously while adopting a variety of stances to find the one he felt suited him best, while 100 metres away mess waiters were unconcernedly laying out silver and napery for his lunch.

He assessed that the time was now right for him to address his assembled forces, before sending them back to Raman and sitting down to his meal.

The Signals Regiment had spent the morning siting speakers round the assembly area in preparation for this moment.

Brigadier Mustapha stepped forward to the microphone, paused imperiously, and then like Moses on the Mount his voice boomed over the air, bidding his attendant army to sit.

There came a susurration as the 15,000 men settled cross-legged on the gravel plain to await their Deputy Commander's next words.

Only one sound could be heard. An approaching aircraft.

The Brigadier looked up and saw a lone Air Force helicopter bearing down from the sky towards him. It hovered a few hundred feet ahead of the bluff on which he stood. It was either bearing an important message or had been sent to fly him back to Raman. Whatever its purpose, he resented the intrusion. Its *thwocking* rotors and the dust storm they created played havoc with the stage-managed delivery of his address. He and his aides had to lower their heads and shield their eyes from the sand and grit being lashed against them. The sudden *rat-a-tat-tat* of firing that followed was barely audible.

From the open door of the helicopter sustained bursts of machine-gun fire smashed Mustapha and his aides backwards onto the rocky ground. Their bodies kicked and bucked as hails of bullets tore into them, ripping them to shreds.

As the entire Army rose aghast from the valley floor in an uproar, the helicopter banked swiftly away to the north. Before any of the horrified soldiery could react it was out of range of retaliatory small-arms fire.

Five minutes later the hi-jacked helicopter landed in a large wadi where 500 rebel forces were camped.

Leaving a guard holding a pistol to the pilot's head the young separatist leader, Hilal al-Bakri, dropped to the ground and loped across to rejoin his subordinate chieftains.

It had been a daring initiative, pursuing the Army into the field. Hilal had known the Grand Council would never countenance such a bold move, and he had instigated the action on his own initiative.

"Our informants were right," he reported to his commanders, taking deep breaths to suppress his jubilation. "The entire Army is drawn up on an open plain not fifteen kilometres south of here. I personally tore apart their Deputy Commander and a group of his aides. They were sitting targets. The opportunity was too good to miss. I think the Army will thank me – no? Everyone knew what an inept figurehead that man was. He is no loss to the future of our country."

"You did well, Sayid," said Majid Zahir, the oldest of the commanders, using the respectful address accorded to senior personages. "It is a shame your brother Suleman has not the same decisive nature. If the execution of this coup had been left to him, we would still be sitting at home talking about it. What happens next, Sayid?"

"What we do now, Majid Zahir, is capitalise upon our advantage. We have located the Army, yet the Army doesn't know who we are, or that we are here, straddling their main access back to Raman. There are 15,000 of them and only five-hundred of us, but that is no matter. They will be strung out in convoys. They will be reeling with what just happened. We retain the advantages of mobility and surprise. We can harass them with flying pickets every metre of the way from here to Raman. We will not remain in one place long enough for them to retaliate. We will engage in a series of guerrilla strikes to their flanks. It will impede their progress and buy time for our brothers in the north to make their move. Come –

"We must prepare to ride . . ."

Lt-Col Hamad Musalam, the dynamic commanding officer of the Ras-al-Am Frontier Regiment had been standing 20 metres away when the Deputy Commander and his aides had been massacred by those lunatics in the helicopter.

He stepped forward and righted the toppled microphone, praying that it still worked. When he tapped the mouthpiece a sound like a tom-tom reverberated round the plain below. He spoke calmly and precisely.

"You have all seen what happened. Brigadier Mustapha and three of his aides have been killed. We do not know who is responsible for this outrage, or why it was carried out. We shall shortly be returning to Raman in compliance with our original orders. You are to prepare to move out in fifteen minutes. Will all commanding officers or their representatives report to me here now." He switched off the microphone and stepped back. "Cover those bodies," he instructed a young officer. He headed for the Signals tent.

"Get me Headquarters in Raman," he commanded the duty operator. "I wish to speak with General Stubbs."

When he came out of the tent he found fellow commanding officers drawn up outside waiting for him.

"Thank you, gentlemen." He smiled. "One of us needed to

take decisions, and I was the closest. I have just spoken with General Stubbs and told him about this terrible affair. He is coming by helicopter to join us as soon as possible. General Stubbs said he will inform His Majesty. We should now coordinate our routes and timings for the immediate withdrawal of all troops from the field. It will take some time to clear everyone in an orderly fashion, so the first regiment should leave as soon as possible. Any questions?"

"Yes," said Lt-Col Khalfan Khalifa of the Border Defence Regiment, placing his clipboard on the ground. "We know about this mounting unrest, the woman in the Palace, the oil tanker incident and the ammo depot going up - and now our Deputy Commander and his party have been cold-bloodedly murdered. With something as serious as this erupting all around us, shouldn't we conduct a tactical withdrawal, rather than dashing pell-mell for home?"

"We *are* an army," put in Lt-Col Saoud Alhabsi. "There'd have to be an awful lot of boys with bows and arrows out there to take us on. You really think there's a threat? Let's get on with it, I say. If we get a move on there's a chance I could still attend a dinner party tonight."

The other COs smiled, implying little serious concern on their part.

"Right." Hamad Musalam finalised the briefing. "We should aim to have the first regiment away within ten minutes. Let's go."

SIXTEEN

"You got my message - that I'd be late?"

David Marks apologised to Ferguson, Hans and Chuck Henderson, waiting for him gazing in the gift shop windows round the Tasa Hotel's atrium.

"I had to go to a funeral."

"Anyone we know?" Ferguson asked.

"In the normal course of events you would no doubt have met them, yes – but you hadn't arrived here in time."

David told them about the tanker incident in which Simon Pritchard and Tony Fanshawe had been shot, and how Simon's wife, Jenny, and Jack Hargreaves had later been impaled and killed by flying glass in the hospital when the ammunition dump exploded.

"Bit of a crazy place to build a hospital, right next to an ammunition depot, wasn't it?" Chuck remarked.

"Yes, unfortunately," David agreed. "It was blast, from half-a-mile away. Tragic. One hell of a nice family, the Pritchards. Thank God young Jeremy, their son, pulled through from his snake bite and one of the nurses flying home on leave escorted him and his twin sister, Susan, home to Jenny's sister. We could have repatriated their parents and the other two chaps for a UK interment, but their respective families OK'd us conducting the burials here at the Christian cemetery in Raman. Ironic, really; we have about one funeral a decade, yet only three days ago they buried Roxanne Duprés there as well.

"Who's she?" Ferguson asked.

"Roxanne Duprés? You don't know about her?"

"Oh, yup: Prince Fahad's 'English mistress' – right?"

"Correct. I'll brief you more fully in the car on our way out to Masela Camp. Ready? We go."

The four men walked to the car park and climbed into David's Toyota Cressida staff car with its Armoured Regiment pennant fluttering from the bonnet.

"Cracking piece of goods she was, too. Lovely redhead. Superb figure. Didn't give a shit about anything or anyone. Used to drive a black Trans-Am about the place. I was out jogging on one of the deserted beaches once when I glimpsed the thing parked in the dunes. Thinking she might have got herself into some sort of trouble, stuck in the sand or something, I trotted across for a look. She was lying spread eagled on the ground beside it, sunbathing."

"Anything wrong with that?" asked Chuck.

"Not at all," David chuckled. "If you like that sort of thing; and most of us do - stark naked? Here in the heart of Araby? Give her her due, she lay without flinching, amusedly watching me check that she was a genuine redhead, then started stroking herself. It was the most blatant come-hither I've ever known."

"And did you?" asked Hans eagerly.

"No way, José. More than my life was worth. It was a dicey situation. She could have cut up rough for being rejected, but all she did was wave a 'no hoper' sign at me before turning over to tan her bottom. Mind you, she made sure to wriggle it about a bit, settling into the sand. As I said, cracking piece of stuff, but I'm not sure I should have wanted to breed from it. Slightly dubious antecedents, I've heard."

"A piece of ass in my book's a piece of ass," Chuck opined with a sniff. "Say, David – is that right you're the commander of the armoured regiment here?"

"Yes, I am."

"How come with the country in such an uproar you're not out there with your tanks and stuff on these manoeuvres?"

"I have an extremely competent Ras-al-Ami 2i/c," said David, "and . . . oh, *shit*."

They were approaching the Fallen Warrior roundabout when a Ras-al-Ami motorcycle patrolman, resplendent in doeskin breeches and black riding boots, stepped from his parked machine and signalled them to pull over onto the hard shoulder.

"We can't have been here long enough to have broken any law *yet*," Chuck laughed.

"No – it's HM," David explained.

"His Majesty? The Sultan? Where? Coming specially to greet me; that's nice." Chuck laughed again. "That's real nice of the man."

A queue of traffic formed behind them. They were grateful for David's air-conditioning. Used as they were to tropic climes, even through the brown tinted windscreen the sun's glare was making them squint.

The main road was now devoid of moving traffic except for clusters of police cars at points along the route. Out of the heat-hazed horizon behind them came a convoy of flashing lights, rapidly preceded by a red Volvo estate car with motorcycle outriders.

"That's Colonel Jeffs, the commander of the Royal Guard Regiment," David explained. "He's the Sultan's personal bodyguard. Must be a millionaire twice over by now. He eats, sleeps and lives the job. Bachelor. Early fifties. Used to be a colonial policeman. The outriders aren't police. They're Royal Guard Regiment motorcyclists," he went on as the motorcade whooshed past them through the roundabout with perilous haste.

"Here's the Sultan now," said Chuck as a flag-bedecked, metallic-blue, smoked-glass Mercedes-600 came towards them cocooned by a phalanx of motorcyclists.

"That's what you're meant to think," David said, "but you're wrong. The Sultan will be in one of the unmarked vehicles bringing up the rear. There he is now. See? In this car, here."

"You mean, that's him - sitting in front?" Hans enquired earnestly.

"Yup; that's him."

The car swept past so quickly that they caught barely a glimpse of Ras-al-Am's Ruler sitting erect behind the windscreen of an insignificant vehicle, an austere expression on his grey-bearded face. He was followed by five more cars, an ambulance and a breakdown vehicle.

Moments later the motor patrolman stepped back into the road and beckoned David to proceed.

"Why was he sitting in front?" Hans asked.

"In this part of the world dignitaries like to sit in the front of a car rather than the back. Only underlings and women sit in the back."

"Thanks a bundle," Hans acknowledged from behind.

The Baluch guard at the gates of Masela Camp saluted David's car as they entered and drove up to the NATO-like Headquarters building. Parking outside the main entrance, David led them through the doors and up the wide staircase to the heart of the building.

Walking along the grey-tiled corridors towards the General's offices their ears were assailed by the sound of Indian and Pakistani staff jabbering away in Hindi and Urdu, the opening and slamming shut of Beamsteel and Godrej filing cabinet drawers, and everyone clattering away noisily on typewriters and answering the constantly jangling telephones, while Indian and European carpetbaggers strode the corridors to appointments with the heads of the various military branches in their identical offices.

Other officers passed, going about their business singly or in groups, laden with files from conference to working party to committee meeting, all engaged in spending or saving the Sultan's money.

"Who's *in* all these offices?" Chuck asked, bemused.

"Two or three officers, a calculator, a bit of horse sense, a clutch of Pakistani clerks, a prayer and a whistle," David told him. "The hard-pressed, under-manned Directorate of Purchasing; the Finance Branch; the Colonel Logistics and his staff; the Force Ordnance Services; the Directorate of Mechanical and Electrical Engineering; the Signals Regiment; the Force Medical Services, each one a grandiose sounding title, all of whom spend their days entertaining or fending off the world's ingratiating salesmen of military impedimenta who turn up in expectant droves for a slice of Ras-al-Am's annual $2billion defence budget.

"Ever since Ras-al-Am first opened its doors equipment has been pouring in to us from a whole range of sources.

"We've had Russian 130mm artillery pieces built by Koreans but purchased via Egypt: American M60 tanks: Austrian Pinzgauer one-and-a-half-ton wheeled section vehicles: Austrian Steyr rifles and bayonets: Swarovski binoculars: Chinese ammunition: boots made in Hong Kong; chicken bits canned in Singapore; Indian cholera serum; Mercedes . . . Land Rovers . . . the inventory is endless. That's what goes on in all these offices along the left hand side of the corridor here. That one over there, on the right, is the map store. Next door to that's a gent's loo. Things are quiet at the moment because everyone's out on the manoeuvre, but normally it gets fairly hectic in here."

"You've gotta be kidding," said Chuck. "It's bedlam. "I'd go out of my mind in five minutes, working in a place like this."

"It happens." David laughed. Last month the wife of one of our loan-service colonels chased him round their garden at midnight in her nightie, brandishing his 12-bore and calling him a cunt. Most of the camp turned out to cheer her on. They reckoned there was some justification – but she was a known alcoholic and he was a hard-working old sod so nobody minded very much, least of all the pot-smoking poofter colonel who lived next door."

"That's a point," said Chuck. "This being an Arab army, do you have much trouble with homosexuality?"

"None at all," David said. "There's as much of it as you want. Here's the General's office now. He's expecting us."

General Wally's outer office contained four leather armchairs and a long coffee table stacked with copies of the *Defence Journal*. These were laid out each morning by his ADC, a brightly be-medalled young Ras-al-Ami captain, who now sat at a large empty desk with the General's diary opened in front of him – and aspirations.

He rose politely to shake hands with the guests.

"The General is expecting you, sir," he said to David. "I'll let him know you're here."

Walking over to the closed door opposite he peered through a spy-hole, to see if the General was playing carpet golf or haranguing someone on the telephone. The coast was clear. He knocked, and opened the door.

General Wally was standing at the far end of the room with his back to them as they entered, studying a wall map of Ras-al-Am while smoking one of his ever smouldering Silk Cut cigarettes.

The ADC cleared his throat. "General . . .?"

"Harrumph." Stroking his chin General Wally turned from the map. "FERGUSON," he roared: "Hans; Chuck." He hurried across the carpet to greet them with outstretched arms, pumping their hands vigorously and thumping them on the back with exuberance. "Gosh – it's great to see you chaps, it really is," he enthused. "Not bad. Not bad at all. The system works, after all. It's been too long since we last used it, don't you think? Well, we've got our chance this time. There's a big one brewing, chaps, which is why I've called you in. The best team I ever had. Great. How have you been? Tell me – Ferguson . . . it's some years since you've been out this way, isn't it? Changed much, has it?"

"One hell of a lot, as a matter of fact, General. The development's unbelievable. I hardly recognise the place. And as for you, sir; if I may say so . . . it's obvious you've kept taking the pills."

He grinned happily. It was really very good to see this tough old bugger again, to be reminded that men like him were still around.

General Wally was also chortling with pleasure. Bright lights darted from his eyes.

"I expect David has already told you most of what we know," he said, "but settle yourselves down and let me brief you fully. What is it *now?"* he snapped.

"I am sorry, Sayid. You are needed urgently in the radio room. An important transmission . . . for your ears only."

"Bugger it. Alright, Ahmed. I'll come right away. Fix these

guys some coffee, will you? I'll be right back."

He stonked angrily out of the room.

"Nothing's changed." Ferguson laughed. "Still the same old firebrand."

The ADC returned carrying a tray of coffees which he was just placing on the table when the General burst back in.

"No time for coffee, chaps. Sorry – we're off. The shit's really hitting the fan now. My Deputy Commander, Mustapha Said's gone and got himself murdered. Bloody fool. Had a rush of blood to the head and decided he'd Troop the Colour up a wadi. He was just priming himself to take the salute when some shite-hawk in a heli flew up and zapped him and his aides with a heavy calibre machine-gun. Hamad Asalam's stepped in and assumed command. He's a good man, but I'm flying down there just in case something else brews up. You chaps'll have to come with me. Might turn out you can be useful. I'll brief you on the way. Go and drink your coffee. I've got to take a leak first anyway."

A string of sand-coloured Jebel Recce Regiment vehicles was wending an erratic 30kmh course along the floor of Wadi Siddiq. The jundees packed into the backs of these dust-shrouded vehicles had their heads wrapped in their shemaghs, but still the all-pervasive sand and grit covered everything. Men and vehicles resembled ash-smothered mummies in mobile sarcophagi.

Bouncing about in the front seat of his command vehicle at the head of the column, their CO, Lt-Col Rashid Ali worried that he still might not get back to Raman in time for his dinner party that night.

The convoy had started out in packets of five with 20 metres between vehicles, but then the all-enshrouding dust churned up by their tyres had obscured the drivers' vision so much that each vehicle had to put on its headlights and slip back to 70 metres distance. It was a choking nightmare, and this was only the first regiment to move out. Back in the assembly area there were a further 12,000 men waiting to trickle into formation to follow the same route.

Another two hours of this hellish drive lay ahead before the Jebel Recce Regiment would hit the main south-north Raman blacktop highway.

Only two men in the entire Army were enjoying clear vision: Colonel Rashid Ali and his driver in the lead vehicle – and their flanks were as much obscured by dust as everyone else's . . .

. . . and it was from the left flank that Hilal al-Bakri's rebel force launched its first lightning attack.

A rocket-launched missile caught the colonel's vehicle clean amidships, slicing off his legs at the thigh and decapitating his driver. Their vehicle was hurled into the air and rolled over seven times before erupting into a ball of flame.

After this first strike the rebels galloped their horses along the dust cloud's billowing periphery, firing into the column at random.

As their windscreens shattered the vehicles swerved and crashed into each other, crushing and killing many and maiming others.

Five minutes after the attack had begun, it abated. The rebels wheeled off to re-group and await the arrival of the next convoy.

From his seat beside the pilot in the hi-jacked helicopter flying above, Hilal al-Bakri whooped with joy. He ordered the pilot to set down behind the dunes where his force was regrouping. Leaving the pilot under guard he ran across to join Majid Zahir.

"Wonderful; *WONDERFUL,*" he cried. "Majid, that was magnificent; truly magnificent. In one swoop your men have more than decimated almost an entire regiment of the Sultan's army. Can we do it again? There's another dust cloud approaching a kilometre down the road."

"We are ready, Sayid. We shall do it," Majid Zahir avowed. "Truly Allah is with us this day." He swung into his saddle, raised his rifle aloft and cried: "We ride. We ride."

As the horsemen thundered off to meet the approaching convoy, Hilal al-Bakri ran back to the helicopter. Its rotors whirled and lifted it to climb and observe the second ambush.

In the excitement neither Hilal al-Bakri nor the harassed pilot saw another helicopter – approaching 1,000ft above them and a kilometre behind.

"What the hell's all *this*?" General Wally roared into his mouthpiece, almost lifting his pilot's earphones. "Drop lower, man. Bank; bank – I want to see what's happened. Jeesus fucking wept. Have they been nuked, or had the mother of all pile-ups? What do you make of it, Ferguson?"

"Looks like they've run into an ambush. Whatever it was they've been properly duffed up."

"Too bloody right they have: it's one *helluva* mess down there."

"That's our hi-jacked heli ahead, sir," their pilot informed the General.

"*Is* it, by Christ? Let's go and see what it's doing?"

Their pilot climbed to lessen the chance of detection, and the five men continued to observe the unfurling events below them.

Drunk with their first success and having no reason to change their tactics, the rebels were preparing to re-enact their action plan a second time. Although unaware of it, they were about to engage Lt-Col Hamad Musalam's Frontier Force.

With a burst of flame the rebels' first rocket left its launcher and *whooshed* away to score a direct hit on the convoy's lead vehicle, which immediately exploded, killing the regiment's 2i/c and his driver.

Colonel Hamad Musalam was not there with his regiment, having elected to stay behind in the assembly area until the bodies of the Deputy Commander and his aides had been collected, and the last convoy departed.

The rebels had not been aware of the significance of this second attack – that Colonel Musalam's Frontier Force was considered to be the best trained force in the Army. Nor could they have been expected to know that the young captain in the convoy's second vehicle was one of those trained at Sandhurst. Today's action gave him the chance to repay part of his debt to the Sultanate, and make a name for himself.

His training had taught him to react to an ambush.

"GET OFF THE TRACK. VEER OFF TO THE RIGHT – *NOW,"* he roared at his driver.

The unsuspecting jundees in the back found themselves tossed against the roof of the vehicle as it bucketed off the main route of advance for 200 metres. Thumping their driver's shoulder to stop, the young captain leapt from the cab and screamed at the jundees in the rear to dismount.

Spreading quickly out from the vehicle they took cover where they could, hurling themselves to the ground on the scrub-covered plateau.

The other vehicles in the convoy followed the same initiative. The 1,000 instinctively alert troops rapidly formed a defensive line two kilometres in length, and cocked their weapons.

When the rebels galloped along the line they wondered why this convoy's dust cloud had gone in so many directions, but blindly fired into it.

They were met with retaliatory fusillades which sent their broken horses and men stumbling back in disarray.

"WITHDRAW . . . *WITHDRAW,"* Majid Zahir screamed at those closest to him, scrambling onto a wounded leg and struggling to mount a riderless horse. Above them Hilal al-Bakri pounded the helicopter's console.

"It's over: IT'S *OVER*; I'll not compromise my men's lives needlessly. Hover above that outcrop," he commanded the pilot. "We can act as a rally point for our brave warriors."

The young Frontier Force captain peered through the diminishing dust cloud and saw that the attacking horsemen were now galloping away.

The dust cloud led towards a ridge of dunes a kilometre distant where a helicopter hovered overhead. It was difficult to estimate the numbers of their attackers, but they appeared considerable.

Blood lust and adrenalin coursed through the young officer's veins. There were senior officers further along their column, but he had no time to liaise with them. This was a battle-heat situation. Time was crucial. His regiment needed to know the strength and identity of its enemy.

The young officer leapt up from behind his cover of rocks, quickly detailing six men to accompany him. They clattered with their equipment across to the nearest vehicle and clambered aboard, the young captain at the wheel.

He slewed off in the direction of the dunes, struggling to keep to the hard ground and avoid getting bogged.

It was a bold action. They had no cover and were in full view of the helicopter hovering quarter of a kilometre away.

He wasn't sure what to do. If he didn't crest the dunes he would discover nothing and his mission would fail. He stopped his vehicle, and the decision was made for him.

The helicopter was descending when one of his jundees in the back of the stationary vehicle opened fire with a burst from his GPMG. The weapon's 7.62 rounds smashed into the helicopter's cupola, riddling the Air Force pilot. The craft spiralled out of control. Seconds later there was a loud *cruuump* from behind the dunes and a giant fireball unfurled into the air.

The jundees cheered and stamped their feet on the floor of the vehicle. The captain thought: Well, at least we've downed the thing. No more heroics now. Time to leave.

Gunning the engine he swung the vehicle in a circle to retreat, but then it stalled just as a large group of horsemen appeared silhouetted along the crest of one of the dunes.

Frantically the captain pressed the ignition, but the engine would not re-start. His jundees held their fire. There were only seven of them, and at least fifty horsemen up on the dunes with more appearing all the time.

The engine still refused to fire. They smelled diesel.

What the *hell* should he do? It would be ignominious to surrender: equally to run – and they would be cut down by small arms' fire if they tried.

A group of around twenty horsemen detached itself from the main body and slithered down the dunes, across the plateau towards them.

Someone from the regiment must *surely* have observed

their plight and would come to their assistance?

The horsemen were now less than 50 metres away.

The six jundees behind him climbed down from the vehicle and laid their weapons on the ground.

The horsemen were cantering towards them. Suddenly the vehicle's engine caught and fired. The jundees turned to scramble aboard but the horsemen fell on them, cutting, hacking, putting each one of them brutally to the sword.

The young captain screamed with bitter rage as he swung the truck round and roared off, forced to desert his fallen comrades. His moment of glory had turned to acid in his bowels.

Seconds later a bullet smashed into the back of his skull. His head and torso slumped over the bloodied wheel and the vehicle stalled to a juddering stop.

Two horsemen rode up to heave his body out of the cab, sending it thudding to the ground. One of them handed his beast's reins to the other and pulled himself into the cab. He re-started the engine and drove the vehicle back towards the dunes.

Hilal al-Bakri had survived the helicopter crash by hurling himself clear and had landed unharmed in the soft sand.

He was elated with this unexpected booty. Now he would have his own command vehicle.

SEVENTEEN

General Wally had his pilot set down behind the Frontier Force's defensive line. Watching the entire debacle from the air he had recognised the rebels' ploy.

"Now they know we've got their measure they won't try that again," he shouted at Ferguson and the others as they spilled out of the helicopter. "Who's in command here?"

"I am, Sayid," cried a harassed Ras-al-Ami major, hurrying across and saluting him.

"Ah, yes – I know you: Abdul Mustapha. Tell me what's happened and what you're doing about it."

"We were attacked, Sayid. Ambushed . . .".

"Yes, dammit man, I know that already. Tell me properly."

"Sayid, Major Saleh Moosa and his driver were killed. Captain Ahmed Haroon was in the second vehicle. He pulled off the road and formed a defensive position. The rest of us did the same. A group of horsemen started firing at us. We returned their fire and they went away. Then Captain Haroon and six men very bravely – or perhaps foolishly, followed them. They have not yet returned."

"Nor will they, Abdul Mustapha. We saw them getting killed, I'm afraid. The rebels have taken their vehicle. Where's the rest of my army?"

"Behind me, Sayid."

"That's nice to know. Must make you sleep better at night, does it? Abdul, where are they?"

"Sayid, they are spread out over many kilometres. I have radioed back what's happened. They have halted and are awaiting further instructions."

"Right: well my instructions are that they are to break out and high-tail it back to Raman to their unit locations with all speed, *without* incurring any more casualties. Send that message, will you?"

"Yes, Sayid."

"Good. Now how many wounded have you here?"

"None at all, Sayid – apart from Captain Haroon's detachment. We adopted good positions and repelled the attackers."

"Right, well there's one helluva mess back down the route where the Jebel Recce Regiment's had a mauling. Stop there on your way and do what you can to help them. Have you heard anything from them? Over the air?"

"No, Sayid."

"Their radios must be down. Raise the medics and have the Field Ambulances move up there. Get this show back on the road again for me, Abdul. I'm depending on you."

"Yes, Sayid. It will be done." He saluted the General's back as he hurried back to the helicopter.

"Ferguson, you boys wait here for me, will you? Do what you can to assist. I want to get those buggers on horseback, see if we can't find out something about them. I'll be back soon. Stop looking so damn' miserable." He grinned. "Now this thing's blown there's going to be plenty for you three boyos to get your teeth into . . .

. . . follow that camel," he yelled at his pilot, clambering into the helicopter seat and buckling himself in.

"Sir?"

"Well – horse, then . . . dammit, the marauders. Get after them. They went that-a-way. I think. Or was it the other way? I don't know, let's find them anyway. Get this damn' machine into the air and then we'll be able to see, won't we!"

The helicopter rose and set off to the north, its pilot struggling to suppress a grin. Everyone in the Ras-al-Am forces knew that their General's jocularities and displays of bellicosity were facades. His military acuity and consideration made him a joy to serve with, unless incompetent, in which case you didn't serve with him very long.

"There they are," he growled into his mouthpiece, pointing. "Christ – there's enough of 'em too, aren't there!"

Five kilometres ahead billows of dust rose into the air where the withdrawing rebels were cantering northward across the plain like a herd of wildebeest.

"Nice fellows," grizzled the General. "I suppose they've left their dead and wounded behind for the vultures. What in hell's behind all this, I wonder? They're normally such placid people. Something or someone's stirred 'em up pretty good, that's for sure. We'll have to get to the bottom of it." He fingered his mouthpiece. "Bear off to the right, Laddie, will you, and drop your height. I want to get ahead of them and then come back low. Not so much dust that way, and the sun'll be behind us. We'll get a better view of what we're looking at. In fact, let's do some dune-hopping. That way we'll come upon them before they see us."

The helicopter veered to the right, beating ahead for five kilometres until General Wally indicated to the pilot to turn round again.

"There's their dust cloud. Head straight for it at fifty-feet. Don't aim for them head-on when we get there, keep slightly right so I can see them out of my side of the window."

Sweeping low across the plateau they approached a range of dunes like foothills. A central dust cloud revealed where the rebel horsemen were clambering up. Each dune was an massive wave of sand rising to 400 feet.

The pilot reduced his speed and eased the helicopter up the forward slope of the first dune, almost clipping the top of it as he dropped down the other side to approach the next.

"This is like a giant roller coaster," General Wally guffawed. "I reckon that dust cloud's now about three dunes away. The sand must be muffling the sound of our approach. We're going to take them by surprise."

Now that they were off the gravel plain Hilal al-Bakri's driver had reduced their new command vehicle's tyre pressure to navigate the dunes more skilfully. They were off to a flank, one dune ahead of their horsemen.

As they reached its crest their world exploded into a rending, splintering nightmare.

A helicopter . . . a *helicopter* was coming up the other side of the same dune. It loomed in front of them like some giant infernal insect. The point of its skis tore through the windscreen and superstructure ripping the vehicle completely apart. The driver was instantly decapitated. What was left of the vehicle hurtled backwards down the dune.

"HOLY *SHIT*," General Wally and the pilot yelled simultaneously. "Nice one, *Cyril*," the General then added. Now touch down quickly."

"What? Are you sure, sir?"

"Just do it. That's one of our vehicles. There might be someone still alive in it who knows a thing or two."

"You really think so, sir? After that impact? No chance."

The helicopter touched down between the two dunes and General Wally leapt out and scrambled across to the shattered vehicle.

Fifty metres away the seemingly indestructible Hilal al-Bakri lay groaning half slumped out of the smashed vehicle, confident that his men would be with him at any moment. He could still hear the helicopter somewhere off in the distance, but knew that Almighty Allah was protecting him. Less than an hour ago he had survived a helicopter crash, and now this. It was miraculous. His leg was shattered, and probably some ribs as well, but he was alive.

A shadow fell across him. He had to squint to keep the blood out of his eyes.

Then a gruff English voice rasped, "Right, y'bugger. Let's be having you out of there, shall we!"

Pain sliced in waves through Hilal al-Bakri's body as he was dragged from the vehicle and hoisted onto the Englishman's back. Certainly his ribs were broken.

A shot rang out. A spurt of sand erupted a metre away, as the first of his men crested a dune and saw what was happening.

He heard the helicopter's revs increase, but then he blacked out with the pain of being jolted across the Englishman's shoulders. General Wally heaved him in through the open door like a sack of potatoes, screaming *"GO,"* to the pilot while scrambling up beside him. A hail of small arms' fire *zipped* beneath the helicopter as it surged into the air and away out of the dunes.

"If I may say so, sir," said the pilot, grinning, "you are one very hands-on general, General. A bit close, that one was, sir."

"Nothing to it, laddie. Well, yeah . . . s'pose it was, a bit, really. I wonder what we've landed for ourselves back there – a buckshee *A*-rab, or a person of substance?"

"Is he alright, sir?"

"He's in one helluva state. No trouble though. Out like a light. Let's get back to the convoy quick as you can, shall we?"

"Right Ferguson, you're on," said the General. "Something your team can do. There's a broken body in the back of that heli. Take it back to Masela Camp, hospitalise it, semi-mend it and grill it as soon as you can. I don't know who he is but he knows more about what's going on than we do. Find out what you can, even if it means plucking a toe-nail or two. The Army's lost face today, so I'll travel back with the convoys . . . kick some arse and bolster their spirits. I'll catch up with you later. Take the heli. Now – go."

Ferguson, Hans and Chuck climbed into the back of the aircraft and gave a thumbs-up to the pilot. The great whirly-bird rose into the air once more and headed off across the plain to Masela Camp.

The body slumped on the floor groaned as the helicopter banked, making it roll over face upward. They could see that several of the man's ribs had burst through his chest wall, like snapped rattan cladding. His scarlet right leg was a mass of protruding shards and bone splinters. His face was a bruised and bloodied mask.

"Poor sod must be in agony," Chuck bellowed.

"He will be when he regains consciousness," yelled Hans.

Leaning forward Ferguson used the man's shemagh to wipe some of the blood and grime from his bearded face.

"Christ, I think I know him," he said. The others raised their eyebrows disbelievingly. "No – I do. He was one of my corporals when I was out here in the Army. Bright boy. Studied hard, left the Army and went off to university somewhere . . . the States, I think. Bakri – . It's coming back now. Hilal al-Bakri. If he'd applied himself he could have got a commission, but he was something of a maverick. I'm not surprised he became mixed up with this lot, whoever they turn out to be."

He plucked a headset from the wall and spoke to the pilot. "Can you radio ahead to have an ambulance waiting on the pad when we arrive? Our boy here's in bad shape. He's just started coughing up blood."

"Affirmative," came the reply over the headset. "Already been done."

"Thanks, pal: good thinking." Ferguson hung up the headset. "He had an older brother too, I remember. Suleman al-Bakri. Flight-lieutenant in the Air Force. Also left to go to university."

"Hey – this bloke really *is* coughing up blood," said Chuck. "I'm not sure he's going to make it."

Ferguson knelt beside Hilal and spoke to him in Arabic. "Hang on, Hilal. We're getting you to a hospital as fast as we can. Not long now. You're tough. You can fight it."

Hilal's eyes opened and gazed vacantly round the cabin. He focused on the faces peering down at him, then attempted to smile through his pain. "Major Ferguson. I remember you. You saved my life on the jebel once, many years ago." He paused as stabs of pain shot through his battered body. More blood frothed from his mouth. "Are you saving my life this time, too?"

"Looks that way doesn't it, Hilal. No – you're not going to die on us. Where's your brother, Suleman?"

"My brother? Suleman? He is with our . . . glorious Liberation Army - at Wazin."

Ferguson stiffened at what Hilal's quick relapse into delirium was allowing him to impart, but then the helicopter suddenly lurched and seemed to be experiencing difficulty righting itself again. The pilot's voice crackled over the headset on the hook. Chuck grabbed it. "Say again?"

"Make sure you're strapped in back there. There's a Shamal blowing up. We're going to catch some of it. We should be landing in about five minutes. Out."

A Shamal did not waft inquisitively round a girl's skirt and then chase off down the road in pursuit of a Kleenex. A Shamal started as a dusty idea in the hot desert interior, built in intensity and then unfolded towards Raman.

A fulvid sky full of sand heralded the arrival of a Shamal.

Doors banged, awnings snapped, small boats bobbed at their choppy moorings and a sense of impending dissolution filled the air until the Shamal unleashed its full howling ferocity at everything it could find, hurling sand through keyholes and flattening curtains against the ceiling.

If you ventured out into a Shamal it could whip your eyeballs out, remove loose teeth and lodge small rocks up your nostrils. Terrified pye-dogs would be plucked up and whisked away like Baron Műnchausen across the jebel. Roofs ended up on the far side of town, ships bashed up the high street, cyclists went through shop windows - and it could play havoc with ladies' hair-do's.

They buckled their seat belts tighter. Ferguson hoped Hilal wouldn't receive too much of a buffeting where he was on the floor. The helicopter bucked about like a dinghy in a whirlpool, losing and gaining height sickeningly at five second intervals. The three of them began to feel queasy. Hilal al-Bakri was ashen, bringing up gobs of blood-red vomit.

Ferguson looked out at the ochre sky. The pilot must be battering on by the seat of his pants with instruments going crazy. They'd owe him a beer or three for this.

The engine noise eventually reduced to a whine, the helicopter settled and they heard the rotor blades swishing above. They had touched down successfully.

They unbuckled their seat belts and Hans jumped down to allow Ferguson and Chuck to lower Hilal al-Bakri's body into his arms, but two white-coated ambulance men with a trolley appeared through the swirling sand and handled him professionally. They wheeled the trolley away and slid his

125

stretcher through the open doors of an ambulance.

Ferguson was impressed with their speed and slickness, and it did not occur to him that something might be irregular until he noticed that the ambulance was a Police vehicle and not an Army one.

"Who did you radio for an ambulance?" he shouted up to the pilot.

"Force Base Hospital at Masela, who else?" was the reply.

"So why should he be met by a Police ambulance?"

The pilot shrugged. Lowering his head against the screaming wind Ferguson staggered across the tarmac towards the ambulance. There was a *cluunk* as its doors were closed and he drew close enough to see its receding tail lights glowing through the murk as it drove away.

"*Shit*. For Christ's sake . . ." He whirled on the other two. "We need a vehicle and a telephone. We don't even know in which direction to walk in this bloody sandstorm. Are we slap bang in the middle of the airstrip, or what? Right – let's go: this way . . ."

They struck out, unable to see more than six feet in front of them, until a lull in the wind and swirling sand showed a cluster of lights off to their left. Seconds later the wind and sand enveloped them once more, but the respite had allowed them to see in which direction to head. It took them several minutes, but eventually they saw steps ahead and staggered up them to tumble into 1 Squadron's Ops Room.

"Hi, there – can I help you?" cried a cheery voice from behind a desk. "Nice day for a picnic. I'm Peter Irwin. Who are you?"

"Three little lambs who have lost their way," Ferguson quipped.

"I can see that."

"We came in on that chopper that's just landed. And – yes – you *can* help us if you will - to save me messing around with a telephone system I'm not familiar with? Can you get me through to the Casualty Department at FBH?"

"Sure – no problem," the Air Force officer said, picking up his phone and punching in a number. "There y'go. Force Base

Hospital. Got straight through." He held the receiver out to Ferguson who took it, and said: "Hallo."

"Doctor Changra Singh here. May I help you?"

"Doctor, did your department receive a message twenty-minutes ago to have an ambulance waiting to meet a casevac being brought in by helicopter?"

"Yes we did."

"Why wasn't it sent?"

"It was sent. When it arrived they were informed they were no longer required."

"By whom, Doctor?"

"The Police, who had an ambulance of their own there already. A police inspector said the casualty was a civilian, so they would handle it."

"So he's been taken to the Police Hospital."

"I would assume so, yes."

"Thank you for your help, Doctor; goodbye . . . Police Hospital - ?" Ferguson raised his eyebrows enquiringly at Peter Irwin who quickly stabbed out another number for him.

"Police Hospital? One of your ambulances left the airstrip a few minutes ago with a casualty just flown in by heli. Can you tell me who authorised that?"

"Who wishes to know, please?"

"I do. I brought the casualty in myself and he is under military jurisdiction."

"We've been otherwise informed, sir. We were told to ensure that he was taken into police custody."

"Where did that instruction come from?"

"The Ras-al-Am Intelligence Directorate, sir."

"The casualty was in a bad way. Coughing blood. Has he arrived there with you yet?"

"Er . . . actually, no sir. I understand that he is to be taken directly to Madan Prison."

"Christ-all-bloody-mighty, the condition he was in he'll be dead on arrival." There was a pause on the other end of the line. Ferguson slammed the telephone back onto its cradle. "General Wally's going to hit the fucking roof over this," he railed. "The Police and Army have always been at loggerheads in this place. Tell me . . .," he turned to Peter Irwin – "who heads up the Intelligence Directorate?"

"Man called called Giles Carrington," said Peter, "which for what it's worth suggests that your casualty should expect to find himself undergoing something ominous 'ere long. I don't think I'd put much money on his chances of finding himself on the mend any time soon."

"I agree." Ferguson grimaced. "I remember that gentleman's name from last time I was here, so trying to get more information's going to be impossible. Right -," he turned to Hans and Chuck, "we've got some fast thinking and faster moving to do now, so let's go."

Hilal al-Bakri lapsed into unconsciousness again in the ambulance, unaware that it had turned into the gates of the forbidding concrete and wire-enmeshed Madan Prison and was now driving round the inside perimeter to a palm grove in the prison's furthermost eastern corner. The doors were thrown open and despite the ambulance men's protests two burly prison warders hefted Hilal roughly from his stretcher and out of the vehicle which was then sent bumping back to the Police Hospital.

Hilal's broken body was dragged across the grove to a hole already dug in the hot sand. The two warders tied his feet with wire and bound his hands behind his back.

Dribbling pink bile and groaning, Hilal shook his head in disbelief at the absurdity of what was being done to him. It was hardly likely that he would escape. His leg and chest looked as though he'd been fired from a cannon into a mangle, and his lungs were a bubbling red cauldron.

The two warders heaved him up excruciatingly by his armpits and lowered him into the hole. They picked up shovels and started piling the excavated sand in around him, packing it tightly up to his chin.

Then they walked off and left him.

His addled brain whirled and eddied in a scarlet fog. The Shamal had blown itself out now, but despite the hot sun beating down onto his skull, he felt cold.

He urinated. That, too, was painful in the tightly packed sand.

A scorpion wriggled up to investigate his nose, but unprovoked it moved disinterestedly on. Flies, ants and a wasp stung his face. His nose ran into parched and broken lips, and now his body felt like a fired clay furnace.

His heart thudded against the restriction of its sandy tomb.

A man in light khaki strolled up through the palms towards him and sat down in the shade. He was carrying a fly-whisk.

For a moment through the mist Hilal thought he recognised the man. A boyhood friend from school. Now an Inspector of Police.

Despite explicit personal instructions from the Director of the RID that he was to be disposed of without interrogation, the Inspector of Police began to question Hilal.

They had been instructed to shoot him, but felt the severity of a live burial might induce some loquaciousness on Hilal's part.

It did not.

Uncaring about the extent of his injuries, the Police were indifferent to death and the fact that nothing made sense to Hilal any more.

His boyhood friend, this Inspector of Police, shrugged and turned to stroll back through the palms. He was sad. It was very hot and it was obvious that whatever he had done to deserve it, his old school friend was suffering greatly.

Ten minutes later three other men appeared, walking through the palm grove towards him, like cruel children come to prod a sick animal.

They stopped ten feet away, muttering to each other, then one of them bent to pick up a stone, drew back his arm and threw it at Hilal. It landed inches from his face, knocking a puff of dust into his eyes.

One of the other men picked up a larger stone and threw it, not forcefully, but this one found its mark and bounced off the smashed bridge of Hilal's nose.

A third stone came towards him. Instinctively he closed

both eyes. This stone hit the top of his head and he felt another blinding flash of pain cours like lightning down through his bowels to his heels.

An unerringly aimed fourth stone tore into his left eyelid, pulping the eyeball beneath. A fifth and sixth then crushed his cheek bone and broke off two of his teeth.

His head was throbbing and singing anew. His mouth tasted even more bitter with fresh blood and mucus.

For a moment they stopped stoning him, but when his blurred vision cleared he saw three pairs of boots standing in front of his broken nose. One boot was slowly raised, and then its toecap connected viciously against Hilal's right ear, another crushed his right temple and the heel of the third drove into his chin.

The sand subdued the sound of the *CRAAACK* as his neck snapped. Hilal was distantly aware of soft, plumb-like oedema erupting about him, then he disappeared into a long flaming tunnel to oblivion.

Several miles offshore the tail end of the Shamal had swung round to return.

When it reached the palm grove and rattled the coarse fronds of the surrounding trees the three executioners sought shelter in a nearby stone sangar. One of them ran out to place a green canvas bucket over Hilal's broken head in an attempt to save what was left of him for later.

While they sheltered, the wind whipped the bucket off into the trees. If he'd been able to breathe his blood-drenched lungs would have clogged with sand. But he was no longer breathing.

At the age of twenty-seven Hilal al-Bakri was now dead.

EIGHTEEN

"The rebels have re-grouped and are having *another* go at the Army?"

"'Fraid so, Ferguson," said David. "They're a determined lot. Home-grown whirling dervishers. They've got the bit between their teeth. Two good points about it though, the Army's got General Wally out there with them, and they're also getting excellent training at the real thing. Some manoeuvre *this* turned out to be."

The four men were sitting in David Marks's office at Masela Camp.

Repeated calls to the Police had failed to elicit any information about the fate of Hilal al-Bakri. They were confronted with a wall of silence.

"It's a bit of a running battle out there at the moment," David went on. "I've had General Wally on the air twice. He's happy as a sand-boy playing soldiers. They've suffered a few casualties, but by sheer weight of numbers the Army must win through. It's really no more than an elephant being harassed by mosquitoes. I couldn't hazard a guess as to when they'll all arrive back though. There's no point in you three honchos going out there now, so what do you want to do in the meantime?

"Find Suleman al-Bakri," Ferguson said. "In a moment of delirium his brother Hilal let slip that he was with the Liberation Army at Wizan."

"Well, if the al-Bakris are connected with this whole thing, why not call on their father – old Sheik al-Bakri? He's up at Wadi Besim. It's on the way to Wizan. He's an educated and understanding old boy. At one time he was Ras-al-Am's ambassador to London. He's also very pro-military, and since you saved his son Hilal's life all those years ago . . .?"

"Yeah, I heard him refer to that on the helicopter," Chuck intervened. "What was that all about then?"

"Nothing really," said Ferguson. "He went somewhere out on the jebel. He'd fallen down a crevasse and broken his leg? He'd also received a couple of nasty scorpion bites. I found him and hauled him out. That's a good idea, David . . . can you kit us out with a couple of Land Rovers?"

"No problem."

Although it had been years since he was last there, the view from the lip of rock overlooking Wadi Besim never ceased to thrill Ferguson. He felt transported back to the sixteenth century - and even beyond.

The wadi was like a cattle rustlers' hideout in the Old West. Trees and thick foliage on the natural rock walls camouflaged the village nestling below. The silence in these mountains, and their echo, allowed each sound from the valley floor to reach them as a gift-wrapped package on the clean air.

They heard a dog bark; the clatter of cooking utensils being washed; the voices of women chattering as they performed their ablutions beside a rock pool; the gurgling sound of running water; a young boy's shout, and exotic birds chirruping in the branches.

To reach the village below they had to descend a series of well-worn rock steps and broad stone slabs hewn out centuries before.

When they reached the foot of these steps they were confronted by a goat stretching up to nibble the leaves of a red-flowering pomegranate tree.

They walked along a path to the heart of the village, Hans and Chuck following Ferguson's example and offering elaborate greetings to everyone they met. Shy young women averted their gaze, while the more confident older ones flashed gold-toothed grins as they glided by with an assortment of loads precariously balanced on their heads.

They passed the village's one-room school just as the morning's class dispersed for their midday meal, and were overrun by thirty or so barefoot little brown figures who erupted like chattering monkeys through the open doorway, feet flashing beneath their dish-dashas, laughing and thrusting their grubby hands up to be shaken as they hurtled homeward. The three tough mercenaries chuckled to see such exuberance. Every third world country they'd been to seemed to have got it right where their children were concerned.

To get to Sheik al-Bakri's house they entered a warren of wattle-stanchioned stone passageways unchanged since the days of the Prophet.

The higgledy-piggledy houses, built like a Spanish pueblo village on prehistoric foundations were linked by erratic steps and pathways, one house's front door blanket opening onto the neighbour's kitchen window, and so on.

A dignified old man stood leaning against the wall of his house as they passed below him.

"Hallo, Major Ferguson," he called. "I remember you well. How are you? Praise be to Allah. Welcome to Wadi Besim. Welcome to my house. Come, you and your friends must join me for coffee and dates."

It was Sheik al-Bakri himself, retired statesman, now revered village elder, magistrate and mayor.

For Ferguson and his friends not to have been invited for coffee would have been an insult. In the Middle East even police coming to arrest a murderer were compulsorily offered and accepted the obligatory hospitality by the man's family before making an arrest. For Ferguson to decline the invitation would give rise to even greater offence.

The three of them climbed the steps and shook hands with Sheik al-Bakri who led them inside his small stone abode, kicking off his sandals and leaving them at the door of his simple majlis, the austere reception room where men convened and conversed away from their womenfolk.

In Raman the Sheikh had a grace-and-favour villa the size of a small palace, but preferred to live here in the village of his ancestors.

He clapped his hands to gain attention behind the scenes, calling for refreshments for his honoured guests. Female voices and a flurry of activity could be heard from an adjoining room as the three men sat cross-legged on a large colourful rug, like Red Indians preparing to pow-wow. Their 70-year-old host did likewise, tugging his dish-dasha over his knees like a girl kneeling on a lawn.

The room had a series of cushioned recesses set in its walls, few decorations other than an Indian trader's garish calendar nailed to the wall, with a faded postcard of Mecca, an incense burner and a portable cassette-player and radio on a shelf.

Inside it was cool despite its lack of a fan or air-conditioning. These houses had trellised plaster woodwork and subtle arched chimneys developed down the centuries to exploit the slightest breeze in hot weather.

"So, Major Ferguson – tell me some things," said the elder, and for five minutes they exchanged pleasantries about the crops and the weather.

One of the Sheik's sons by his third wife appeared like a genie in the doorway, bowed and padded in barefoot bearing a tray the size of a dustbin lid which he set on the floor between his father and his guests.

Ferguson and his companions inwardly groaned. The tray contained a plate of segmented oranges and salt, bananas, a pile of sticky dates smothered in flies, four plastic beakers and a water jug.

Malaria was rife in Ras-al-Am, as was infectious hepatitis which they knew could be contracted from conditions such as these, but they dare not offend the Sheik. They brushed away the flies and stuck their fingers into the gooey mound of dates.

The Sheik's son returned with an ornate coffee pot and four small cups which he held in his left palm. Deftly he poured a jet of thick black coffee into each of these and offered them first to the guests. Ferguson politely indicated the Sheik who insisted that his guests should take the first cup, and not until this time-honoured ritual had been conducted three times did they sip the hot, bitter liquid.

The Sheik's son, standing with the pot ready poised, promptly crouched to refill the cups. After their third cup Ferguson assessed that the Sheik was content with the range of their small talk, and ventured lightly: "I understand that your

134

son Suleman is now with the Liberation Army at Wizan?"

There was a silence while the old Sheik's face struggled to conceal a range of emotions. He tapped his fingers together and chewed his lower lip.

"You know about this?" He raised one bushy eyebrow and Ferguson nodded. "I see. Well, it was bound to become common knowledge sooner or later. My younger son, Hilal, is with them too, you know," he said, a hint of pride in his voice.

"Sheik, it would help us if we could find out something about this Glorious Liberation Army. Why has it been formed? What are its aims? Are you able to tell us any of these things?"

"I can tell you all of these things," the old man replied. "For many months my loyalties have been divided between the ideals of the Sultan and the Sultanate, which I have always upheld – and these new revolutionary ideals of my sons, which I have listened to, which I understand and which I try to respect. At my age I shun violence, but every generation seems to create its share of it. When there is so much of it around in the modern world there is no reason to expect that Ras-al-Am should be spared. From my vantage point here in the hills, detached from the day-to-day life in the Capital, I am well placed to view my country's affairs objectively.

"Because of our petro dollars Ras-al-Am has leapt from medievalism to super-sophistication in less than two decades. It is ruled by a progressive monarchy and run by a government of ministers, most of whom are members of the Royal Family. Sultan Hamad has created a considerable national pride, identity and awareness. Everyone flies our country's distinctive flag above their homes and has a picture of the Sultan in their parlours, yet we are still a nation of haves and have-nots.

"The hill people are witnessing the concentration of growth and urbane development of the Capital Area around Raman with its expanding suburbs and tree-lined, neon lit tarmacadamed roads where previously there were only dirt tracks. They see the shiny cars, the plush homes and high-rise government buildings. They see this explosion of wealth, and so not unnaturally ask themselves If I am Ras-al-Ami too, then

135

where is my share? They are good people, but people of limited intellect. Our history is riven with incidents of the hill tribes taking up arms to ride down on the more affluent city-dwellers on the coast to exact retribution for all manner of slights. What's to prevent them doing the same sort of thing today? Line up their simmering discontent that I've just described with a twentieth century catalyst – and you have trouble."

"What exactly *is* that catalyst?" Ferguson asked.

"Simple," the old man said. "Higher education – but no jobs. For the past few years a whole crop of suitable young Ras-al-Amis have been encouraged to go away to study and qualify abroad in the United States and Europe, in UK especially. This had to happen if Ras-al-Am was ever going to develop into a self supporting nation with its own doctors, dentists, teachers, bankers and so on. After being subjected to western liberalism and acquiring their degrees our first generation of graduates has returned: and what do they find? No careers and no jobs. The country is expanding rapidly, but not fast enough to accommodate the aspirations of these bright young men. My own two sons are cases in point. The number of unemployed Ras-al-Ami graduates has become several hundred, and increasing. And none of the Ras-al-Ami Old Guard has yet died. Add to this the discontent caused by the Royal Family's monopolistic stranglehold on ninety-percent of the selected businesses that reject gate crashing young entrepreneurs trying to break into their game, and you have a potentially lethal impasse.

"You won't have seen them when you were here before, Major Ferguson, but since you have been away all the bright young graduates have to do all day is cruise round Raman in their Mercedes and BMWs drinking Heineken, taking drugs and killing time while they await some sort of opportunity to arise. All sound reason for frustration. It has been inevitable that sooner or later the pressure would have to burst. Because of their breeding, education, background and sympathies my sons were approached to organise an effective expression of this national discontent. They accepted the challenge, and the

Liberation Army was formed."

Hans, Chuck and Ferguson sat spellbound while the old Sheik expounded the reasons for these recent events.

"Your sons run the whole thing?" Ferguson asked.

"Certainly." The old man nodded. "I assumed you knew that, and that it is the reason you are here."

"Well – we knew that Hilal was involved in some capacity, and we had reason to think that Suleman might be as well, but we weren't sure of the extent of their involvement."

"They are the Liberation Army's joint commanders," the Sheik said.

Ferguson didn't feel he could break the news to the old man that he was unlikely ever to see his younger son alive again. "What will be their next move?" he asked.

"That I cannot say." The old man smiled.

"I understand. But can you confirm that Suleman is currently at Wizan."

"I believe that to be so – yes."

Ferguson could see the Sheik was getting tired and that when they left he would doubtless indulge in soul searching about the amount of information he had divulged, but they all had the best interests of Ras-al-Am at heart. The more each party knew about what the other was thinking, the greater chance of reaching a less bloody compromise.

"Although my sons command the Liberation Army, you should be aware that they are not its principal instigators."

"Really?"

"Not at all. I don't know who *is*, but I am led to believe that it is some very senior personage in the Royal Court," said the Sheik.

"You are as well briefed as I am," Ferguson told his friends after the three of them clambered back up the cliff path out of Wadi Besim and were back beside their two Land Rovers. "We now have two priorities; make contact with General Wally and relay everything Sheik al-Bakri has told us, plus we need to track down Suleman at Wizan and see what he's up to. Think you and Hans can handle that, while I get on back to Masela?"

137

"No problem," Chuck affirmed: Hans nodded agreement.

"Good. We'll now go our separate ways, and meet up in Masela later – right?"

They clambered aboard their vehicles and set off in different directions, bouncing across the copper-coloured rock-strewn bundu to pick up their routes from the hills back down to the coastal plain below.

An hour later Ferguson was in the valley driving through Basira Oasis, prior to striking south-east for the 200 kilometre high-speed trek back to Masela Camp.

Not many people outside Ras-al-Am knew about Basira Oasis. Its name conjured an image of a palm-fringed pool with hawk-nosed Sons of the Desert bartering gold and guns while their camels took on water – but Basira Oasis was not like that at all.

Its population of 50,000 was spread between two sprawling townships of mud and wattle shacks interspersed with high-rise offices, hotels and a hospital.

Basira Oasis was on the border between the United Arab Emirates and Ras-al-Am. The Ras-al-Am Army, Police Force and civil populace worked and mingled with their UAE opposite numbers. There was a riot of currency and car number plates, dust, dogs and businesses, as well as dark and perspiring itinerant Asian labourers.

After negotiating the town's chaotic traffic Ferguson hit the blacktop eastward, his jacket sticking to the seat of the Land Rover.

Summers in Ras-al-Am were months of enervating heat and humidity. Raman, the capital, was one of the hottest cities in the world, where frying an egg on your car bonnet to prove it was now an outmoded party-piece. Most of its offices were air-conditioned, but out here in the jebel the hills glowed like grills, baking the valley floors in oven temperatures.

The new road through the hills curved through glaring bright white sand and gravel on either side. Here in this barren expanse sunglasses were a necessity, to reduce migraine and accidents, despite other vehicles only passing every ten minutes or so.

Oily blobs and lines flashed and darted across Ferguson's windscreen as he drove.

The gravel plain, the rocks and scrub hovered in what appeared to be shimmering pools of water.

Mirages were a common sight, but the image that suddenly presented itself to Ferguson now seemed unlikely to be true. He pulled his vehicle onto the hard shoulder.

Reaching across the seat beside him he grabbed his binoculars. Three-hundred metres ahead a water standpipe was clearly outlined on the gravel plain 50 metres from the roadside.

These overhead pipes are a common sight in the Middle East. They are outlets for artesian bores sunk into the water table beneath the surface.

Despite the high mineral content and brackishness potable water bowsers refilled at these pipes, where concrete stands enabled them to park without sinking into the wet sand.

Whilst taking on water from the green PVC hose which dangled from the pipe, the bowser driver usually used the waiting time to refuel and then dump his empty diesel drums nearby, so the concrete slabs became black and greasy from all the spillages. The soiled area dried in the hot sun, but the randomly discarded drums gave the site the appearance of a mechanic's yard in the Australian outback.

In this unlikely setting, for a moment Ferguson thought he could see . . .

. . . a naked woman . . .

. . . silhouetted, on tiptoe, on the concrete slab beneath the standpipe . . .

. . . gazing skyward, her arms raised like an Inca princess offering exultant praise to heaven.

Was he going nuts? Heatstroke? Hallucinating? What was the matter with him?

He focused his Swarovski binoculars and zoomed them in on a flame-red BMW 320 parked just off the otherwise deserted highway.

Darting his arc of vision off to the left he brought the lens to rest by the standpipe, where there undoubtedly stood a naked woman. She was European, with long brunette hair and a bronzed and shapely body glistening beneath the cascade of water gushing from the hose.

Ferguson could not decide whether to continue feasting his eyes on this tasty sight, or drive closer before she covered herself like startled prey frightened by his approach.

His pulses raced, not just from the excitement and disbelief, but also from concern for the woman's safety.

The naked body is anathema to Muslims. Ras-al-Ami policemen were volatile and unpredictable. They would not react with the same sang-froid as their British counterparts. In a place as remote as this they would probably shoot the girl on the spot for being mad.

Ferguson decided he should tell her . . .

. . . but just at that moment she stopped washing herself, crouched – and froze.

Like Ferguson she had seen three Toyota Land Cruisers approaching from the opposite direction.

They slowed down, paused, and pulled off the road to bump over to the standpipe.

The woman did not flinch, but brazenly resumed an erect posture beside the cascading hose. Ferguson admired her chutzpah.

For 30 seconds nothing happened . . .

. . . then the Land Cruisers' doors opened and a dozen Arabs clambered out to form a group which moved hesitantly across the intervening space towards her.

Ferguson could almost sense licking of lips. He pulled his Land Rover back onto the road and accelerated to cover the ground between himself and what was about to occur.

Damn the stupid woman. As though he didn't have enough on his plate to worry about.

Neither she nor her would-be assailants saw or heard his approach. When Ferguson was still 50 metres distance he saw one of the Arabs tentatively reach out and stroke the woman's shoulder.

She did not flinch, but fetched him a resounding slap across his face that sent him reeling back with amazement.

This inflamed his companions who moved forward en masse to manhandle her. As they grabbed at her she slipped onto the wet concrete slab.

Ferguson knew that if he was going to do anything to help this young lady he needed to act quickly.

Ramming his foot onto the brake he slewed the Land Rover around and stopped in a shower of shale. Swivelling in his seat he swiped his shotgun out of its rack, leapt from the cab and loosed off a shell into the air.

The tangled group at the standpipe whipped their heads about and froze as the shot's echo reverberated around the jebel.

With the gun's stock resting against his groin, feeling like Gary Cooper in *High Noon* Ferguson walked slowly towards them. The Arabs knew he looked like trouble.

They got up and dusted themselves down.

Someone still sitting behind the wheel of one of their Land Cruisers peeped the horn three times. Responding to the signal the Arabs hurried across and clambered aboard their vehicles which moved back onto the hardtop.

The last vehicle swung out of line and headed towards Ferguson. The sun on its windscreen prevented him seeing who was driving.

He dropped to one knee to present less of a target. The Land Cruiser paused 10 yards from him, and a voice shouted in English: "I don't yet know who you are, Mister – but this is the second time our paths have crossed. Don't let it happen a third."

As the vehicle accelerated to catch up with the rest of its small convoy, Ferguson glimpsed a man with a black eye patch.

Drongo Horne.

What the hell was *he* doing here, he wondered as the three vehicles disappeared into the distant haze.

He turned to attend to the young woman, now sitting on the wet concrete with her arms across her knees.

"Hallo again," she greeted him. "Thank you. I'm impressed.

141

You're a very unusual photo-journalist, I must say."

It was the nurse they'd sat next to on the plane from Bahrain. What was her name -? Julie Adams. He remembered she had said something about having to arrange to be driven to Basira Oasis to collect her sister's car.

"You're a bloody little fool," he barked. "What the *hell* do you think you were playing at?"

She bridled. "I felt hot, tired and sticky. A shower out here in the desert seemed daringly delicious, and . . . thank God you arrived when you did. You looked pretty good you know, zooming in from the wilderness on a swirl of dust and a gunshot. It was very silly of me, I know. I'm sorry."

Ferguson could see her heart still thumping heavily beneath her naked breast.

"You're covered in sand and your bum's smeared with dieso. Look - why not finish your shower and stop wasting all this precious water?"

Julie registered the softening tone of his voice. "While my new bodyguard continues to keep all the aspiring rapists at bay, you mean"? She laughed. "Good thinking. You're right. Why don't I do just that!"

She rose to her feet and padded back beneath the pouring water. "Care to join me?" she called, coquettishly.

"No. Thanks."

"You really should, you know. It's glorious. Hey – gung-bunging, sorry – gang-banging a white woman, is that the ultimate fantasy for a bunch of Arab wankers?"

"You certainly invited the possibility. They're not even 'in' to bikinis in this part of the world yet, let alone 'out' of them. You should know that."

" . . . Oh I *do*. But, God, I did so want to strip off and get under this water."

"Well, I suggest you hurry up and get out of it," Ferguson bellowed, despite enjoying watching her lissom torso under the cascade.

"Wassamatta now?" she called, peeping out from beneath the spray and wringing out her hair.

"Just get a move on, that's all," he growled, glancing up and down the road.

Julie stepped from beneath the water, slapping her firm belly, flanks and shoulders with her palms. Smoothing the droplets from her breasts she reached for the scruffy towel she had left draped across one of the dieso drums beside her clothes.

"I'm sorry about all this." She pouted, then smiled with mock contrition.

"'s alright," said Ferguson, reaching up to turn off the tap. "It's just that one doesn't often get to see many naked women disporting themselves hereabouts."

"I can imagine." Julie giggled, hopping on one foot while stepped into a skimpy pair of white briefs. She wrapped a light cotton skirt around her hips and pulled on a man's shirt which she knotted across her midriff, leaving her nut-brown navel bare. Flicking up the shirt's collar she turned back the sleeves, slipped on a pair of ethnic sandals, scooped up the towel, and said: "One clean girl, who's ready to go now, please."

"Do you know the way?"

"Sure. Follow my nose."

"Pretty much – yup. It's quite a long haul, so you'd better burn off now in that farty little BMW of yours, and get a move on."

They walked back to the road together and Ferguson opened her car's door for her. Julie squealed when the heat on the front seat burned her bottom.

Quickly she started the engine to enable the AC to kick in.

Patting Ferguson's hand on the windowsill, she winked at him, saying: "Hey - thanks again, Big Boy. You know? Be seeing you . . ."

She let off the hand brake, shifted in to second gear, depressed the throttle and waved a cheery farewell as she went roaring off.

Ferguson smiled to himself, kicked a stone and carried his shotgun back to the Land Rover. Ejecting the spent case from the barrel he was just moving to open the door and replace the gun in its rack when he sensed an in-comer, yelled *"SHEEEIT . . ."* and hurled himself as far from the vehicle as he could.

With a *Whoosh* and a *Cruuump* the Land Rover disintegrated before him in a sheet of flame.

"*Drongo* Bloody *Horne* I'll get you *yet*," he hollered, bowled even further from the vehicle by the rocket's blast. They had doubled back, hidden up behind some rocks higher up and taken a bead on him with a launcher.

Now what the hell was he to do? It was a three-hour drive to Masela, and he needed to get there quickly. He could wait hours here for a lift.

Then he heard another sound . . . could it possibly be -?

It was -. Zipping back towards him from out of the shimmering haze over the undulating blacktop came an unmistakeable little red BMW.

Spunky lass – that had taken some doing.

"One good turn deserves another," Julie Adams screamed out to him, squealing in a savage U-turn on the road. "Don't hang about. Come *on* - leap *in*."

Darting from his skimpy cover Ferguson slithered down onto the road and threw himself through the door Julie flung open for him, just as a stream of machine-gun bullets started *spanging* off the stones around them.

Julie let out the clutch and tore through the car's gears, achieving the manufacturer's best-claimed time for 0 – 60.

"My would-be assailants?" she asked.

"Guess so."

"Yours too now, huh?"

"Looks like."

"I heard the explosion. Thought I'd better nip back and check, that's all."

"I'm very glad that you did. Thanks." He glanced into the rear-view mirror, adding: "You're one ballsy lady."

"We'll have to wait and see about that, won't we! Masela next stop?"

"Right on, lass. Oh, by the way . . . I'm impressed."

NINETEEN

"Where the hell do we start?" Chuck grumbled.

Hans shifted the toothpick from one side of his mouth to the other, sniffed and shrugged.

The two men had arrived at the dusty fishing village of Wizan and parked their Land Rover inconspicuously behind a crumbling white building. They were now strolling through its market place, the suq, getting the feel of the place.

Each man spoke and understood a fair amount of Arabic, but unless they got a lucky break this was going to be one hell of a difficult assignment.

Wherever they looked they saw traders sitting cross-legged beside the produce on their stalls, the all-pervasive heat drawing out the bouquets from their fruits and spices.

The air was filled with the aroma of cardamom, pepper, and dried peas, coffee and sweetmeats, curry powders, ghee and sizzling goats' meat on spits over open fires tended by gold-toothed vendors with flies crawling round their blind eye sockets and suppurating ankle sores.

Mangy pye dogs sniffed at cuts of raw meat while scrawny cats investigated blood-streaked catches of fish.

Bearded, grave-faced Ras-al-Amis cast Chuck and Hans curious glances while visiting the barbers' shops or chatting with friends. Brown-skinned Indians and Pakistanis mingled and bartered with people of a blacker colour, denoting their African ancestry and origin. Women in multi-coloured clothing clustered round the cloth stalls, the silversmiths and goldsmiths, seeking out gaudy bracelets and pendants, fondling them and asking their price.

"This is kinda like wandering through the pages of National Geographic," Chuck said.

"There's something in the air though; can't you sense it?"

"Nope," said Chuck "Unless it's those dates we ate at old Sheik al-Bakri's place. Used to be their ambassador to UK? What the hell's he doing living in a medieval hovel?"

"Opted for a return to the simple life," suggested Hans. "Gone back to his grass roots. Gott in Himmel – what's that smell?"

They had entered a small square where a battery of wooden tables had been set up.

It was the fish market. Fire-blackened pails filled with that day's catch were arrayed on the hard-packed ground strewn with leather buckets of water and crude wire and bristle brushes.

"This place reeks worse than a whore's crotch," Chuck grimaced.

A three-legged dog with puss congealed round its opaque eyes sniffed its way blindly from pail to pail. A scabious white cat leapt onto one of the tables where it yawned and licked its lips.

The whole market shrilled with the harsh prattle of men exchanging a cross-fire of local scandal while they skinned and gutted the fish. Hans watched fascinated as one of them tore his knife adroitly through a fish's neck and hacked off its head before switching his attention to its belly which he slit open with equal skill. He withdrew the shining blue viscera which he plopped into one of the pails. Wiping the sweat from his brow he held the knife aloft for a moment, then plunged his hand into another pail to withdraw another fish.

"I used to like fish," said Hans.

"Still do," said Chuck. "In tins – as soup. Let's get out of here. Cut through between those two old houses."

It was then they got their break.

"Holy shit," gasped Chuck, in front, leaping back and crashing his arm against Hans to sweep him back in against

146

the side wall of one of the two houses."

"Man alive," Chuck hissed. "Take a look out there and get a load of what's going on. If they're not making a film and it's not World War Three, then I reckon we must have found what we're looking for."

Keeping to the shadows Hans edged forward into the gap between the two low houses where the alley spilled onto the beach. *"Phew,"* he whistled between his teeth.

"There must be two-hundred vehicles and as many again horses and camels," said Chuck. "There's got to be upwards of a thousand men."

"Yup – and all raring to go."

Ahead of them the sea lapped the shore fifty metres away, but the hard-packed sand between was crammed with vehicles, horses, camels and men, drawn up in formation along the beach as far as the eye could see.

"They're spread out for well over a kilometre at least," said Hans.

"All armed as well by the look of it. They've even got machine-guns on some of those vehicles."

"We suspected it wasn't going to be a carnival parade," said Hans, "but it never occurred to me they'd be this close to whatever they're up to. I thought we were just going to arrange a nice little chat with Suleman al-Bakri, try to persuade him to change his mind, but what we've got here is the whole bang shooting-works ready to roll."

"Where to though, and what to do - that's the point?"

"They're not pointing towards Mecca, chum. They're aimed at Raman."

"So what do we do? Sit tight and see what happens – or high-tail it back to Raman and tell them what's coming?"

"Tell who, Chuck? The Army's in the field. Who's going to hold-off this lot?"

"The Police?"

"They'd be stretched if they tried. These guys intend ploughing along the beach to avoid detection," said Hans. "It'll take some hours. We can get back to the Capital by road in two hours. I reckon we should hang about and see what happens."

"Good idea," rasped an ominous voice from behind them. "That's what I reckon, too,"

They whirled about to find themselves facing a dozen or more Arabs pointing rifle barrels at them, with Drongo Horne leering at them, thumbs hooked in his belt loops as he stepped forward and surveyed them menacingly.

"I still don't know who you people are or what you think you're doing," he said, "but I did promise that we'd be meeting again, didn't I. I've already had a confrontation earlier today with your big friend in the jebel, who just missed being killed – who *are* you?" he barked.

"Tourists," said Chuck.

Drongo Horne spat derisively at the ground. "What are you doing here?"

"Sight-seeing," said Hans. "We just slipped through here to see the fishing boats. Imagine our surprise when we saw all these tribesmen and armed vehicles. Is some sort of carnival about to start?"

They could see Drongo Horne mentally tussling with himself. Although unlikely, they might have been legitimate tourists – but then he made his decision. "Okay, wise guys – you're coming with me," he snarled.

"Who says?" asked Chuck.

"I do."

"On whose authority?" Hans enquired.

"This," Drongo smirked, indicating the surly cut-throats behind him, brandishing their weapons and blocking the alley. Chuck and Hans glanced at each other, and shrugged. There didn't seem much option at this stage. At least they would be getting themselves closer to the heart of the matter.

"Lead on then, McDrongo," said Chuck as the Arabs surrounded them and edged them back along the beach towards the convoy's centrepoint.

"How did you find us?" asked Hans, after they'd scuffed through the sand for a few minutes.

"Don't be naïve," Drongo said. "This entire village is

sympathetic to the Liberation Army. Two curious white-eyes wandering about the place - what did you expect? You should have kept your snooping until after dark."

"We told you, we weren't snooping – we were sight-seeing," Chuck insisted.

"Sure you were." Drongo Horne spat into the sand again. "Tell that to Suleman al-Bakri. That's him over there."

Suleman al-Bakri was obviously a leader. Wearing lightweight Air Force combat kit he stood taller than those about him, all of whom instinctively deferred to his commanding presence.

"Majid Zahir; you have done well, old friend," he cried out resonantly to an exhausted tribesman with a bloodstained tourniquet wrapped around his leg who stood holding the reins of a foam-flecked horse. "You have ridden hard to bring me this news. You have fought well. Your achievement is great. Now you must rest."

"No, Sayid; I ride with you," the horseman replied, so fatigued he could barely stand.

"As you wish, my brother; you have earned the right." Suleman smiled and patted the other man's shoulder. "Mister Horne . . . what have you there?" he called.

"Sayid – we caught these two men spying on us," Drongo Horne reported. "What would you have me do with them?"

"Whatever you think is best, Mister Horne. I don't have time to consider the matter."

Flanked by his lieutenants Suleman turned and strode down the beach. One of his group leapt onto the back of a command vehicle and activated a switch. His voice boomed along the foreshore.

He cried out to the Liberation Army - "Our glorious leader, Suleman al-Bakri, will address you. Gather round now."

Hordes of men left their vehicles and hobbled animals and made their way as close as they could to the centre-point.

"Quite a turn-out," hissed Chuck. "Isn't this what that

149

British General Montgomery used to do with his Eighth Army, those Desert Rat guys who fought the Afrika Corps in Libya?"

"Don't be a prat: how would *I* know? Mine were Rommel's people," Hans retorted.

"Sorry, I forgot." Chuck grinned. "Hey – Drongo Horne - whatever you call yourself: what's the programme?"

"As far as you're concerned, American shit, you'll be kept under close guard in my vehicle until I decide what to do with you both." He spat, and one of his henchmen jabbed his rifle barrel into Chuck's ribs.

Suleman al-Bakri climbed onto the back of the command vehicle and the hubbub along the beach stilled to attentive silence.

"My brothers," he began – "We have rallied the tribes and prepared the horsemen. Our time is nigh." He paused and a thunderous cheer burst upon the air.

"Majid Zahir, my brother's trusted friend and commander has ridden hard to inform me that Hilal's army is marauding the Sultan's forces south of Wadi Banud. By these brave actions they have detained the government troops in the field. Raman and Masela Camp are now devoid of opposition. WE RIDE TONIGHT."

Again a great cheer rent the air.

"The Grand Council has ordered that at dawn . . . we unleash the horsemen. Tomorrow, my brothers – WE RIDE ON RAMAN."

Amidst cheers that had not been heard since his grandfather's time, Suleman al-Bakri watched while his Liberation Army dispersed to their vehicles and animals and prepared to mount. They would travel that night along the 200 mile stretch of beach, arriving at the outskirts of Raman by dawn.

The morrow would be an historic day.

TWENTY

"My apartment's just over there, behind those trees."

"Very nice too." Ferguson smiled. He and Julie had just driven through the main gate to Masela Camp and past a block of living quarters, having made the journey back to Masela in under two hours. Julie was a sassy conversationalist with a keen wit; he had enjoyed her company. Although it must be obvious to her that a bone-fide photo-journalist would hardly be toting a shotgun to ward off armed tribesmen and then make a dash for it back to Army HQ, Julie had not remarked on this, for which Ferguson liked her all the more.

"Where to now, Chief?" she asked.

"I'd be grateful if you could drop me outside the HQ building."

"My pleasure, sir. And then what?"

"Er . . . sorry?"

"Oh, come *on*," she shrieked, banging the wheel with mock desperation. You saved my *life*, for chrissakes."

"You saved mine too, remember."

"Ex*act*ly. That's what I mean. We saved each others lives, so wouldn't it be a waste of time just to leave it at that? Couldn't we *celebrate*, or something?"

"What did you have in mind?"

"Don't be difficult," she snapped. "Here's your wretched HQ. We missed lunch. Do you think you could find your way across to my apartment afterwards?"

"I should think so. Behind those trees . . ."

"At least let me offer you a cup of *tea* when you've finished."

"Sure. That would be nice."

"Nice, eh. Big deal." She snorted. "How long will you be?

"An hour?"

"See you then."

Hair bouncing, she swung the little car round in the car park and shot off back to her apartment near the base hospital. Ferguson went through the glass doors of the HQ and bounded up the stairs to David Marks's office.

"I owe you one Land Rover," he said, as soon as he went in.

"Y'what?" David squinted up at him from a paper-laden desk.

Ferguson threw himself back into a chair and started to relate the entire day's events, at the end of which David grinned and said, "Yes, I have seen her a couple of times, in the mess. Damned attractive young woman: one of the classiest items we've had here in a very long time. Drongo Horne, you say? He's Giles Carrington's henchman . . ."

"*Is* he, by Christ. Things begin to look even more ominous."

"That's for sure," David agreed. "It's fascinating stuff old Sheik al-Bakri told you, though. General Wally's going to be interested in that. The Army's still having its progress impeded, harried by rebels like terriers round a lion's ankles."

"Last time it was mosquitoes up an elephant's arse," Ferguson grinned.

"Might well have been," retorted David with embarrassed huffiness. "I tend to think analogously. Can't help it. It's the poet in me. By my reckoning the Army will get back sometime tomorrow afternoon. Your debrief will . . . keep till then? It's pretty classified stuff, after all. I'd rather not have it go over the air, especially when the Old Man's got a battle on his hands."

"Agreed."

"You say Chuck and Hans have gone in search of Suleman. Interesting to see what they come up with. What do you want to do now? Go back to your hotel and check in here again tomorrow?"

"Eventually." Uncrossing his legs Ferguson stood up to leave. "But first," he said, tapping the side of his nose and

152

giving David a wink, "I shall be 'taking tea' with a certain young lady of my recent acquaintance . . ."

An hour – Julie thought. I've got an hour. In an hour that extremely tasty killer-diller will be appearing within my four walls. The place is an absolute *tip*. What shall I *do?* I don't think I've even *got* any tea - dammit.

After their two-hour dash and now her ten minutes frenetic domestic activity she was sticky again. Was there time for another quick shower? Tearing off her shirt and unwrapping her skirt she peeled off her briefs and stepped into the shower cubicle.

"Oh, my *GOD*," she screamed.

A Bombay-Runner, one of Ras-al-Am's big brown cockroaches, had somehow lifted the heavy grille of the shower's waste outlet and climbed up the plumbing into the ceramic well.

"Oh, my *God* . . . I cannot abide those things," Julie screeched, clenching her fists against her chattering teeth, while the giant drain beetle scuttled about her ankles waving its six-inch feelers in the air.

"I've never even seen anything so big and brown and horrible as that before, even when I was living in Africa. What am I going to *do?*"

Drumming her heels against the tiles she shifted her position at the same instant the cockroach changed direction. With a *scrunch* that made her retch with nausea, Julie felt her heel crush down with a crackle of smashed, dark brown, hard, horny wing covers, and a *squelch* as her weight completed the job with the rest of the creature's ghastly mushy body.

"*Ohhhh,*" she shuddered, and leapt from the shower to rip off half a loo roll to scrape up the slimy mess. Screwing it into a bundle she flung it into the pan and flushed the horrid thing straight into the Indian Ocean. She didn't think she'd ever be able to sit on that loo seat again in case its ghost came up to get her.

With her heart beating madly Julie turned on the shower and stood frantically lathering herself. She shampooed her hair, rinsed her fanny, turned off the hot tap and realised the cold was just as hot, gave up and towelled herself dry.

Staring at the shower's wall tiles she noticed that they were convex, and poking out from behind the gap in one of the tiles she saw . . . oh, *no* . . . the tips of two more questing brown feelers.

She reached out timorously to tap the tiles with her knuckles. The feelers withdrew, but the hollow sound told her that the cement and grouting had become so brittle that the tiles were only hanging there by self-supportive imagination.

Julie just *knew* that lurking in some disgusting grotto behind these tiles was another bloody great cockroach and that she, Julie Adams from Buckinghamshire, had been put on Earth to be its executioner.

She bashed the tile to crush the cockroach hiding behind it.

The unexpected result almost turned her hair white.

With a *craaash* like a hundred falling dinner plates every tile erupted from the wall and cascaded to the floor in a smashed heap around her ankles.

Crying out with horror Julie saw that not only had there been *one* concealed cockroach, but the entire surface of the wall was their spawning ground. It was smothered with a seething brown colony of eggs, and babies, mothers and fathers, uncles, aunts and grandparents all leaping into a frenzy to escape their rude exposure. They darted onto her shoulders, down her naked breasts and body, onto her thighs and down her legs to burrow through the pile of crumbled tiles at her feet and seek hasty egress through the grille of the waste outlet from where their forebears had first arrived.

Julie didn't know whether to scream, flee, or remain rooted to the spot.

Naked, her feet and ankles buried, bruised and blooded with rubble, with a tight cold band squeezing her head she thought that perhaps her lovely afternoon could now be deemed to have been spoilt.

Stepping from the shower she staggered in search of a bucket to start scooping up the tiles, which she then took outside to pour with a *clang* into the dustbin.

Returning, she ran the shower once more and hosed every nook and cranny that could harbour eggs, scrubbed the walls, scrubbed the well, and once more scrubbed herself.

She dried herself on another big towel, combed out her hair, applied lipstick and perfume, slipped on a pair of high-heels, wrapped a flowing housecoat about herself . . . then the doorbell rang.

Sheeeit, she hissed, knowing she should have dressed properly, but what the hell – it was infernally hot, he'd already seen her starkers anyway, so it didn't make much difference - and there was no time.

Outside, Ferguson enjoyed the late afternoon sky glowing like a sheet of peach-coloured silk. Inside, he heard a door bang, an unladylike oath and the sound of high-heels clacking along a tiled corridor.

"*Hi*," Julie carolled, smiling brightly as she flung open the door. "Am I ever pleased to see *you*," she cried and flung herself sobbing into his arms. What the hell had come over her? She'd had no idea she was going to react like this, but – oh, God – those ghastly cockroaches . . . and a delayed reaction to her ordeal at the water hole . . . "Whatever must you think of me? I'm so sorry . . ." she sniffed, patting his chest and dabbing her eyes.

"That's alright," he smiled. "I enjoyed it – what*ever* it was in aid of."

"I've just had a dreadful experience," she explained, and told him what had happened.

"Poor old you." Ferguson chuckled. "You women never cease to amaze me. You can drive your car into a rocket launcher's field of fire and not bat an eyelid, but then you become hysterical over mice or spiders or cockroaches. Scrub tea. Got any brandy?"

"I think I have, yes," Julie said disengaging herself, brushing back her hair with her fingers. "Medicinal, of course – yes? Meanwhile, why not go out on the balcony?"

Ferguson's spirits darted about like kites in wind. This girl was definitely getting to him. His senses reeled from her perfume and the feel of her flimsily-clad body against his. That was no cheap, tarty ploy. She had been genuinely overwrought by those cockroaches, and was now embarrassed.

He sat down in one of the sun-bleached cane chairs on the balcony, with a view of the cobalt blue ribbon of the Gulf etching the horizon. These past few days he'd had no time to keep abreast of international news, but he assumed this Iran/Iraq War thing was still developing into a major calamity. Only last week US warships had poured 1,500 five-inch shells into an Iranian observation platform, and still the Iranians were bleating for more, sending their young men out in tin-pot boats to provoke a superpower: crazy. Where would it end? *Would* Iran acquire a nuclear capability? *Would* Russia become involved. *Were* they witnessing the dawn of . . .?

"Why so pensive? Penny for them?"

"Whether we are witnessing the dawn of Armageddon . . .?"

"*I* think."

"Do you – why's that?"

"Because I can't find the brandy. Will this do instead?"

She stood in the doorway showing a lot of leg, holding a chilled bottle of champagne on her shoulder like a classical beauty with an amphora.

"The girls gave me this as a flat-warming present. Shall we open it?"

"I can think of no reason why not," he smirked happily.

"There y'go, then," she said, handing him the bottle and placing two flutes on the rickety bamboo table. She sat cross-legged in the chair opposite him, watching attentively while he eased out the cork.

"*Whoosh* – there it goes, you clever old thing," she cried, clapping her hands, leaping up to catch the bubbly's gushes in one of the glasses while the cork shot over the balcony wall to land in the sand below. "My father always told me it should come out with a sigh, like a duchess passing wind," she giggled, "but I much prefer it going off with a *bang* . . . which is why I shook it up a little first, of course."

"Oh, every time," Ferguson agreed with a grin, feeling closer to her with each word she uttered. "What shall we drink to?"

"How about . . . a lovely new friendship?" she suggested, with a twinkle in her eye. Ferguson noted that over the rim of her glass one eyebrow had risen a fraction.

"I thought you were meant to be a hard-working angel of mercy," he said, "not roaring around the desert in a BMW, throwing champagne parties."

"Why not, dammit; we only live once. When have I been able to sit out in the setting sun like this on my own rent-free balcony overlooking the sands of the desert on one side and the Gulf of Ras-al-Am on the other while vultures fly overhead, listening to the muezzin calling the faithful to prayer, guzzling bubbly with a divinely handsome, *definitely* taboo older man – who's some sort of a mercenary to boot, too, if I'm not very much mistaken – Why, it's the most romantic thing I've ever done in my life before. Want to pour us some more?" She waggled her empty flute at him.

"What's with this mercenary tag, then?" he asked as he leaned across to refill her glass.

"Well - you are. Aren't you?"

"How would you know about things like that, may I ask?"

"I've lived in Africa. Recognise the breed."

"Well, you may be right – but then again you might not, so shall we just leave that one alone for a moment?"

"Only on one condition."

"And that would be?"

"You let me wrap my arms around your neck and kiss you."

"Julie." He laughed. "I hardly know you. What about my reputation?"

"Is there one?" she enquired.

He proffered his hand, palm upwards, and was thrilled when she walked her fingers tantalisingly into his grip. Too much sun? The champagne? Was she playing with him? They raised their eyes to hold each other's gaze.

"I mean it," she said.

"But why me?"

"Chemistry, I guess. You're powerful stuff, Ferguson, I told you," she said with a catch in her voice. "I'm a big girl now. We're out here in the Middle East. We've shared an adventure.

You saved my life. I've been scared witless by cockroaches. We're drinking champagne. We're alone. Do I need to go on? Ferguson – surely you can see? I *want* you, for chrissake. I've never come on as strong as this in my life before. Is there any reason why you . . . ?"

"Afraid there is," he said, gravely.

"Oh my God – what?" she clapped a hand to her brow. "Don't tell me. You're diseased? Impotent . . .?"

"Neither. I'm filthy, and need a shower."

"Oh, you *beast*," she shrieked, She leapt across and pummelled him with her fists.

He mauled her affectionately.

"It wasn't easy for me, struggling to say all that, you know. I think you could have helped me along a *little* bit."

"I did."

"You didn't. How?"

"By not interrupting."

"Ferguson – go and get your damned shower, will you," she commanded, raising a fist threateningly. "Everything's in there. Use the red towel. It'll suit you. What was it you said to me out in the desert?" she called after him as he got up to go through to her bathroom, " . . . and bloody well get a move on?"

Climbing out of his soiled clothes he stepped into the shower, grimacing at the mess left by the falling tiles. When the Pakistani workmen got around to re-tiling, the whole place would be like a chalk quarry on a wet day.

He doused himself with her shampoo, lathered up, rinsed off, dried himself with the red towel, and used her comb to sort out his dark curly hair, still wondering why a beautiful 23-year-old woman should be thrusting herself at him like this. He was forty-five. Julie could write her own ticket with a host of eager young bachelors who would fight tooth and claw to get her. *Any* woman in Ras-al-Am was a bonus. One like Julie was a dream come true. Ferguson knew some young women preferred older men, but even so . . .

"Remember, you're meant to be shaking a leg in there," he heard her call. "You're keeping an impatient lady waiting."

Wrapping the towel around his loins he walked with barely concealed excitement through to the bedroom.

Julie lay naked on her big double bed.

Kneeling on one leg beside her he caressed her shoulders and stroked her hair while she gazed at him with liquid eyes and opened her arms. In one fluid motion he whipped off his towel and they subsided into their first full embrace.

"Don't wait," she begged, clawing his broad shoulders. "Come straight into me now."

Turning onto her back she drew up her knees, allowing Ferguson immediate entry.

Julie shuddered and groaned. "I've come already," she confessed, chewing her bottom lip.

"Me too."

"Why don't you turn me over,?"

"Is that how you like it?"

"Any which-way but loose."

Ferguson slapped her rump as she moved, making her yelp. Sitting back on his haunches his tumescence resembled something on the frieze of a Greek vase, while Julie knelt forward and wriggled herself back into position, waggling her bottom at him in an insistent invitation.

She groaned and slumped submissively forward, burying her face in the pillows as though snuffling truffles.

His fingers dug into her hips while he wrenched her body against him.

She bucked in response to each of his thrusts, their bodies slapping together with a sound like wet canvas.

The bed shook under its onslaught. It swung round on its castors, enabling them to see each other's reflections in the wardrobe mirror.

Their eyes met and locked in the glass.

"Darling, I'm coming," Ferguson roared.

"Let me have it," Julie cried. "Give it all to me. Oh *noo* . . ."

Their strokes were so violent they became uncoupled.

Gazing back between her legs Julie saw that Ferguson was twitching like a rogue fire hose. His hot pulses of semen jetted between the backs of her thighs to splat against her quivering

159

belly, across her breasts and up into her face.

"*Wonderful,*" she cried, cupping her palms against her body and massaging her skin. "Give me *all* your drops." She turned to fondle his testicles with one hand while milking him with the other.

She lowered her head, gazing up at him adoringly while bending to her task.

When his tumescence subsided they paused and smiled, Julie releasing him to slip with a *plop* from her lips.

"I feel like the cat that's got the cream."

"And I feel . . .", said Ferguson, stroking her wet tendrils of hair, "well and truly . . ."

"Fucked," they both cried joyously, collapsing into a laughing embrace.

"That, my darling Ferguson . . ." Julie flicked the end of his nose with her finger, "is what I'd call one hell of a bonk."

"And if that . . ." Ferguson retorted, "is the shape of things to come, then I'd say we've got a hectic season ahead of us."

"And I'd say . . ." Julie leaned forward to nibble his ear, "that I made the right choice."

"And I'd say . . . I'm glad I didn't play hard to get," Ferguson replied, tickling her.

"Oh, no . . . *Stop* it," Julie cried, writhing about on the bed, slapping her thighs squelchily together. "I can't stand it. Honestly I can't. *Stop it*, darling. I mean it. Please. Really. *Stop it*," she shrieked.

With a final slap of her rump Ferguson pushed her away and stood up to stretch. When he glanced back at her she was curled on one corner of the destroyed bed sucking her thumb, looking up at him with her big green eyes.

She removed her thumb from her mouth, and with one arched eyebrow and a mew, asked – "More?"

"Certainly not. Come along now, hassle ass. I'm taking you back to my hotel for dinner."

"I'm all for that. T-bone steak for me, please."

She bounded from the bed and then paused. Looking coyly at Ferguson she gave a short yelp, bit her lower lip and clutched one hand front and rear.

160

"Whoops - I'm afraid this has suddenly become rather a senior bathroom job," she gasped. "Excuse me: back in a jiffy."

Ferguson laughed as she scuttled off to the bathroom, trying to keep her knees clenched on the way.

He was delighted that she had eschewed any pretext at modesty.

He followed her to the bathroom to watch while she stood beneath the strong shower jets, bending at the knees to whip a lather of suds between her legs.

"You smell like a musk ox yourself," she shouted, arching her pelvis forward to rinse away the soap. "Come here, I'll wash you."

Ferguson stepped in to the shower beside her.

She poured a blob of shampoo over his head and lathered his whole body with it as it ran.

"This is being done purely for professional reasons, I presume," he teased while she fondled him. "All part of a nurse's role, is it? Big boy's black-belt après-bed bath."

"Course not." She laughed. "It's terrific fun, that's all, having another body to play with – especially such a lovely one as yours. You're big, brown and brawny, Ferguson. Macho gone mad. You're good to be with. I like it. You can stop soaping my breasts now. Grab that green towel and start drying yourself."

Ferguson took a green towel from the rail and dried off while Julie did the same with a big fluffy yellow one.

"What would you like me to wear?" she asked.

"Me – I shall have to put all my stinky clobber back on," he said, "but I don't know what you've got."

"Better go and see then, hadn't we."

Grabbing his hand she led him back along the corridor to her bedroom.

While he put his clothes back on Ferguson enjoyed watching Julie's posture as she sat erect before her mirror combing out her thick hair and applying makeup. Opening her jewel box she slipped two gold bangles over one wrist and a slim Tissot watch on the other, put a ring on one of her fingers and a pair of earrings into pierced ears.

"There," she said, swivelling on her stool to face him, seeking his approval.

"Perfect," he said. "But shouldn't you be wearing a dress or something?"

"Blast." She snapped her fingers in mock annoyance. "*Knew* there was something."

She skipped across the room and flung open her wardrobe door. Swiftly bending down she selected a pair of red high-heels and put them on, then reached up to remove a skimpy white dress from its hanger. She slipped this over her head and let it unfurl to her knees.

"Okay?" she enquired.

"*Gorge*ous, but . . .?"

"What?"

"You're not wearing knickers."

"Rarely do."

"You're a guinea-a-minute, you know that," Ferguson chortled.

"More than that usually sir, but for you it's free. Perfume?"

Hurrying back to her dressing table she removed the stopper from a small bottle and dabbed something expensive behind each ear, across her throat, inside her elbows and wrists and then quickly behind each knee. Re-stopping the bottle she opened her jewel box again and took out a small gold chain. Flicking up her dress she placed her right foot on the stool and fastened the chain around her ankle.

"Right: all set, I think," she said, smoothing the dress over her thighs and standing ready for Ferguson's final approval.

She looked sensational. The dress was nothing but a simple shift with a low bustline and two slender shoulder straps. With her suntanned figure Julie looked absolutely ravishing.

"Ras-al-Amis get hot under the collar about women's bare arms and shoulders," Ferguson explained. "Might it be a good idea if you were to wear some sort of a shawl?"

"Whatever my lord and master suggests: one shawl coming up."

Quickly she opened a drawer and pulled out a black shawl

which she slung with a flourish round her shoulders.

"Suitable?"

"Fantastic. Let's go."

Ferguson sat grinning behind the wheel of Julie's BMW as they drove towards the Tasa Hotel together. He felt the most chuffed buck in Islam.

Julie rustled in the seat beside him, emitting a glorious waft of scent. "Penny for them?"

"Fancying you all over again."

"Nice." She reached a hand along his thigh. "Do you think your friends will have arrived back by the time we get there?"

"I hope so."

"Wonder if they've been having as good a time of it as we were?"

"That I doubt." He chuckled, and felt her dig in her nails.

At the hotel he went straight to Reception.

"I'm sorry, sir," the clerk told him, checking the rack behind him. "Their keys are still here, and there've been no messages."

"Thank you. If they come in will you please tell them I'm in the restaurant.?"

"Certainly, sir."

Leaving Julie to wait for him with a gin-and-tonic in the bar, Ferguson went up to his room to change before joining her.

Two hours later Hans and Chuck still hadn't shown.

"That was a lovely dinner, Ferguson. Thank you so much, I did enjoy it," Julie said, finishing her second cup of coffee. "But I really *should* be getting back to camp now. Tomorrow's my first proper day at work, and I think I've earned a good night's rest."

"Okay." He chuckled. "I don't like the idea of you driving home alone though. Stay the night?"

"M'sieur Gallant: don't be daft – I'll be fine. I mean, I'd love to stay the night, of course I would, but I think I'd better go. Will you call me?"

"Course I'll call you. There are still one or two positions we haven't tried yet."

"Oh, you. Stop it. You'll make me blush."

"Come on. I'll see you out to your car."

When the BMW's tail lights disappeared through the gates and turned right, Ferguson went back inside the hotel. He was worried about Hans and Chuck still not being back yet.

He felt he should be doing something about it, but until they returned there was not a lot he could do. It was stupid of him to have got involved with Julie. She was an adorable creature who, he suspected, was going to become extremely meaningful to him.

He went off to the bar and ordered himself a whisky.

TWENTY-ONE

A pair of vultures circled in the shimmering currents of hot air above the Gulf of Ras-al-Am's coastal belt.

White with black-tipped wings and ghastly yellow heads they had glided over the parched scrubland in search of carcasses, but for the past hour the sound of gunfire had kept them aloft.

Now the shooting had stopped they swooped down to confirm that what awaited them was that rarest delicacy – human flesh.

One of them dropped from the sky to land with a puff of dust in the scrub. Dislodging flies and sand it folded its wings and waddled across to the nearest body . . .

. . . like a fussy diner arranging his cutlery the scavenger appraised the uniformed remains of a Baluch sergeant before darting its long slender bill forward and jabbing out and gobbling the corpse's left eye.

The sergeant, near dead, groaned and twitched his head sideways.

The vulture opened its wings and hopped back. Emboldened by the lack of any further response it darted in again deftly to tear out and swallow the sergeant's other eye.

Shifting its weight awkwardly it sank its talons into the man's distended belly, gaining purchase to rip out a piece of raw flesh and lay bare the glistening viscera.

Thirty or more soldiers of the Masela Camp Guard Company lay dead or dying in the searing dunes beside expended cartridge belts and brass cases glinting like gold in the bright sunlight. Heavy machine guns lay toppled in the blood-soaked sand, dusty barrels still hot from their sustained fire.

Swarms of flies clustered round the sword-hacked flesh and oozing bullet wounds of this detachment of the Sultan's army. Singly and in pairs a dozen more vultures flapped down from the sky to claw and rip the other bodies.

Soon all that remained of the unit were tatters of uniform, slimy white bones and undevoured entrails plopping in the heat. Fully sated, the last of the vultures rose heavily into the sky to find a crag upon which to savour its gluttony and sleep.

Yellow ghost crabs large as a man's fist now began burrowing into the residue of a corporal's open thigh. The warm Gulf waters crept inexorably closer towards his bullet-smashed suede green desert boots, flushing the crabs in and out of the gaping wound.

As the tide continued to rise, the corporal's carcass and those of his comrades were soon awash and then afloat. In due course the ravages of salt water immersion and fishy predators would complete the process started by Ras-al-Am's crabs and vultures. Within a month the men's bloated body segments and tendons would wash ashore on the beaches of Goa a thousand miles to the east, but it was unlikely that any Goan fisherman or paddling tourist who found them would guess from where they had come.

This would be the gruesome aftermath to a scenario that had taken less than an hour to unfold . . .

Raman's International Airport was built on a coastal belt two kilometres from the sea, running parallel to a 10 kilometre stretch of sand known as Schmidt's Beach, eponymously so called after the nearby German construction company's labour campsite on the far side of the dunes.

The intervening wasteland of salt flats and scrub was an open flank which even in normal times presented a security risk to the airport. To counter potential terrorist threats, once a month the Masela Camp Guard Company practised an exercise called *Op Barood*, to secure the airport's flight paths, which they played for real whenever a visiting or departing dignitary was present.

That morning's detachment of the Guard Company's Baluch soldiers had gone to Schmidt's Beach to set up and man their barriers, while overhead a helicopter scoured the area like a giant dragonfly, seeking swimmers, sunbathers, and the occasional bonanza of a courting couple in the dunes. It could be a disturbing experience for lotharios, locked in a meaningful embrace in a secluded sandy enclave, to see a helicopter hovering above like a hawk spotting its prey, and a Land Rover full of Ras-al-Ami soldiers staring down at them. Some never performed properly ever again.

Although it seemed unlikely that picnickers lobbing Frisbees could or even would want to down an intercontinental airliner, the area was cleared as a periodic safety precaution to deter any determined activist smuggling a Sam-7 missile into the dunes.

Helicopters plied the perimeters approach routes, and police launches stood a couple of kilometres offshore.

So far as anyone knew, this month's exercise would be no different to any other. Just another military rehearsal: over by lunchtime.

The Rhodesian pilot, Bas McLaughlin, banked his helicopter seaward and circled to beat a clearway back up the beach.

After two years in Ras-al-Am Bas had only a week left to serve before his contract expired. Now he had been detailed to fly this latest air safety mission.

It was a drag. He had flown it many times before and nothing ever happened.

But, hallo . . . what was that down there? A few kilometres along the coast he glimpsed a series of large blob formations moving down the beach, churning up an enormous dust cloud in their wake.

He continued on course, radioing back to Control that he was proceeding to investigate. When he got closer he saw the formations were made up of bodies of men cantering along on horseback, on Ras-al-Ami racing camels and a vast armada of vehicles. Hundreds of them.

He flew back along the route their line of advance had

taken. The sand had been churned up and furrowed by hooves and tyres so that it resembled a haphazardly ploughed field receding many kilometres into the distant haze.

Who on earth were these guys? What the hell were they up to?

Perplexed, Bas circled again and set off to try to discover who they were and what they were doing. They looked like 7th-century Muslim warriors bent on spreading the word of Islam by fire and sword.

Unless they stopped within the next kilometre they would enter the restricted beach zone; there was no way the detachment from Masela Camp Guard Company would be able to hold them. Even if he was fired on the junior officer commanding the detachment would be unlikely to offer retaliatory fire without a superior's order, and right now all his senior officers were 200 kilometres away in the desert, disengaging from a battle with rebel dissidents.

The riders continued pell-mell along the beach with no indication that they were aware of the fact that they were approaching a no-go zone.

Bas increased his air speed, intending to overtake them and hover over the beach ahead of their line of advance. He skimmed along, nose down, above them.

It was an amazing sight; one he expected to remember as long as he lived. Suddenly the controls leapt in his gloved hand.

The helicopter yawed and slipped.

"NO - ," Bas screamed. "Oh, sweet Christ . . . _NO_ . . ."

A shot from one of the riders below had removed Bas's tail rotor. The smashed blade tore through his fuel tank, exploding into a giant fireball. Burning debris fell amongst the riders on the beach below, killing two horses and three tribesmen, but the rest carried on unchecked . . .

The young commander of the Baluch Guard Company detachment on the beach, Lieut Dil Murad, had observed the helicopter's unusual aerial activity, and listened to the pilot's messages over the air to Control.

He was standing on a sand dune looking intently through his binoculars. He had seen the cloud swirling towards him along the beach, and assumed it to be a dust storm.

He saw the helicopter try to outrun the cloud, and then it exploded into a ball of orange flame, its *CRUUMP* thudding into his ears seconds later.

Lieut Dil Murad had thirty jundees and six vehicles under his command, patrolling the area and manning three checkpoints. He knew he should continue to keep the checkpoints covered, but he recalled the two patrolling Land Rovers to his present location.

Within minutes he saw them come tumbling across the dunes towards him. He ran down from his dune onto the beach, beckoning them to follow. With hand signals he indicated where he wanted them to take up station, facing up the beach, engines running and headlights on full beam.

Other armed soldiers he sited tactically in the dunes. Then he and his sergeant stood-at-ease on the open beach in front of the two Land Rovers, trying to look threatening.

The massive cloud rolling towards them took shape and the young officer realised with horror that his initial fears had been well-founded.

There were horsemen, camel riders and vehicles, doubtless with many more behind creating the dust cloud as they came.

He had no idea who they were or what their intention was.

He desperately wanted to trust that the authority of his presence would stay their advance, but having seen the helicopter disintegrate in mid-air he doubted the strength of his position. He hoped he wouldn't be forced to make an ignominious dash back into the dunes, allowing them to thunder past unchallenged.

Surely somebody must have seen them and be sending reinforcements? The Police launches offshore would have seen the helicopter blow up. They must have radioed what had happened back to their headquarters.

The approaching private army was in clear view now, 500 metres away and closing fast. A crackling rent the air and puffs of sand erupted from the beach a few metres in front of where

Dil Murad and his sergeant were standing. Another 200 metres and they would be within effective range.

There was a *claaang* and the tinkle of smashed glass. Dil Murad swung round to see a spiralling wisp of smoke where one of the Land Rover's headlights had been shot out.

Instinctively he drew his pistol and fired three shots into the air. It was the only retaliatory gesture he could think of. The horde was now using them as target practice.

"Back to the dunes," Dil shouted, and as he hurled himself onto the scrub beside one of his jundees, he screamed the order *"OPEN FIRE."*

If Lieut Dil Murad had not given that order, Suleman al-Bakri might have passed them by. Their aim was to storm the airport, and to do this they had to turn inland at this particular point along the beach.

Their horses and camels were tired, their vehicles overheating, and Suleman knew that they should rest, but also he knew that if they rested they would reduce the momentum they had built. To rest would also reduce their element of surprise, allowing the Police and other agencies to organise resistance.

He had planned to consolidate briefly at this point, confident that his fifth column detachments would concurrently be infiltrating Masela Camp, Police Headquarters, the Ras-al-Am Television Studios and other key installations. Now they had encountered this unforeseen detachment of the Sultan's forces.

In the area ahead of the dunes where the soldiers had gone to ground, Suleman's riders had left a hundred-metre zone of clear beach, apart from the two Land Rovers which stood there with their engines still running.

Who *were* these soldiers? Suleman puzzled. Why were they not out in the desert with the rest of the Army? Had they been waiting for him?

Why were there not more of them? The helicopter had had a radio. These soldiers had radios. The Police launches riding at anchor offshore had radios.

All of them now knew that Suleman al-Bakri's Army of

Liberation was approaching Raman. Was no one going to attempt to halt his progress?

Had his other units managed to take over the Army camp at Masela and the Police Headquarters? Had his meticulous planning fooled all these professional units, and he was riding towards an unchallenged victory for their cause – and for Ras-al-Am's history books?

They should now proceed to take Raman International Airport, but Suleman realised that despite his superior numbers this small detachment of Government soldiers in the dunes would still offer token resistance. Because this would slow the speed of his advance, the detachment had to be disposed of quickly.

Suleman's horse reared and pawed the air, then he spurred the great white beast forward and crested the dunes at a gallop, his followers close behind.

The ensuing fire fight was short, bloody and effective.

Suleman lost twelve of his men. Lieut Dil Murad and his 30 jundees of the Masela Camp Guard Company were all killed.

When the firing stopped the vultures circling above dropped one by one from the sky while the Liberation Army proceeded across the salt flats towards Raman International Airport.

TWENTY-TWO

Aboard Gulf Air's Tristar Flight GF001 to London (Heathrow), passengers on the port side were able to view the Raman control tower and the usual activity of the airport's ground crews.

Passengers on the starboard side however, scanning their in-flight magazines awaiting take off, were startled to glimpse, through the condensation on the portholes, hundreds of horse and camel-mounted tribesmen accompanying an armada of Land Rovers and Land Cruisers approaching erratically across the salt flats between the airport and the sea, the riders brandishing primitive hand-beaten swords and more recent rifles and machine-guns.

With no surcease to its wild advance the forerunners of this terrifying mob broke from the scrub to clatter across the main runway, loosing off fusillades of shots and ululating Koranic invocations.

In the shimmering heat at the end of the runway a Hercules C-130 military transport plane was landing, tyres emitting blue smoke from its touchdown.

The reverse thrust on the Hercules' engines made an awesome sound, but the maniacal warriors were not to be deterred from their intent to storm the airport buildings.

When they and the Hercules made their inevitable collision, vehicles were sent careening into the air like Dinky Toys, the catapulted rebels bouncing along the concrete to lie like piles of laundry discarded in the breeze.

Camels and horses screamed as their legs were cut from under them and their chests stoved in. Decapitated riders' brain matter atomised across the airstrip like pink aerosol spray.

"Come ON, this is our CHANCE" Chuck Henderson yelled at Hans Ehrlich. "GO; GO; *GO."*

For the past hour Drongo Horne sat in the front of their vehicle. Bored by his self-appointed chore guarding the two men through the night, he had delegated the duty to one of his Arabs.

Their vehicle was one of those that narrowly missed the Hercules, but in the evasive dash their guard had been hurled from the back to crack open his skull on the concrete. Drongo Horne was screaming abuse and directions at the driver.

Hans and Chuck vaulted over the vehicle's tailgate into a para roll on the airstrip and weaved their way through the mass of vehicles around them. The slaughter was dreadful, but the main body of Suleman's forces continued to push inexorably towards the airport buildings.

"Make for the perimeter fence," Chuck yelled.

The Hercules finally came to a stop, seeming to shudder with remorse at the carnage it had wreaked. Its tail section opened and a man with a Bergen jumped down from the ramp to zig-zag hell-for-leather across the airstrip, bullets ricocheting round his ankles as the rebels fired at him.

When Hans and Chuck reached the perimeter fence they hurled themselves against it, their flying leap taking them half-way to the top. They scrambled over the wire, dropped to the ground on the far side, and laughed hysterically to see Ferguson standing there giving them a derisory slow hand-clap.

"I said you were always an hour late and a dollar short. Quickly now, give the General a hand."

"The General," Chuck gasped. "Where?"

"Behind you. That's him belting across the tarmac. The Army's beaten off the rebels in the desert, and he flew back in that Hercules. I've just come from Masela Camp to meet him. I bet he didn't expect this sort of reception, though. What happened to you two, anyway?"

"We got here, didn't we? Just as the balloon's gone up . . . Come *ON*, General – you can make it," Chuck yelled as

General Wally's Bergen came sailing over the fence. With a rattle the General scaled the wire and landed beside them.

"Not bad for an old guy," he gasped. "Got a fag? Left mine on the plane."

"Only Marlboro," said Ferguson.

"Forget it. Don't like their advert." He tweaked out and discarded a flattened lead bullet lodged in the rigging of his Bergen then swung round to grip the mesh of the fence and gaze across the airstrip.

"Not thinking of going back for them, are you, Sir?" Ferguson asked.

"Daft bastard," chuckled the General. "No – I'm looking to see what those buggers think they're up to. Right bloody mess, isn't it. Know who they are? What's going on?"

"Yes sir, we do. That is the Army of Liberation," Ferguson told him.

"Army of *Liberation?* What the hell's *that* when it's at home?"

"About a thousand strong," Chuck explained. "The guy you dragged out of the crashed helicopter was Hilal al-Bakri . . ."

"Old Sheik al-Bakri's son? the General cried.

"The same. He was heading-up the rebels harassing you and the Army," said Ferguson. "After we got him back here on the helicopter, we lost him. The Police got hold of him. I think it fair to assume he's no longer with us."

"This lot mobbing up the airport is the Liberation Army's main force," Chuck explained, "led by Hilal's older brother, Suleman – and some no-good piece of bad-ass nasty work called Drongo Horne."

"*He's* with them, is he?" Ferguson remarked, surprised.

Chuck and Hans nodded affirmation.

"We stumbled on their main force up at Wizan yesterday," Hans went on. "They gave us a ride back here during the night. A couple of groups peeled off along the way, but we don't know where they went to."

"Know what it's all about?" the General barked.

"Yes, sir, we do," said Ferguson. "It has to do with some massive social unrest we'll tell you about later."

"Well they're obviously hell bent on taking over the airport. Done their homework, too. Classic first move. Come on -" General Wally snapped. "Let's get out of here. There's nothing we can do while chaos reigns. We must get away and plan our next move."

While General Wally and the Zeta Team hurried away from the airport, the horrified passengers on Gulf Air's stationary Tristar realised that what was happening was not a film stunt, but a real and terrifying incident that looked likely to crash through their presumed invulnerability. They willed the captain to leave as quickly as possible, but it was obvious he would be unable to get the plane airborne until the runway was cleared of camel and horseflesh, broken bodies and smashed vehicles.

The flight had already been delayed three hours because of mechanical failure. Some of the passengers had slept in the airport lounge, some had drunk steadily at the small duty-free bar despite the earliness of the hour, and others almost finished reading the paperbacks they had bought for the journey.

For the past hour they had heard distant gunfire, but assumed it was the Army practising on their ranges. A rumour circulated around that a helicopter had crashed on the beach, but no one knew any more about it.

Dieter Ritter was livid about this delay in take-off. For a whole month he had been stuck in the Middle East, trying to finalise a truck order for his firm, Magirus-Deutz. It had taken two years of negotiation to arrive at this point, and his customer was still giving him the run-around. The specification was spot on; the spares backing package was right; delivery was right, and the price was ever better than right. They were so close in the running against their sole competitor, Renault of France, that it would have be ridiculous to pull out now, even though the air fares, hotel bills, dinners and goodies they had expended over the past 24 months amounted to more than $½million. Nevertheless Dieter was so frustrated by his treatment that he had considered recommending to his Managing Director that they withdraw on principle in the hope that this might force their customer's hand to a decision in their favour. A meeting was scheduled in Düsseldorf tomorrow afternoon, but he would stop-over in London to complete some business there first.

A sigh and a rustle went round the departure lounge when it was announced that the plane was ready for boarding. Passengers gathered up their personal hand luggage and formed queues at the tinted glass door. A smiling Zanzibari airport official checked their boarding cards and they filed out to climb aboard the airport buses.

As soon as he got aboard the plane all Dieter wanted to do was sleep. He stowed their hand luggage in the overhead compartment, removed his linen jacket, loosened his tie, strapped himself in with his seat belt and patted his wife's knee. Heide was reading a paperback biography of Julio Iglesias. He had left her to her own devices a lot in recent years, silly romantic woman – but apart from nearly getting herself raped at the hotel pool that afternoon, she had seemed content enough with him this trip, swimming and lazing every day and rooting about in the suq each afternoon. She looked rested, tanned and healthy. Five minutes later Dieter was fast asleep.

Then he woke again, with all this damned racket going on.

The captain's voice, commendably calm, cut above the taped music being played in the cabin.

"Ladies and gentlemen, this is Captain Danile speaking. I can't tell you what's happening outside, but as you can see it doesn't look healthy. We're as much in the dark about what's going on as you are – but I don't think you should place too much hope on getting back to London today. We seem to be in the wrong place at the wrong time. I expect we shall hear . . ."

His voice was cut short with a choking cry. The plane shuddered from raking bursts of machine-gun fire. Streams of heavy calibre bullets ripped and zipped through the fuselage, crackling a dance of death and injury through the cabin. The passengers scrambled to avoid this rain of fire, swiping the air as though fending off mosquitoes. Dieter Ritter scored an instant hit with his left palm and stared with disbelief at the bloody hole that appeared. His wife whimpered beside him when he stopped waving his arm and slumped beside her with a more surprised expression as a little black hole like the one in his hand appeared between his eyes.

The cabin crew huddled together helplessly at the forward entrance. The door was smashed open from outside. The stewardesses screamed when bearded Ras-al-Ami tribesmen burst through the jagged opening into the plane, brandishing swords and small arms.

"ALL OF YOU – OFF *NOW*," one of the swordsmen barked.

Heide Dieter thought she should be screaming, but found it easier just to smile instead. She realised this was her reaction to shock. Julio Iglesias slipped from her lap to be trampled and skidded away by a gnarled sandaled foot. Heide drifted into a faint.

Some of the passengers were fat-cat Ras-al-Amis from Raman flying to Knightsbridge and Bond Street shopping, or going on holiday at one of their luxury European apartments. Voluble exchanges ensued in Arabic while they demanded their aggressors tell them what was happening, but all they received by way of response was an impatient buffeting. They were hustled from the plane alongside the Europeans with their briefcases, their lightweight suits and sun-bronzed wives.

Heide Ritter awoke on a bench back inside the airport lounge. "May I get you anything?" a man next to her asked solicitously.

"No – thank you. Where is my husband? Where's Dieter?" she cried. "My husband's been killed, hasn't he? He died on the plane. I saw him. He was shot through the hand and then in his head, wasn't he . . .?"

"I believe . . . I'm afraid he was – yes," the man affirmed calmly. "I'm very, very sorry."

"Where is he? Is he still on the plane?"

"I think so. There's not a lot that anybody can do just yet, until we know what is happening, you see."

"What *is* happening? Have we been hi-jacked?"

"That would seem to be the case, yes."

"I must have fainted on the plane," said Heide. "How did I get here?"

"One of Allah's Army humped you across his shoulder," the man told her.

In Masela Camp Bob Davidson, a contract officer or 'mercenary' in this Britons' Foreign Legion, to which he and 200 other kindred spirits belonged, was sitting at his desk in Northern Raman Brigade's Headquarters, preparing handover notes for his successor.

Bob was not going on leave. He had not gone on the ill fated Army manoeuvres either.

Captain David Berry, his successor, in Ras-al-am only a fortnight, had been thrown in at the deep end and gone into the field in his place. Tonight Bob was flying home to England for good. He was now fifty-three and had been in Ras-al-Am seven years. Many of his peers, some of them divorced, inebriates or in debt, but good guys for all that, when they retired chose to hang-up their swords in Spain, or Cyprus, ex-mercenarys' seemingly appropriate last resting places. But Bob had opted for Folkestone. His house was paid for, he had £80,000 in the bank, a British Army pension, and he was going to grow tomatoes and see more of his long-suffering wife, Mary, than he had throughout his life as a soldier.

He was disappointed that his chums were away in the field, because traditionally he would have been wined and dined from the mess tonight, or else they would have clubbed together to take him to the Airport Restaurant and pour him onto the plane afterwards. Now he would just have to slide out quietly by himself, without the bunting. The only blessing was that on arrival at Heathrow's Terminal Three tomorrow it would be the first time in seven years that he wouldn't have a thick head.

It was now 8.30 a.m. Time to finish up here and go back to his bayte, take his uniform off for the last time and finish packing. He had cleared his desk and finished his handover notes. Reading through them he made one or two corrections and then took them through to the orderly room next door for

178

Sultan Shah, the Pakistani clerk, to type. Sultan Shah -? Bob smiled: what grandiose names some of them had – like christening someone Top Dog or Prince Regent. When he pushed open the orderly room door Sultan Shah looked up at him with a crestfallen expression.

"What's up, Sunshine – gone and got yourself another problem?" Bob asked jovially.

"Oh, sir – I am receiving some *wery* bad news, sir. It is bad that we are to lose you, sir, and that makes me *wery* sad, but to compound my unhappiness I am just now receiving telegram from my cousin in Rawalpindi. All at home is *not* good, sir. It is pretty damn critical that I now must go there for compassionate leave, sir. If you will so kindly approve, sir - please sir. Perhaps sir would like to perceive the telegram to confirm verification of my statement?"

Bob took the proffered telegram and read the two well-known sentences he had seen many times before which never ceased to amuse him. Would the Pakistani mafia never give up this transparent ploy to gain extra leave?

"What is it this time, Sultan; somebody having a Big birthday party?"

He scanned and handed back the telegram on which were printed the immortal words: *Mother serious sick. Come quick for last look.*

"Oh no, sir. Absolutely genuine this time, I assure," the harassed clerk insisted, turning-in his most moving performance of profound filial concern.

"As I recall, Sultan, you've been for last looks at your mother three times this year, in addition to your normal leave entitlement. Last year you nipped back for a couple of last looks at your uncle, as well. It's a remarkably resilient family you've got. Can't *any*thing be done to kill them off once and for all? Then you could concentrate on earning your salary for a change, without all this dashing back and forth to attend all these family sick beds."

"Sir, you are mocking me, and this is *wery* serious matter. This time my mother she is really dying, I think. I must ask for your decision, sir – now."

"I'm flying back to England tonight Sultan, and . . ."

"Yes, sir. I know, sir."

"I know you know. What you must also know is that you are an important fellow, Sultan Shah. You are the only clerk left in headquarters until the brigade returns from manoeuvres. Surely you understand that if you drop everything and fly to Pakistan for another last look at your mother, I should have to stay behind to do your job for you . . ."

"You are most kind, sir. Thank you, sir. Thank you *wery* much."

"Wrong – Sultan Shah. Listen to what I'm saying. I cannot do your job for you, because for one reason I do not type. The other reason is that I am being officially discharged from the army today. In a few hours time I shall be a civilian, my Ras-al-Ami visa will be cancelled, and I shall be leaving Raman. Another reason I wouldn't do your job for you is because you have cried wolf too many times for me to believe you now. I think you understand my position quite clearly. I'm afraid that on this occasion I have no option, therefore, but to decline your request for last-look leave."

"Sir, that is *wery* unreasonable."

"Unreasonable or not, Sultan Shah, it's no use you pretending to look shocked, because that's the size of it. Now I'd like you to type these handover notes for me please, and put them into Captain Berry's file ready for when he returns from manoeuvres. Okay? I'm sorry if your mother really is due to pop her clogs, but you've brought it on yourself. I'll shake hands with you now, and say goodbye. Thank you for all the help you've given me while you've been my clerk – and the very best of luck in the future."

"Thank you, sir. Thank you. Sir – please can you give me reference, before you go sir, please?"

"Not now Sultan Shah – no. If you knew you wanted a reference you should have asked me for one before. If you ask Captain Berry in due course, I'm sure he will be pleased to oblige you with one."

"That means I shall have to work *wery* hard for him sir, because he does not know me yet like you do."

"I think you're beginning to catch on to the size of things, Sultan Shah. Now I must be off."

"Goodbye, sir. Goodbye. Thank you. And may God go with you, sir, and put blessings on your family."

Christ – they're like children, Bob thought, picking up his beret and leaving the office for the last time. Walking to the end of the balcony he leaned over its stone balustrade. He took out his pipe and lit it, reflecting on this closing chapter of his life, smiling at the prospect that this time tomorrow he would be wearing his favourite slippers and cardigan and having tea with his wife, Mary, in their drawing room at home. It was a shame the camp was so depleted. He would like to have been able to say a proper goodbye to one or two folk.

Unaccountably Bob felt a premonition of danger from behind, but before he was able to turn a violent blow knocked him forward, winding him as his solar plexus thrust at the stone balustrade. The pipe shot from his mouth and arced down with a small shower of sparks to bounce off the roof of his car parked on the sand below.

His first thought was that a sheaf of tiles must have rushed off the roof and smashed into the back of his neck, but he knew the roof was flat and had no tiles.

He regained his breath and tried to flex his shoulder blades, which were burning and wet.

Things were happening to him. He began to worry that he might really be hurt. Despite excruciating pain when he flexed his shoulder blades, he tested them once more.

The axe that had thudded into his back loosened and dropped onto the stone balcony floor.

Bob laughed at the absurdity of it. A spurt of blood gushed from his mouth and splashed the whitewashed wall.

He stumbled like a felled ox. Blood welled from the wedge-shaped wound in his back, dyeing his dark uniform darker still. His arms, chest, stomach and groin, trouser legs, socks and boots were sopping with blood. He collapsed slowly onto his knees and tried to wipe his eyes to clear his blurring vision.

The flyscreen door to the orderly room swung open.

Sultan Shah came out, studying files. Glancing up, he saw

181

the blood on the wall and then his officer pitch forward onto his face on the stone floor. A further rush of blood frothed from Bob's mouth as he raised his hand to try to say something.

Then he died.

The barefoot Ras-al-Ami tribesman who had padded noiselessly up the stone steps from the courtyard below and hurtled along the balcony with the upraised axe-blade glinting in his brown fist, fled to rejoin the rest of Suleman al-Bakri's Liberation Army.

He had been instructed to gain access to Northern Raman Brigade's Headquarters to assess the strength of its rear party. Its strength had been this one white officer and a Pakistani clerk.

Sultan Shah telephoned the hospital, but after that he lacked further initiative.

He ventured onto the balcony again to see if Captain Sahib had got better. Flies were clustering round Bob's vacant eyes. This was a wery terrible thing that had happened. Who could have done such a thing? What a wery great tragedy too, that the Captain Sahib's Memsahib, poor lady, would not have time to come from England to see her husband, Captain Davidson Sahib, for one last look.

TWENTY-THREE

Masela Camp usually boasted a population of 10,000, but because of the Army's manoeuvres that strength had become more than halved.

The Transport Regiment's vehicle parks were empty. The Electrical and Mechanical Engineers' workshops were empty. The large Ordnance Depot was operating on a skeleton rear party. Most of the arms had been withdrawn from the armouries.

A few elderly staff officers had been left behind to run the Headquarters Building, and the Navy's and Air Force's central staffs were still operating in their respective wings. The Force Base Hospital was operating, its principal task today being to conduct an autopsy on the late Captain Bob Davidson, who had so cruelly been axed to death earlier that morning.

The military band was rehearsing for its appearance at the country's National Day Parade in three weeks time, and staff were running the messes around camp.

The unsuspecting inmates of Masela Camp were going about their daily business in the usual way.

Many of those off duty were swimming with their wives at the Aqua Club, or had gone into Raman shopping, or had played a round of golf and were now locked in a traffic jam that had built up throughout the capital area.

Unaware, at this stage, what was happening, they were also unaware that when they got back to Masela Camp they would be unable to get in.

Those who had remained in camp playing tennis, lounging around the pools, sleeping in their rooms, did not discover that anything unusual was happening until they got into their cars to drive somewhere else and saw columns of dusty vehicles crammed with armed tribesmen roaring round the camp's road network, or parked commandingly at road junctions.

In his office on the first floor of the Headquarters Building, David Marks's telephone started to jangle incessantly with people ringing to ask what the hell was going on.

'David didn't know that anything *was* 'going on. He was waiting for Ferguson and the General to get back from the airport.

He had no idea yet that 30 Liberation Army vehicles had driven straight through the main gates, running down three open-mouthed Baluch guards, had secured the Guard Room and fanned out to complete their mission to take over the camp, at the same time that Bas McLaughlin in his helicopter was sighting their main force galloping along the beach.

Just before Bas screamed *"Mayday"* and his fuel tank exploded, the rebels' Masela Attack Group swept into the Headquarters Building to take over the Air Force and Naval Ops Rooms.

While Lieut Dil Murad fired his three ineffectual pistol shots into the air, they took over the Army Control Room, so that none of Dil Murad's frantic radio messages were heeded.

Three minutes later David Marks knew what was 'going on' alright, when his door burst open and two rifle barrels and a Ras-al-Ami fighting sword were thrust at his chest.

Majid Zahir was now Masela Camp's new supremo, although the camp and its inmates were not fully aware of this yet.

The British naval lieutenant-commander on duty in the Naval Ops Room was allowed to make some tea which he shared with his captors. Majid strode in flanked by three aides.

"You are to contact the Naval Base down on the Raman coast immediately," he barked at the Englishman.

"Certainly, old chap," the Commander replied, to buy time and display some of the British phlegm he had read about his forbears possessing in stirring tales of embroilment in similar situations in the past. "And what should I tell them?"

"Suleman al-Bakri, the Commander of the glorious Liberation Army, orders that they are to send Patrol Boats to collect a group of men waiting by the beached dhow at the harbour wall in Raman. They are to be taken round the headland and landed at the bay beside the Sultan's palace. Do you understand?"

"Perfectly, old boy – but it's a bit of a tall order, you know. I don't command the Raman Naval Base, I have no authority to order anyone there to do anything. Even if I relayed it as a request they would still think I was barmy – or pissed. As far as I know the Naval Base doesn't know your lot are trying to take over the country. In any case, the harbour wall is reinforced with concrete dragons' teeth to prevent the waves smashing it up. No boat could get alongside there. Your chaps would have to swim from the wall to the boats. Whereabouts are they waiting? Are they expecting these boats to come for them? The whole thing sounds sloppy to me, you know. I don't think you appreciate the complexity of what you're trying to do. Putting a blunderbuss up my nose won't help matters either, so please stop it." He pushed the barrel aside with his finger, as though brushing away a bee. "Do you understand what I've just said to you?"

Majid understood enough to realise there might be a problem, nevertheless he barked "DO IT."

"Very well," the Commander sighed. "And what would you have me tell them when they say no?"

"You can tell them we are holding many British hostages at the Airport."

"I agree that might put a different complexion on things."

"And if our demand is not met, they will be killed."

"I see. What – all of them? Gosh, that's a bit steep. You'll be getting your pictures in the paper if you do that sort of thing, you know. Very well then, I'll see what I can do."

The Commander was now the sole representative of the Sultan's Navy.

Nothing would be gained if he died bravely with a bullet up his nose, having refused to cooperate – so the best course for the moment might be to do what he had been instructed to do,

185

slowly; if hostages' lives were at stake, and he had no doubt they might be, what he did next had to be as right as he could get it. Useless trying to persuade the Raman Naval Base duty officer to act on these crazy instructions.

He picked up his telephone and dialled the Duty Officer's number: not at the Naval Base, but at the British Embassy. Miraculously, the line had not yet been tampered with, and he got through.

"Duty Officer."

"Hallo, Lieutenant-Commander Nick Mair here, Naval Ops Room at Masela. Do we know one another?"

"I don't think so. Rodney Glendenning. What can I do for you?"

"Rodney, we've got a bit of a problem on our hands. Wondering if you could possibly help? I should tell you that this is going to seem like either a hoax or the most amazing phone call you've ever had, but I assure you it's kosher. Tell me – have you heard that there is an armoured insurrection taking place?"

"I can't actually say that I have. When, exactly?"

"Now, as a matter of fact. I'm sitting here with a local war lord breathing down my neck and a rifle in my back. Masela Camp appears to have been overrun, and I am informed that other rebels have taken over the Airport and are holding European hostages there."

"Good Lord."

"Exactly."

"No one's told us anything. But then they never do. One of our chaps has just telephoned in to say he'll be late on duty because of a humongous traffic jam along the Corniche. I also understand there's a bit of a fracas going on outside Police Headquarters."

"Good man, Rodney. All this seems to authenticate what I'm talking about – right?"

"Oh, absolutely. Right."

"Well, my wallah here, the one who keeps jabbing his rifle in my slats, wants the Naval Base to launch some of their Patrol Boats round to the harbour wall to collect a group of his chums and drop them off in the bay outside the Sultan's palace. There's no way the Naval Base would accept my authority, and right now I have no access to somebody senior. If you would contact the Naval Base and explain the situation - coming from the Embassy, they might spark. Y'see, if they don't, chummies at the Airport are going to start wasting a few Brits, and as my wife and kids are amongst them, I'd like to stop that happening and get this business sorted out. Got the general picture have you, Rodney?"

"I believe I have. You are absolutely sure this is not some sort of hoax, aren't you?"

"Absolutely not a hoax, Rodney. I'm sitting here trying to remain calm and collected and present the situation to you comprehensively. Can you do it?"

"Yes – of course. I'm sure I'm taking the most fearful risk though. If it backfires, I suppose I'll see you on the next plane out."

"Better than the next box. You're a star, Rodney – thanks. Champagne on me afterwards."

"Righty-ho;– cheerio for now then."

The phone clicked and Nick Mair muttered, "Rodney – one day I hope they make you an Ambassador." Replacing the receiver he swung round in his chair, and said: "Right, General. What's next on the agenda?"

"It will happen?" Majid Zahir asked anxiously.

"Don't know for sure, sport. We've done all we can from this end. Just have to wait and see, won't we."

Majid Zahir swung out of the Naval Ops Room with his three aides hurrying beside him, left the HQ Building and roared off in his Hiace van to report back to Suleman al-Bakri at the Airport, 10 minutes drive down the road.

TWENTY-FOUR

Lying in Bed Number One was an overweight British sergeant groaning over a hard-earned peptic ulcer, and in Bed 2 a cavalry type recovering from an accidental gunshot wound on a weekend hunting trip.

In Bed 3 was a chewed-up Ras-al-Ami subaltern, who like so many of his countrymen had a navigational error on Raman's new flyover and taken an Acapulco dive off the top, landing on his head amongst the crumpled Toyota machinery in the scorpion-infested rocks at the base of one of the flyover's stanchions.

Threshing about in Bed 4 was a major with DTs, and in Bed 5 a syphilitic sergeant wondering, as did everyone else in celibate Raman, just how he could have caught it.

A young Ras-al-Ami, freshly minus his appendix, was missing his mother in Bed 6. The remaining beds in Ward 7 were empty – but not for much longer.

"You've heard the Army's taken a bit of a mauling in the desert?" the Matron was saying to Julie as they completed her introductory tour. "We're expecting a lot of gunshot wounds and fractures to be brought in this morning. We don't know how many yet, but you can bet your life we'll be busy. Good job you've had a few days to prepare, eh?" She smiled. "Coffee?"

"Please; love some," said Julie.

They went back to the older woman's office where a percolator bubbled on a shelf.

"Oh, blast – look, help yourself," she was told, as the telephone rang.

"Matron speaking. Casualty? Yes? Captain Bob Davidson?

Bob Davidson? *Dead?* You can't possibly mean it. Oh, my God – *how?* The *poor* man. His poor *wife.* He was flying home tonight for good. Well, thank you for telling me. Oh, how *dreadful . . . "*

Replacing the receiver the Matron turned to pour her coffee. Opening a small cupboard she took down a small bottle of brandy and sloshed some into the mug. "Purely medicinal," she said to Julie, replacing the bottle. "Bob Davidson was one of the nicest men you could ever hope to meet. We all called him Uncle. It's so very sad."

"Whatever happened?" Julie asked, shocked.

"It's so bizarre that I can hardly believe it, even out here" the Matron said. "Someone's killed him with – an *axe. "*

"My God. How horrible." Julie gasped, spilling coffee on the white slacks of her new uniform.

"Who in heaven's name would do a thing like that . . .?" the Matron said; "I mean, if . . ."

They both looked up at the noise of rushing feet and banging and shouting.

"What the . . .?" The Matron leapt up and flung open her door. Her hand flew to her mouth.

The corridor outside was teeming with armed tribesmen. She tried to close the door, but a group had already seen her. They rushed towards her, brandishing their razor-sharp khunjars.

The Matron was amazed to see that one of the men was a savage-looking European wearing an eye patch.

"Where is Hilal al-Bakri?" he demanded.

TWENTY-FIVE

Mohammed al-Ajmi, the Sultan's nephew, did not glide in with a fleet of Mercedes, flowing robes and minders. Wearing stonewashed designer jeans and a pink Ralph Loren polo shirt he drove himself through Giles Carrington's gates in an Aston-Martin Lagonda and burst unannounced into the study.

"It is not going well. The situation is extremely grave. What is it you British say? We have a tiger by its tail? In this case, it is our own tiger . . ."

"Mohammed, nothing can be gained by panicking. Calm down," Giles urged him. "Now – tell me what is happening."

"The Police carried out your instructions. Hilal al-Bakri died without uttering a word - I *believe*. Because his group attacked the oil tanker, murdered Roxanne Duprés, blew up the ammunition depot and tried to bring down a Jaguar aircraft we had to bring our entire operation forward. Hilal's preemptive strike in the desert proved to be brilliant. It enabled Suleman to launch the main force without hindrance. So far as we know Suleman and his men have not yet learned of Hilal's death. Hilal's chief lieutenant, Majid Zahir, is now with Suleman, so he will know that Hilal was injured and captured and flown back to Raman in one of the Sultan's helicopters. But Suleman and your Mister Drongo Horne have successfully taken the Airport, Masela Camp and the Television Studios."

"That's *wonderful* news," Giles cried.

"Yes – but the Police Headquarters is still under siege," Mohammed went on, "and this has caused enormous traffic congestion throughout Raman."

"So?"

"So Suleman's Palace Assault Group has been held up by a

TRAFFIC JAM. Can you *believe* that?" Mohammed shouted, throwing himself into a chair.

"The Army has beaten off the last of Hilal's brave marauders in the desert and will now be back in their camps within hours. Suleman is due to announce the coup to the nation on television at seven-o'clock this evening. How can he do that if the Sultan is still sitting on his throne in the Palace?"

"I understand the problem," Giles said, rising from his desk and walking to the drinks cabinet. "Unfortunately -," he went on, packing ice cubes into two crystal glasses and dousing them from a whisky decanter, "unfortunately there is nothing we can do to influence events." He handed one of the heavy glasses to Mohammed, who he knew could easily be a contender as one of David Walker's premier global customers. "Suleman knows what must be done. He is acting on our behalf. Either he resolves the situation for us, or he doesn't. Our futures depend entirely on him, one way or the other. All we can do now, my friend, is sit back and sweat it out. Everything depends on Suleman: Cheers." He took a swig of the amber liquid.

Mohammed al-Ajmi did the same and nearly choked.

"Sorry – went down the wrong way," he said, wiping his chin.

TWENTY-FIVE

"Your Majesty, I fear for your safety. Please won't you consider leaving Raman and fly to a safer location?"

General Wally's first priority on leaving the Airport had been to gain an audience with Sultan Hamad to brief him, to acquire an official proclamation that a state of emergency existed, and gain his authority to impose martial law.

He and the Zeta Team had managed to reach the Palace before the traffic build-up that had brought Raman to a standstill.

"No, General – I shall stay where I am," said the Sultan. "It is most unlikely an attempt would be made on my life, or that they would dare to storm my Palace. In any case, the Palace Guard is on full alert."

Beside him, his son Crown Prince Fahad didn't look too sure on either count, thought the General.

"Very well, sir. If that is your decision I must respect it," he said.

"Thank you, General." The Sultan smiled. "Now tell me, how do you plan to stabilise the situation?"

"I shall need to consider that, Your Majesty. This whole thing has erupted so quickly. We've just heard that Army Headquarters at Masela Camp has fallen under rebel control also. Our first priority is going to be to resecure that and the Airport. Your Army will be back from the field and in their barracks later this afternoon, so there's not much that can be done before tomorrow. In the meantime I shall use the Special Forces camp at Bidi as the centre of my operations. As Your Majesty is aware, your Special Forces did not come on manoeuvres with us, so they are intact and operational. I have my Zeta Team outside with me now. We need to return quickly. As the roads are congested with traffic, may we use one of the Palace helicopters?"

"Naturally, General. And while they're here may I have the pleasure of meeting these famed Zeta Group men of yours?"

"Of course, Your Majesty. They will be honoured. They – er . . . they're not in court dress, Your Majesty."

"Nor would I expect them to be." The Sultan smiled and accompanied General Wally to the door.

Ferguson, Hans and Chuck were sitting outside in a marble ante-room when the door opened and General Wally and the Sultan came across towards them. Ferguson gulped: "On your feet; quick," he hissed.

"Holy sheeeit. It's the Main Man himself, isn't it?" Chuck gasped.

"Your Majesty, please may I present three gentlemen of Zeta Group," General Wally intoned, winking at them all as he did so, enjoying their discomfiture. "Mister Chuck Henderson, an American ex-Green Beret. Herr Hans Ehrlich, late of the French Foreign Legion – and Mister Don Ferguson, an ex-Royal Marine Commando who at one time served in Your Majesty's own forces here in Ras-al-Am."

The Sultan smiled and raised one eyebrow with interest. "*Did* you, Mister Ferguson? That's most interesting. I should like to talk more about it with you, but needs at the moment are pressing. I know something of the reputation of you Zeta Group people and am most grateful to you gentlemen for coming to the service of my country. Let us hope for a successful outcome to your endeavours on our behalf. Thank you. I will not detain you further."

With a swirl of his gold robes the Sultan turned and left the room.

Their unscheduled audience was ended.

"Jesus," Chuck guffawed, slapping his thigh. "I didn't know whether I was meant to bow or curtsy, but I'm certainly going up in the world," he cried as their helicopter rose from the Palace forecourt and headed away from Raman. "Ol' Chuck

Henderson from Lincoln, Nebraska, hobnobbing with kings. Wow*ee*. I liked his aftershave, didn't you?"

"I thought he had a beard," said Hans.

"It was some very expensive cologne," said General Wally. "Christ, just look at that traffic down there. We've got to get aboard this situation and sort it out quickly chaps, before we lose any more of the initiative."

Ten minutes later their helicopter landed at the Special Forces HQ at Bidi, 15 kilometres down the road from Masela Camp.

Now that the opposing forces had made their opening moves, the Zeta Team was ready to respond.

TWENTY-SIX

With the Army away from Raman, Suleman al-Bakri knew that the Police were the sole obstacle to overcome before he could establish overall control of the country.

The twenty or so police on duty at the Airport spent their lives strolling about with loaded guns to menace the public, but when they needed to use them professionally in their own defence to make an assertive stand against the rebels, they were chary about taking them out of their holsters. Suleman's men had quickly disarmed them and they were now squatting disconsolately on the Customs' Hall floor, hands locked behind their necks, displaying a range of emotions from disillusionment to fear. Six of Suleman's men were guarding them with sub-machine-guns.

Another team guarded the passengers, held as hostages to secure demands Suleman might otherwise not obtain.

A third group had taken over the Control Tower and was explaining to the air traffic controllers what they should do, while a fourth and larger team was outside the Airport buildings securing perimeter defence.

The Airport was now effectively under Suleman's control. He set up his Command HQ in the air-conditioned comfort of the Airport Restaurant, on the first floor.

The restaurant's smartly-dressed Indian and Pakistani waiters, who had come on duty to open the bar and set the tables for lunch, were bemused by the takeover, but uncomplainingly went on to do as they were told when ordered to gather in the kitchens and stay there.

When Majid Zahir roared up in his Hiace van, accompanied by an armed escort, the situation did not prevent the habitual exchange of courtesies between them. These concluded, Majid reported excitedly, "The military camp at Masela is now under our control, Sayid. There are some families there, doctors and nurses, civilian engineers, the military band, the Naval and Air Force headquarters staff . . . but the majority of the camp's inmates were off duty, ill-prepared to offer resistance. We have taken over Northern Raman Brigade Headquarters and the Armed Forces Headquarters building, the Power Station and the Ammunition Depot, and have put a guard on the Helipad. The camp is secure. The Naval Ops Room has ordered the Naval Base on the coast at Raman to send Patrol Boats to collect our Palace Assault Group held up on the Corniche by the traffic there."

"Well *done*, Majid. Suleman smiled. "And what have you done with the prisoners?"

"We have not taken prisoners."

"Why?"

"The camp is sealed. No one can enter or leave. We have control of their telephone exchange. It is only a minor exchange, and our people have control of the main Ramantel exchange in town. If we took everybody prisoner we would have to guard and feed them. By leaving them in their quarters and messes they can continue to fend for themselves. They will be less trouble to us that way."

"I agree. Let us see . . ."

A clattering of feet across the mezzanine floor outside heralded the arrival of more emissaries . . .

"The Television and Radio Studios are secure," Suleman was informed.

"The Police Headquarters is still under siege," reported another. "The Police are offering resistance. Many of our men have been killed or wounded. We have the whole complex surrounded, but civilian traffic is still grid-locked and the roundabouts are choked."

"Why *is* this?" Suleman demanded angrily. So far this ludicrous traffic jam was his first setback.

"It is a busy time of day, Sayid," he was told. "Everybody has stopped and got out of their cars to watch. They think

196

they're witnessing the rehearsal of some Police extravaganza for the forthcoming National Day Parade. Shots are being fired, people are being killed, but still the public is lined up gawping beside the roads. The tailbacks are becoming worse every minute. The whole of Raman and its approach roads are at a standstill. Nothing can get in or out. We were barely able to reach you here to report to you. Certainly we won't be able to return. We *must* get the traffic moving again, but none of us knows how."

"It is also crucial for our Palace Assault Group to have achieved its aim before your TV broadcast can take place," another emissary reminded him.

Suleman was aware that up to now each stage of the coup had been effected faultlessly. He had taken the Airport, the Army Camp and the Television and Radio studios, and was holding the Police Headquarters under siege. There could be no question now of withdrawing back to Wazin, as though their venture had been nothing but a half-hearted romp. Men had been killed. He was holding an airport full of hostages. Outgoing flights had been grounded. International incomers were being diverted to Dubai, Qatar and Bahrain. By now the whole world knew what was happening in Ras-al-Am . . . yet the completion of this whole glorious mission was being foiled by a traffic jam. He *had* to take over the Police Headquarters and the Palace, otherwise the whole operation would grind to an ignominious halt. His mind raced like a computer, frantically seeking a solution. The restaurant Command Centre was filled with Ras-al-Ami warriors anxious to resume action.

"I have the answer," Suleman announced. "We shall use the Police to help us, the same way that we have with the Navy."

The Police Air Wing hangars adjoined Raman Airport.

By threatening the hostages' deaths, it had been easy for a group of Suleman's men to commandeer a Police helicopter and its pilot.

Suleman was now flying towards Raman, following the main road below. Kilometre after kilometre was choked with immovable traffic. It was unbelievable that the bottleneck at the Police Headquarters' roundabout should have produced such congestion. Suleman's priority had been to finalise the takeover of that headquarters and then to get the traffic moving again. Now he had the use of this Police helicopter his priorities had changed. He could see that his men on the ground appeared to have the Police HQ securely surrounded. By the time dusk fell the traffic might clear by itself. Suleman knew it was imperative to make his scheduled TV appearance at seven-o'clock. Before that it was crucial to take over the Palace. He had to reach Raman to see if Majid Zahir had been successful in getting the Navy to come and lift-off his Palace Assault Group from the Corniche.

It was the first time any of Suleman's three aides had ever been in a helicopter. They sat behind him, glued to their seats in terror, glancing down with wary fascination at the ground flashing by below. Suleman could recognise key points along their route. They were flew over the sports stadium, heading above the Raman suburbs. Suleman's intention was to head for the sea and turn right, knowing the Corniche would then be below them. He recognised the Raman Hotel, the great green dome of the Central Mosque, the Darsan Roundabout with its adjoining fire station, the appliances glinting in the sun, and then they were approaching the sea and banking across the harbour. He signalled the pilot to reduce air speed and altitude to hover above the Corniche while Suleman endeavoured to locate his Assault Group. It seemed an impossible task. The Corniche was packed solid with stationary vehicles and thousands of people milling about the exit to the suq, or sitting dangling their legs over the harbour wall as though awaiting the commencement of a regatta. Suleman could see several police with hand radios, who had long given up trying to untangle the mess, while still being aware of the event that was the cause of it.

Beside Suleman, the pilot was talking into his mouthpiece. Suleman realised that the Police on the ground must have contacted the helicopter in the air, assuming that some Police superior was coming to their assistance. Above the noise

Suleman strained to hear what was being said, but then his attention was diverted by the most wondrous sight of all.

Three Naval Patrol Boats creamed powerfully round the headland and slowed to turn into the harbour.

Suleman was elated. Their principal setback had now been overcome. Majid Zahir had worked a miracle. Allah was with them.

Now the problem was that he did not know where in the throngs below his Palace Assault Group was located, and the Group was unaware that Naval craft had come to collect them. Nor did they know that it was Suleman al-Bakri hovering overhead in the Police helicopter. When they saw the boats and helicopter closing in on them, the Assault Group might assume that everything had been aborted and it was the authorities closing in pursuit. They would probably disperse into the mass of lanes in the nearby suq. The only way to claw success from this phase of the operation would be for the Assault Group to be able to see Suleman, and for him to convey what they should do by some form of signal. He turned in his seat and saw that the helicopter was carrying a winch. Much to the pilot's consternation he clambered back over the seat, shouting to his aides what he intended to do. They struggled to help him into the harness. When he was ready he thumped the pilot's shoulder, indicating that he wanted to be lowered to the water. The pilot shrugged and released the winch.

Displaying more courage than he felt, Suleman swung out of the cabin and hung on grimly while the pilot lowered him towards the sea. He was surprised by the noise and buffeting he received from the wind. He began to feel vulnerable and foolish, swinging like a rag doll on the end of a hawser with seagulls cackling all around him.

He shouted but couldn't even hear himself as his words were whipped away by the wind, so there was no hope of rallying his warriors from the middle of a traffic jam 500 metres away. The pilot stopped lowering the cable, leaving Suleman suspended 50ft above the harbour wondering what to do. The three Patrol Boats moved slowly beneath him, guessing that he was trying to land on one of them. He could see the harbour wall lined with police and thousands of curious onlookers. Suleman seethed with fury, frustration and indignity.

Amazingly, his plan then worked.

The helicopter pilot released the winch and lowered Suleman onto the aft deck of the nearest Patrol Boat beneath him. He released his harness and instructed the young Ras-al-Ami Naval lieutenant to edge his boats in towards the harbour wall. Windswept, Suleman stood on the prow like Sinbad, scrutinising the grinning faces staring at him from across the harbour wall 50 metres away. Many were waving. Some were stern-faced policemen. Children scampered dangerously along the top of the wall hurling banana skins and orange peel at him, and then a voice cried out clearly on the breeze: "Suleman!"

His Palace Assault Group appeared and began clambering up onto the wall. Suleman signalled that they should manoeuvre themselves across the dragons' teeth and swim out to the boats. More armed figures swarmed over the wall and plunged into the choppy water to strike out towards the boats. Suleman could see policemen forcing their way through the crowds, trying to prevent the final detachment of men jumping off the wall, but before they could be reached the entire Assault Group was into the sea, floundering with rifle slings caught round their necks, and their dishdashas ballooning in the water behind them. One or two had forgotten they couldn't swim, and these had to be manhandled towards the boats by their fellows. The bedraggled bunch clambered aboard, grinning and soaking wet.

Suleman's euphoria at regathering his Assault Group now waned. The sailors went about their business with a detached professionalism, obeying his instructions to be landed at the bay beside the Palace, yet Suleman got the feeling he was being humoured; that these same sailors were aware of an unforeseen force that was gathering in the wings to be unleashed against him. His problems were by no means over. The Police Headquarters was still under siege. He had lost the commandeered helicopter with his aides still on board. He had the Palace to storm and a television broadcast to make. The time frame for his operation had been knocked completely awry. He had no contact with his Command Headquarters, and as the patrol boats bearing him and his 70 man strike-force rounded the headland into the cove in front of the Palace, Suleman's sinking heart told him there was worse to come.

As the glittering façade of the Sultan's Palace came into view, Suleman realised he must be mad. The Palace was daunting, an architectural masterpiece that symbolised all the power that he had undertaken to usurp, and he wondered if he could go through with it. What had possessed him to allow Giles Carrington and Mohammed al-Ajmi to persuade him to become the instrument of their power struggle? Sultan Hamad had done them no harm. He was not a tyrannical oppressor. He was the instigator of Ras-al-Am's renaissance, and had re-invested his country with national pride and a sense of destiny. How had he, Suleman al-Bakri, allowed himself to be swept so far along such an absurd path, a path that could lead only to his own shame and damnation? Yes – his name would ring through the history of Ras-al-Am; but as a traitor.

Gazing about him he saw that the awesome reality of the Palace had affected his men. They also were subdued. Could he now call up reserves of determination to rekindle their fervour and mount a successful attempt to take the Palace? What other course lay open to them? Surrender, and ignominious defeat? Should he stir them to die alongside him in one final attempt to achieve what they had set out to do? Men standing near Suleman were shivering, if not from their swim in the harbour, from faltering resolve. Would they now swim ashore for him, with their rifles to sweep all before them and raise the flag of liberation? He knew the Palace was guarded by soldiers of the Royal Guard with their distinctive maroon berets, bandoliers and bombast. For all their Ruritanian regalia no one but the Sultan held the Royal Guard in high esteem, but Suleman knew they were waiting there in the Palace grounds behind the Palace walls, prepared to repel his attack with an arsenal of modern weapons. If he saw his plan through now and went ashore, any of his men who were not killed would be taken prisoner. Their cause would be jeopardised if he allowed such a situation to occur. Better to live to fight another day.

The reverberations through the timbers at the soles of his feet had stopped. The boats' engines were ticking over now, the three craft riding the swell 300 metres offshore. The Assault Group stood silently watching him, waiting. He peered shoreward again. In the failing light he was able to perceive tell-tale movements along the Palace's sea wall telling him that the fully primed Royal Guard were also becoming restless. Suleman knew that he faced the death of himself and his men if he persisted with what he now realised was an ill conceived plan.

He turned and addressed his Assault Group. He said: "It would be a folly. We shall not go ashore to storm the Royal Palace."

There was a short silence while each man considered the implication of their commander's pronouncement. There rose muted dissent from some of them, followed by a numbed silence. Despite their previous fervour each of them knew that this phase of their coup had been destined to fail. The consequences of this failure eluded them, but when Suleman spoke again there was a rustle of acceptance for the decision he had made.

"You will return us to Schmidt's Beach as quickly as possible," he instructed the Naval lieutenant.

The young Ras-al-Ami officer nodded and gave the appropriate orders. With a roar of engines the three boats turned and surged out through the cove entrance back to sea, bearing westward towards Schmidt's Beach.

Suleman's intention now was to land at the point along Schmidt's Beach where they had killed Lieutenant Dil Murad and his Baluch Guard Company soldiers that morning, wade his men ashore there and cross overland by foot to regroup back at the Airport. He knew where everything had gone wrong. Ever since the bedevilling traffic jam he had made up his plans as he went along. Now it was almost dark and he would be unable to reach the Television Studios in time to make his broadcast at 7-o'clock. The Liberation Army's credibility was almost completely lost.

As the leading patrol boat cut a phosphorescent swathe through the Gulf waters Suleman sat cross-legged on its prow mentally striving to formulate a revised strategy.

While Suleman was overseeing the Assault Group's aborted seizure of the Royal Palace, Majid Zahir took the initiative and commandeered a police helicopter of his own to fly to the Television Studios in the hills above Merin Heights. At ten minutes to seven, when there was still no sign of Suleman appearing and no word of what was happening, Majid knew there was an important decision to be made. Whether the Liberation Army ultimately succeeded or not, he, Majid Zahir, would forever be known as one of the prime accomplices in the plot. How crucial was it for their proposed broadcast to go out at 7-o'clock? Majid believed it was crucial, and if Suleman al-Bakri was detained from making it then shouldn't he, Majid Zahir, broadcast in his place? The intimidated studio staff had been standing by to beam the broadcast. For the past three hours television screens throughout the Sultanate had broadcast repetitious gourd music and a superimposed test card proclaiming

All programmes have been suspended in preparation for a national announcement to be broadcast at 7.00 pm.

It was now five minutes to.

TWENTY–SEVEN

Drongo Horne decided that he must have Julie Adams.

Sired of a Polish barkeep out of a Belgian whore behind a battery of bins in a Brussels alleyway after WWII, reared in remand homes and prisons, native cunning had enabled the 39-year-old psychotic thug to ingratiate himself into Giles Carrington's employment as arranger-cum-hit man.

Even Drongo's most charitable acquaintance, a Danish pornographer in Copenhagen, would describe him as a soulless bastard who should have been exterminated before puberty.

Uncharacteristically, Giles Carrington had overlooked investigating Drongo's background too closely when he first employed him for a rush job three years previously. The job had been carried out satisfactorily, other jobs followed which were successfully concluded, and Drongo Horne found himself slotted in as a below-stairs, back-door minion of the Ras-al-Am Intelligence Department.

"I have no idea who you are or what you are talking about," the Matron snapped at him when he crashed into her office that morning. "Nor do I have the faintest notion who this Hilal al-Bakri person is. I can assure you he's not here." She glowered at Drongo.

"In that case lady, you're of no use to me," Drongo snarled, shoving her to the door and into the corridor outside. Locking the door he whirled about and leered at Julie, standing with her back against one of the cabinets. "On the other hand, little lady, you and I have some unfinished business to attend to, haven't we!" he said, unbuckling his combat belt and moving menacingly towards her.

"Not that I'm aware of," Julie retorted, inwardly quaking but jutting her jaw defiantly.

"Oh, I think we do. It was you flashing your backside and boobies at me and my men yesterday, washing your body under that hose in the desert."

Julie gasped, appalled to think that this animal was one of those to have seen her like that.

"My passions were getting quite inflamed," Drongo chuckled, "until that interloper came along to break the party up. Now you're exciting me all over again with your little display of contempt. This time I want a private viewing."

Darting his right hand out like a vicious claw, he ripped open Julie's uniform jacket, yanking it from her shoulders to expose her left breast. "*Very* nice," he chuckled, wiping the back of one hand across his mouth. "Now show me the other one."

Julie spat at him with disgust.

Drongo lashed out his right fist to send her sprawling across the desk. He threw himself on top of her, tearing at the waistband of her slacks as he did so. "Now you're going to get what God put you on this Earth for, you precious English rose," he snarled.

"*Pig*. Utter *filth*," Julie hissed, feeling the stubble of his chin rasp against her throat. She turned her face away, her nostrils wrinkling at the blast of foetid breath from his yellow teeth.

The hospital had been overrun with his cronies. The door was locked. There was nothing Matron could do to help her. There was no one to come to her assistance.

Julie braced herself, preparing to be subjected to the most horrific ordeal of her young life.

Later, his lust still aroused, Drongo Horne left Masela Camp and went to the Airport. When he arrived there he found men of the Liberation Army manning defensive positions at the approach points and along the perimeter, their vehicles haphazardly parked, camels and horses tethered to railings and fences.

A group of tribesmen guarding the steps to the Restaurant Command Centre greeted Drongo suspiciously as he brushed past and went upstairs. Rumours abounded about what this unsavoury European was doing in their company, but their leader, Suleman al-Bakri, trusted him so that was good enough for most of them.

Neither Giles Carrington nor the Sultan's nephew, Mohammed al-Ajmi, intended proclaiming their association with the coup until it was completed. In the meantime, Drongo Horne was fulfilling the role of linch-pin between Suleman's men on the ground and the two provocateurs in their ivory towers.

Drongo was here to tell Suleman al-Bakri that he had failed to locate his brother Hilal at the military hospital, but Suleman was not at the Airport.

"He commandeered a Police helicopter and flew to Raman to supervise the assault on the Palace," Drongo was told by the Ras-al-Ami rebels he found in the Command Centre.

"When's he due back?" he barked.

"We do not know, Sayid. We are waiting here now to be told what to do."

"*Bugger* it," Drongo spat, lashing out with his boot and kicking over a chair. Lighting a cigarette he strolled across to peer over the balcony at the hostages in the lounge below, then smiled to himself.

He recognised one of them.

He continued leaning over the balcony for a while, smoking his cigarette, then went back into the Restaurant. His eye lit on the door at the far side of the room, with the sign BAR lit above it. Drongo strode across the room and kicked in the door.

The Bar was thickly carpeted with easy chairs, pot plants and pictures. The bar itself had a steel grille over the front of it. Licking his lips Drongo drew the heavy combat knife from its sheath at his belt and used it as a crowbar to snap the grille's lock. Rolling up the grille with a crash he vaulted over the counter and helped himself to a can of Heineken from the humming cool tray. He ripped off its tag and hurled the liquid to the back of his throat, dribbling runnels down his chin and onto his clothes. Tossing the can aside he snatched up another, and poured himself a whisky chaser. He selected a tape from a drawer, stuck it in the cassette player and filled the bar with Ipi Tombe music. After three more beers and two further glasses of whisky he stripped off his shirt and walked playfully over the furniture, upending it as he went. Two more whiskies later, enthused by the frenzied African drum music belting from the speakers, he lurched off to get Heide Ritter up from where he'd seen her downstairs in the hostages' lounge . . .

TWENTY-EIGHT

It was 7.00 pm.

"People of Ras-al-Am . . . may God be with you . . . I am Majid Zahir, Deputy Leader of the glorious Army of Liberation, speaking to you from the studios of Ras-al-Am Television, which fell to our control at three-o'clock this afternoon. The Army's camp at Masela is also under our control, as is Raman International Airport. The Airport is now closed for all incoming and outgoing flights, and you should avoid going near it. We are also holding as hostages a plane-load of passengers. The Police Headquarters will shortly be in our control, and our glorious leader – Suleman al-Bakri –is presently engaged taking over the Royal Palace of Sultan Hamad, at Raman.

"Ours is a beneficent occupation of the Capital Area. You have nothing to fear and should go about your business in the normal way. However, any attempt to hinder the activities of the Liberation Army will be met with stern reprisal.

"Our aims are simple. It is our belief that this great nation of ours will benefit from the introduction of a competitive political party to augment the present Monarchic administration, to create greater employment for young people, and to institute a more equable distribution of the nation's wealth. You are aware that under the country's present system no such party would be allowed to form. That is the reason why it has been necessary for us to institute today's events, to seize our own platform from where we wish only to serve you – the people of Ras-al-Am.

"Bulletins will be issued from time to time, so please stay tuned to Ras-al-Am Television and Radio . . ."

Majid Zahir allowed himself a wry smile . . .

"I am sorry: I should have said Liberation Army Television and Radio. Thank you for listening, and – good evening."

Majid's face faded from the monitor screens to be replaced by a new test card and a new selection of gourd music with tambourine accompaniment.

Majid wiped his grubby sleeve across his perspiring brow as the overhead lights clunked shut. He walked to a window and let up the blind. It was a clear, moonlit night. He could see the lights of tankers out in the Gulf; the lights of Merin Heights below him; the lights of the petrol refinery glowing behind the hills; the winking lights of Masela Camp away to the west, and of Raman to the east. He felt that all these lights should be pulsing more strongly after his momentous broadcast.

Majid glanced down at the Raman-Masela road below. It took a moment before he realised that it appeared to be normal. Lights were flashing, indicating, moving . . . at *last* the traffic jam had been cleared.

Alhamdulillah. Praise be to God.

Now he must hurry back to the Airport to see what was happening there.

TWENTY-NINE

Suleman al-Bakri was exahausted.

His aborted Palace Assault Group was exhausted, too. The men defending the Airport's perimeter were exhausted – and those surrounding Police Headquarters and keeping it under siege were also exhausted – as were Majid Zahir's men occupying the camp at Masela.

Suleman knew that advancing armies always marched on their stomachs, receiving water and vittles either through their own supply lines or through recourse to local plunder.

It was 8.00 pm. Suleman al-Bakri's Liberation Army had been riding and fighting for 24 hours, swept along by the enormity of the affair in which they were engaged. Now they were tired and hungry.

Suleman's plan had fallen short of resupply or replenishment arrangements. Horses and camels, tethered along one side of the Airport, needed water and fodder. Vehicles needed fuel. No plans had been made for duty rotation, so those surrounding the Police HQ would have to remain in position throughout the night. Suleman had trusted too much to faith in Allah's support; and luck, but any luck they might have had was now running out.

The Navy had put Suleman and his Assault Group ashore at Schmidt's Beach as planned. Again they'd had to swim ashore before setting off in darkness across the dunes. They stumbled upon the mutilated bodies of the soldiers and their own fallen comrades from their earlier encounter that morning, and then struck out across the salt flats to make their way to the Airport. They managed to gain access through the perimeter fence without challenge from their own outlying defences. Their route had been lit by cooking fires of their piquets who foraged food from various sources and were preparing meals for themselves as though enjoying a celebratory barbeque. The Airport security was now non-effective.

When they reached the main complex Suleman's men went in search of water or slumped exhausted, curling up to sleep in their wet sandy clothes on the main car park. Suleman felt drained. He acknowledged the greetings of those he met as he ascended the steps to the Restaurant. Majiz Zahir rose to greet him with a beaming embrace and slaps on the back, but then realised from Suleman's expression that his mission had not been a successful one. "We don't yet hold the Palace, Sayid?" he asked.

Suleman shook his head.

"It was impossible. A suicide mission. If the Assault Group had been able to get there two hours earlier as planned, when surprise was still on our side, we might have succeeded. We would have suffered casualties, but I believe we could have done it. We have failed to secure the Palace and we have failed to secure the Police Headquarters. The men have lost heart and . . ."

"But Sayid – " Majid flung his arms wide and beamed expansively. "You still have *me*." He wagged an admonitory finger at the dejected Suleman. "We have Masela Camp. We have broadcast – ". He looked abashed when Suleman glanced up at him. "*I* have broadcast our message to the Ras-al-Am people, on your behalf of course, so now they and the entire world know who we are and what we stand for, and know what we have already achieved on their behalf. I explained to them that you, our glorious leader, were engaged in the process of acquiring the Royal Palace and, well, the fact that you haven't is merely a technicality that we can resolve tomorrow, isn't it."

Suleman had to smile at his loyal friend's enthusiasm.

"I wish I could share your confidence," he confessed. "Our success depended on speed and surprise, and now we have lost both. The Palace Guard will be trebled, and the Police will bring reinforcements in from all over the country. We cannot possibly regain the initiative now. Our coup is doomed to failure."

"Defeatist talk, Sayid. You're clearly exhausted. What you need is sleep. Tomorrow is Holy Day. You will awaken refreshed and find that Allah's light will shine upon us anew."

"Majid, how can I sleep? We must revise our strategy. We still hold the hostages. We can't keep them forever. There are women and children and old people amongst them. We have to find fuel for our vehicles, fodder for our animals, food and water for our men. There is much, much to be done."

"Of course there is," Majid agreed, "but you can't do it without food and sleep. You have probably forgotten that we are sitting in one of the best restaurants in Ras-al-Am, so I am going to fetch you something to eat."

"By the way, Majid – where is Mister Drongo Horne?" Suleman asked.

Suleman paused on his way to the kitchen doors. "This morning he went to Masela Camp to try to find your brother Hilal in the hospital; but I am sorry, I'm afraid he was not there. Then this afternoon he returned here to the Airport, smashed open the Bar and became very drunk. Repulsively stripped to the waist he then went lurching amongst the hostages, searching for a woman. He found one to his liking and dragged her back up here to the Bar where he barricaded the door and one can only assume by the noise that ensued, raped her. Because he is such a violent and unpredictable man, no one attempted to stop him. He was in there for about an hour with the poor creature, then he strode out and left in his vehicle. No one knows where he's gone."

"Good riddance," Suleman sighed. "He is a despicable man. I am sorry we have to have him foisted on us like this. What happened to the woman?"

"We returned her to the other hostages. Some of the European women passengers are looking after her."

Suleman nodded and Majid continued through the doors to the kitchens. Suleman remained slumped on the sofa staring out of the window at the grounded aircraft outside, at the fires flickering round the perimeter, and reflected on the hopelessness of their situation. They should have anticipated every phase and devised contingency plans to counter each eventuality. They were disorganised. Their glorious venture had now ground to a halt. He could not see how they could extract themselves from this impasse. They should salvage what they could from the debacle and withdraw back to Wazin for a few days' grace with their families, before the authorities arrived to exact retribution.

When Majid returned, bearing a plate of curried chicken, rice and dhal, he found Suleman fast asleep. Majid consumed half the meal himself and lay on an adjoining sofa to digest it. Soon he, too, was asleep.

One by one the perimeter fires subsided as their custodians slumbered at their posts. In the Departures Lounge the hostages settled as best they could for the night.

Six hours later twelve ghostly figures in black toppled out of an aircraft high above the jebel and fell through the waning night sky . . .

In the pre-dawn light the parachutists drifted down to land on the salt flats beyond the Airport's perimeter wire. They concealed their 'chutes and padded silently in from their individual drop zones to regroup with the Boss.

Ferguson, Hans, Chuck and nine members of the Sultan's Special Forces – known as Hamad's Racing Snakes - were in position to strike second blood for the Sultan.

THIRTY

Hamad's Racing Snakes were drawn from the elite echelons of Ras-al-Am's warrior battalions. Trained by British SAS NCOs, they were equipped with black jumpsuits, black berets with a silver mamba cap badge and, many would have said, a built-in death-wish. Their headquarters and training depot was located at Bidi, in the hills 15 kilometres west of Masela Camp.

As soon as General Wally and the Zeta Team arrived from the Royal Palace, the General said: "All yours, Ferguson. I've got to get these buggers out of Masela Camp. You and your boys sort out the Airport, will you?"

"Better see what we've got first," Ferguson said. "Can't take an airport with a ball of string and a scout knife. Come on Khalfan," he said, addressing the Snakes' popular Commanding Officer, Lieut Col Khalfan Khamis. "Show us what's hidden in that Aladdin's cave of yours."

The Racing Snakes had weapons that fired anything from airgun pellets to cannon balls. Anti-hijack drill was one of their specialities, and they were conversant with the internal and external layout of Raman Airport. When Khalfan Khamis produced the Airport's plans from his safe they studied them closely for half-an-hour and then Ferguson said, "Right – here's what we're going to do."

They were disappointed. It was a piece of cake. A doddle. A walkover. No grappling hooks. No stun grenades. No squirts of Hechler-Koch. No blood.

No hassle.

They sidled up out of the dark to each defensive position round the Airport's perimeter and neutralised its inmates. Then they worked round to the front of the Airport where they quietly located the Command Centre in the Restaurant, and bound and gagged Suleman al-Bakri, Majid Zahir and their aides, and left them under guard.

They overpowered the rebels guarding the policemen dozing on the floor of the Customs Hall, one of the Racing Snakes brandishing a shotgun to indicate that they would prefer it if the policemen remained on the floor a while longer. They didn't want *them* scrambling about all over the place redressing grievances and snarling up the works.

"Good morning."

In the Departures Lounge the hostages and their guards stared up dazedly to see a lone black-clad figure in a balaclava looking down at them from the balcony above. Before they could assess the threat or fire at the figure, the glass doors behind them clicked open, and as the rebel guards swung round each received a bullet between the eyes from four more black-clad figures.

After that it was a formality to release the captive air traffic controllers in the tower.

Although not yet fully secure, Raman International Airport had been retaken. So far it would rank as one of the most effortlessly successful anti-terrorist operations.

Then it began to get messy.

Ferguson heard a *cruuump* and a *craaash* as the plate-glass window behind him disintegrated, showering him with shards that embedded themselves in his black jumpsuit. Hans's voice crackled through his earpiece. "They're using mortars on us. They've found our range. We're pinned down out here on the airstrip. We don't stand a chance."

Holy shit. Ferguson plucked the largest shards of glass from his jumpsuit and whipped off his balaclava to staunch some of the blood. He knew what must have happened. Twelve men trying to do the task of fifty. They had neutralised ten defensive positions round the perimeter, using Magic Glue to bond the inmates' wrists behind their backs. Instead of leaving Racing Snakes troopers, he had left just Hans and Chuck to round the prisoners up and march the sorry horde across the airstrip to the Main Building. In the darkness, one of the defensive positions must have been overlooked. With no regard for the safety of their captured comrades, the rebels in that position were firing 81mm mortars at Hans and Chuck.

Hans was right. They didn't stand a chance, pinned down in the middle of an open airstrip. The shrapnel would slice a man in two, *whanging* up hideously off that flat concrete.

What the hell could he do?

Through the gaping window cavity he could see them in the glare a half-mile away, the finned bombs bursting about them at 15 second intervals. Most of their prisoners lay hugging the ground, some wounded, some dead, others running in all directions with their arms still stuck together behind their backs.

He couldn't make out Hans or Chuck.

Tracing the trajectory of two of the bombs Ferguson saw where the mortar was located, half a mile out in the dunes. Whatever he attempted would be too late – but he had to do something. Blood still welled from a gash on his upper arm, but there was no time to apply a tourniquet. He leapt through the jagged window frame onto the flat roof beneath, and from there onto the ground. He knocked an open-mouthed rebel from the cab of his Land Cruiser, clambered in and gunned the vehicle out across the airstrip. Now that the mortar gunners had found the range of Hans's and Chuck's group, Ferguson didn't think they would switch their fire onto him. He roared past Hans, relieved to see that he appeared to be alright. He was concerned that he had not glimpsed Chuck, but headed on towards the emplacement, from where they were still loosing off their mortars. Christ, how many bombs did they have left? The Land Cruiser bucketed onto rough scrub. The windscreen starred from a rifle bullet. Ferguson punched the glass out with his fist and seeing that he had nearly reached the emplacement he continued steering straight towards it. He roared over the lip of its bank and landed the two-ton vehicle on top of three Ras-Al-Amis and their overturned mortar. One was killed instantly, the other two left with broken backs, necks and legs.

"Oh, SHIT," Ferguson roared when he saw who they were.

They hadn't been rebel tribesmen at all. They were Police. Furthermore, they had just finished their supply of mortar bombs.

"Sorry, fellas," Ferguson bellowed at their contorted bodies. "Someone should have told us. Christ, what a cock-up. I'll do what I can for you when I get back, but as you know . . . there's a small war going on."

Leaving his vehicle straddling the emplacement, Ferguson staggered back across the dunes towards the Airport. His blood was flowing faster now, staining the sand with each dogged step he took. Thank God I'm used to this kind of caper, he thought – aware that if he didn't stem the flow of blood from his arm shortly his strength would soon desert him.

It took 15 minutes to reach Hans.

He recalled the day he had watched his German friend walk off down the beach in Thailand, thinking he should have had a young eagle perched on his shoulder. Now he had a full-grown one. The blond giant was carrying Chuck.

"Tell me?" Ferguson demanded, drawing wearily abreast of them.

Hans said nothing, but stared fixedly ahead as he stamped towards the Airport buildings.

Ferguson knew that Chuck Henderson, their comrade from Central America and Lincoln, Nebraska, would soldier no more.

THIRTY-ONE

"The regiments are all back in their barracks." General Wally was giving a sitrep.

"A company of Frontier Force has moved in to man the Airport and get it operational again after the sterling work you did resecuring it. There's no need for me to say anything about Chuck. Obviously, I feel the same way you do about it. Thank God he was a loner and had no family. Rotten luck getting caught by shrapnel like that, especially after the capers he's managed to get away with over the years, but – I guess it goes with the badge. Went straight into his heart, you say? I have no idea who the hell decided to send a mortar team to the Airport. It was crazy. No doubt it will all come out in the wash-up afterwards. Now, Ferguson – how do you feel?"

"About what, sir? I'm fine. Why?"

"Arm okay?"

"Sure. The Doc's stitched it. No problem."

"Feel up to a bit of jogging?"

"Er . . . go on, sir. What have you got in mind? Some sort of celebratory race?"

"We've got no communications into or out of Masela Camp," the General explained. "I don't know what David Marks's up to. Dead for all we know. The point is, I want to relieve the damn place today, but before we go in it would be useful to know the rebels' dispositions and strength. You and Hans want to tackle it for me?"

"Of course; but how? Slide down a moonbeam?"

"Not quite. But it's important that you leave right away, while it's still dark. This is what I've got in mind . . ."

It was 0430.

Ferguson had changed into shorts, singlets and trainers. He and Hans borrowed a civilian car from one of the Racing Snakes' officers, and drove the few kilometres to Masela Camp.

Just short of its principal access road they turned off to approach the camp's south-western corner via rutted tracks that played havoc with the car's suspension.

Masela Camp was contained within 20 square kilometres of military real estate, with a sturdy 10ft high wire fence surmounted by an outward facing razor-wire barrier running dauntingly along the length of its perimeter. Anyone attempting to scale this fence from the outside would be left dangling in shreds.

The Camp's principal buildings, its offices, messes and quarters had been constructed in the central hub of the complex. The separately fenced ammunition depot had been built in the camp's otherwise empty south-western corner, like a camp within a camp. The ammunition depot had a series of brickbuilt watchtowers erected around it, with searchlights manned by guards armed with rifles and machine-guns. One of the towers had been damaged when Hilal al-Bakri's men blew up part of this depot, but the remaining towers, now manned by the rebels, held a commanding view of the outer perimeter wire, yet General Wally had told Ferguson that this inaccessible, well-guarded corner of the camp afforded his best entry point.

He looked for a shallow gully running at right angles to the fence, excavated six months before to lay a power cable. Soil subsidence had left a gap under the wire through which a man could crawl, and just at that juncture a low hillock obscured the point of entry from the nearest watchtower's field of vision. The General had come across it while walking the perimeter fence one day. Once inside Ferguson would only have to jog round the inside track and, attired as he was, he was unlikely to be challenged, another idiot Brit out on his morning run. But it was imperative to reach the gap outside the wire under cover of darkness.

They had used the car's headlights to avoid plunging into one of the many crevasses they encountered, but they dared not risk taking the car closer for fear of their lights being seen.

Two-hundred metres from the wire they jolted to a stop in a defile below the watchtower's line of sight. Navigating the approach in the dark had taken them longer than they'd thought. It was now 0530 and the sky was lightening in the east.

"Give me two hours," Ferguson told Hans. "If I'm not back, or haven't got word to you, scarper on back to Bidi. I should be able to find this radio ham General Wally's told us about. What did he say his name was? Hearn? Brierley Hearn? That's it. Right – I'm off."

Closing the car door quietly he scrambled up the bank of the defile, scratching his legs on thorn bushes and tripping over boulders. The worst thing that could happen would be to turn an ankle. He could see the greyish blur of the wire mesh fence looming in front of him, with the first of the four watchtowers silhouetted against the lightening sky. He could place some reliance on the guards' reduced attentiveness at this stage of their vigil, but one of the more alert ones might still spy him darting across the rocks. What he needed was black shorts and another 10 minutes of darkness.

It was becoming touch and go. There was half a kilometre of ground to cover before he reached the gap in the fence.

If the watchtower guards *were* awake and observant, and looked in his direction, they couldn't fail to see him zig-zagging across the pre-dawn landscape like a wraith.

If he moved stealthily he would not reach the gap before the sun rose above the horizon. It was 50/50 either way. He went for broke and pounded as hard as he dare along the gravel path outside the fence. He had counted off 30 of its retaining posts and covered half a kilometre, breathing hard. If everything went belly up at least he would die fit, although he would meet his Maker in a lather, sweating like a pig.

He counted off another 15 posts. Fifteen more to go. Another two minutes running time, and he'd be there.

Shit – what was that? He grimaced, and then grinned at his

nervous reaction. A vulture had glided down out of the pre-dawn sky and perched ominously on top of one of the posts he had just passed, glowering at his retreating back, folding its wings and picking its beak with a talon. Fourteen posts, 13, 12, 10 posts . . . he had nearly reached the gap.

The golden orb of the sun burst majestically above the jebel in the east, bathing the plain with the first light of day. Immediately a volley of shots rang out from the nearest watchtower and reverberated around the rocky hillsides. A storm of hot lead *spanged* and whined off the rocks behind him. He plunged headlong to the ground, grazing his arms and legs as he skidded through the gravel.

A cheer went up from the rebels in the watchtower, who assumed he'd been hit. In due course they might send out a vehicle to collect his body, after the vultures and flies had removed his eyes and had their fill of him.

His heart thumped loudly against the ground. His abrasions stung like mad and his arm had resumed bleeding. He turned his head sideways to look up at the watchtower, but it was obscured behind the small hillock.

He was out of their sight, and had been all the while – so how had he been seen? He eased himself into a crouch, looked around and grinned with relief.

The shredded carcass of the vulture lay flapping on the ground 20 metres behind him. If Ferguson had been 10 seconds later it was him they would have been using for target practice – his body now expiring in an Arabian dawn death.

The gap in the wire was now 30 metres ahead of him.

To risk detection at this stage would be absurd; he scurried across the ground on his hands and knees and wormed his way beneath the wire at the spot General Wally had told him the gap would be.

Inside he stood up, swiped the dirt and gravel from his cuts and set off in a jog along the wire's inside track towards the central complex. He glanced once across his shoulder, seeing that this time one of the rebel guards *was* observing him through binoculars from the watchtower. He waved and carried on jogging. The guard lowered his binoculars and waved back before turning to peruse another sector of the camp. Ferguson had made it. The ploy had worked.

He loped alongside the soccer pitches until he hit the blacktop road, then slowed to a walk to regain his breath and conserve energy. His task now was to recce the whole camp, noting the rebels' dispositions to report back to the General.

It was now 0600. The muezzin's voice had already called the faithful to prayer over the speakers of the camp's mosque, and those Asian sons of the Prophet who were not feeling faithful this morning were clattering the pans in their mess kitchens and cookhouses, indicating that the usual breakfast preparations were well underway.

Because today was Friday, Holy Day, nothing stirred in the Brit quarters, where most of the idle sods were probably still all a-bed. The hardest part of his task was to walk past Julie's bayte without stopping to go in. He glanced up at her balcony and saw that the curtains were open. Was Julie in there, asleep? He did hope so. Or perhaps she was on duty. He wished he could surprise her, but if he did his mission would never be completed . . .

He broke into another light jog and continued his survey of the camp. Early morning on Holy Day was not the best time to recce an enemy's deployments. They would be ticking over at half revs, displaying a misleading impression of their strength and capability. He passed one group, half-a-dozen camped on the car park in front of the Garrison Mess beside the main road, which was carrion-infested this morning. Ferguson knew that all camps in the Middle East abounded with feral cats breeding and scavenging in the rain-channels. From time to time their caterwauling became so unbearable that cat shoots took place, when half of them were splattered by .22s and carted off in the dust truck, but compassion for nature in the raw decreed leniency in the cull. This usually meant scores of kittens being left to be squashed by cars. Their remains stayed stuck to the tarmac for weeks, drying in the hot sun and wind until they resembled mummified strips of leather compressed into a dull brown mosaic - but this morning there were more carcasses than usual. The camp must have been visited by a locust swarm. Stragglers with broken wings fell from the sky to lie twitching on the ground, providing a source of fascination to the kittens who were so preoccupied with clawing-up the locusts that they became oblivious to the threat from approaching headlights.

Ferguson jogged down the road towards Northern Raman Brigade HQ. This dun-coloured Beau Geste fort had a refurbished howitzer chained to a concrete plinth on its forecourt, beside an historic brass cannon standing like some medieval sentry, an iron cannon ball protruding from its muzzle like a boar with an apple. The flag had been struck and the building appeared deserted, apart from a dozen rebels parked with their vehicles on the open car park in front.

If this had been a normal weekday the main vehicle park in front of the adjoining HQ building would be filled with ranks of cars, and coaches bringing civilian clerical staff in from Raman. Instead there were dusty rebel minibuses, pick-ups and Land Cruisers parked about the place. Ferguson jogged on down the stretch of road towards the main gates. This was where the main body of rebels had chosen to locate themselves. There were about 20 vehicles parked alongside the road. Fifty or more rebels stood at the gates, or squatted on the ground, waiting, it seemed, for nothing much to happen. Ferguson suspected that if he was going to be apprehended, it would be here, so he retraced his steps up the hill towards the Garrison Mess. He had completed his mental appreciation of the situation, and was formulating a plan to suggest to the General.

It was now 0645. Time for him to locate Major Brierley Hearn.

THIRTY-ONE

Brierley Hearn was a passed-over RAEC major with a speech impediment, a penchant for the grape, and a sinecure of a job in the HQ's Archive Department, cataloguing and committing to floppy disc the sparse but burgeoning history of Ras-al-Am's military achievements.

Brierley was not of the warrior caste. Because he marched to a different tune he didn't have many friends in Ras-al-Am. Apart from his work, and grapes, his principal topics of conversation, especially when in his cups, were his two passions - scouting and ham radio.

Not many of Ras-al-Am's mercenaries were 'into' ham radio, but if any of them stupidly bought a drink for Brierley at the mess bar they were guaranteed to receive an update on the state of amateur radio enthusiasts worldwide, from King Hussein of Jordan, with whom Brierley – like everyone else in the ham fraternity often spoke, to Yugoslav freighters up the Orinoco.

Mercenaries came and went, did a good job (or didn't), crashed cars, paid alimony and school fees, indulged in extra-marital fornication if opportunity presented itself, played tennis, golf and squash, went home on leave every three months, enjoyed adventures in Bangkok and Bali, got cancer, furred arteries and heart disease, earned, saved and spent seriously big bucks, left a negligible or otherwise impression on Ras-al-Am and its army, and then went back to the outside world . . . but Brierley Hearn seemed to go on forever.

He had arrived in Ras-al-Am in 1971, after too much boy scouting caught up with his military career in UK. With no relatives to keep track of him he sank gratefully into obscurity and adopted the Islamic way of life. Some of his peers were unaware that Brierley was an accomplished and fluent Arabist. Those who were privileged to visit his bayte over the years and marvel at its pasha's-palace décor had moved on. Today no one of the current generation knew what made Brierley tick, except that come rain or shine he was immutably there, always friendly but usually inebriated and in cloud-cuckoo land.

It was generally assumed he was in his mid-50s, when he was only a well-worn 47. His staple diet was port and crisps, and although he did not have Aids, his appearance suggested that he might have. He hated his weedy body, and had never done much with it, feeling it was merely a repository for his brain. He sensed that his body, his brain and his very soul were on the wane and scheduled for an early demise, but consoled himself that if he died someone might notice him at last, if only as an administrative inconvenience to be disposed of.

In the meantime he had a pretty shrewd idea what was going on in Masela Camp.

Dresed in Ras-al-Ami national garb, his dishdasha, cap and sandals, which invariably evinced mirth from his colleagues, Brierley had left his bayte to walk the camp the previous afternoon, to glean as much intelligence as he could. It didn't take long for him to realise that some gimcrack Liberation Army was on the march, and what their aims must be.

Ferguson had no difficulty locating him. The roof of Brierley's bayte was a nest of aerials.

When he wasn't talking to himself he could converse concurrently with the Alice Springs postmaster and Austrian shopkeepers in Paraguay, while simultaneously tapping furiously in Morse to someone on Tristan de Cunha, stirring his tea with a pencil and munching a Kit-Kat.

At 0700 Brierley had his microphone clasped in one sweaty hand while the fingers of the other scanned the airwaves for the frequency he sought.

"Can you get through?" Ferguson asked.

"Special Forces at Bidi? Course I can. They're only over the next hill. Christ, this time yesterday I was speaking with a fur trapper in Alaska. How's your tea?"

"Perfect; thanks. I'm sorry I had to disturb you at this ungodly hour, but it was important. I managed to break into camp, but it could prove a time-consuming exercise trying to break out again. If you can raise General Wally for me it will save time for us all."

"No problem," Brierley replied, scratching his tousled head. "On air now for you. There y'go." He stood up and offered Ferguson his place. "Get on with it. Speak up. 's all yours."

"Ferguson?"

"Morning, sir."

"You managed to get in alright then. Bloody good show. Now then . . ."

THIRTY-TWO

Rape!
RAPE.
That was the only word for it, Julie thought as she lay in bed instinctively curled in the foetal position in one of the hospital's private wards, trying not to regress to sucking her thumb.

It was no good pretending it hadn't happened, or dressing it up in any other way.

That disgusting bastard, that BRUTE . . . had *RAPED* her.

He'd threatened her, molested her, attacked her, beaten and assaulted her . . . and then Raped her.

She knew she was a big girl now, and the Middle East hadn't promised to be a holiday camp, but lots of girls managed to complete their tours there without actually being RAPED. Why HER?

Then again, she reasoned – she happened to have arrived just as a revolution was getting started.

An innocent bystander? She was merely another of its inevitable victims. Perhaps she should be grateful not to have been killed.

That beast with the black eye patch was savage enough to have slit her throat when he'd finished. She'd read somewhere that most rapists were inadequate, but he'd been so Big. He'd continued taking her without let-up for Ages. She suppressed a hysterical giggle. After he finished with her he had re-clasped his heavy belt round his waist, and left, leaving her spread-eagled across the Matron's desk like a broken doll.

The other rebels must have left the hospital at the same time because shortly after he'd gone the Matron hurried back in.

"Oh, my dear," she gasped as the sight of Julie confirmed her worst fears. She snatched up the telephone and within minutes four nurses rushed in with a stretcher-trolley. They lifted Julie carefully onto it and wheeled her quickly off to a bathroom where two of them stayed while she lay sobbing and soaking in neck-high hot water for 15 minutes, took a shower and they'd tucked her up in bed. A sympathetic Indian doctor sedated her and she'd slipped fitfully in and out of sleep for the past 24 hours. She was awake now and wresting with the enormity of what had happened, wondering whether she would ever readjust.

The door opened and two heads peered round. It was Jenny and Samantha, her sister's two friends who had met her at the Airport only last week.

"How's our best girl shaping up today?" Jenny asked, sitting beside her on the bed and taking one of her hands, while Samantha leaned against the wash basin. "Anything broken?"

"At least not my maidenhead," Julie heard herself snigger in an attempt at light heartedness, "but that's about all. Certainly my heart and my spirit, for a while. Don't know yet. It's the first time it's ever happened to me. I think I came near to it in a bus shelter at home when I was sixteen once, I'm not sure – but nothing like this. Will I be alright?"

"*Course* you will. I'm sure of it. You, er . . . you couldn't find yourself pregnant, could you?"

"No – but . . . but . . . what about some dreadful disease?"

"*Most* unlikely – but the doctors here would sort it out for you in a jiffy."

"No, I mean – well . . . something . . . unmentionable." She started to shake again just at the thought of it.

"Not a chance; not in a *zillion* years," Samantha reassured her enthusiastically. "For*get* it. It couldn't happen. Erase it from your mind this instant. NOW."

"Thank you." Julie smiled wanly at them. "You're both very sweet. You should be psychiatrists, not nurses. What*ever's* that noise . . .?"

"You're right," Samantha said, going across curiously to the window. "There's one *helluva* racket going on out there.

228

Whatever is it?" She looked out the window, and gasped.
"Holy *shit*," she mouthed, then span round to Julie and Jenny
yelling: "either it's World War Three breaking out down there
girls - or the Cavalry's just arrived!"

THIRTY-THREE

With their tracks clanking, governors banging and flames spurting, the sabre squadron of tanks came bursting out of the jebel onto the hardtop road like angry lions. They converged on Masela Camp, one troop heading straight for the main gates, the other veering off to access the unmanned south western approach gate.

Ferguson's assessment of the situation over the air to General Stubbs had been accepted, and quickly acted upon. The Sultan's Armoured Regiment had been alerted and the squadron of Chieftain main battle tanks loaded onto transporters to be conveyed from their camp for offloading in a laager near Masela.

Only the previous year teams of civil engineers and a sweating Asian labour force had widened the road from the tank barracks to Masela Camp and strengthened its culverts to take their weight, but there was no point having their clattering tracks chewing chunks out of it unnecessarily. Besides, their approaching noise would have given early warning of their arrival.

Ferguson's suggested plan to the General was simple. He considered that the rebels' defence at Masela was so slipshod that a short, sharp shock would send them reeling into disarray and expulsion.

The General liked the idea.

Since its formation the Ras-al-Am Armoured Regiment – known with jocular familiarity within the fraternity as the Life Boys - had had no opportunity to raise its mailed fist in anger, and although unleashing a squadron of battle tanks in this case was like drawing a sword to kill a mosquito, the General was resolved to disperse the rebel forces as quickly as possible. As well as being morale-raising practice for the tank crews, it would be a lot of fun. General Wally had never liked his camp's gates anyway. This way he could get them replaced for free.

General Wally had a soft spot for tanks: iron-clad warships of the high plain, sporting heavy-sounding names like Centurion, Chieftain, and Challenger; Conqueror . . . and the German Panzers, Tigers and Panthers – God he was going back a bit there . . . then there were the WWII Cromwells, Churchills, and Valentines . . . Crusaders – and the German Leopard . . . and their smaller British cousins, carrying lethal stings of their own . . . Scorpion, Saladin, Saracen, and the rest. And the crews who rode in them, commanded them, knew them, cursed them, tended them, loved them and had learned how to deploy them in accordance with set piece drills, sometimes wantonly through farm buildings and the wheat fields of North Germany, at other times bravely and with inspired originality if the occasion allowed. Good pieces of kit – tanks!

Tanks were hot in the desert, cold in the snow and not much different in between. They brewed up easily and cooked human flesh to perfection, but the traditional black-cockaded cap and leather vestments, boots, spurs and ethos of everything that was to do with tanks still had lashings of flash, dash and panache about them. In the General's view Ferguson had got it absolutely right, suggesting that a small armoured *blitzkrieg* was their best way forward. Overdramatic overkill perhaps, but it would teach the buggers a lesson for next time, squash a few toes, make 'em wince, bring tears to their eyes and spoil their day. Good stuff. Sod 'em – unruly Nig-Nogs. No man should have to practise constraint all the time. What good was power if you were unable to exercise it occasionally? A quick burst on his banjo like this might even blow his tubes clean, help him give up smoking . . .

The Battle Captain of the lead tank had his orders and knew what to do.

After the tanks had broken through and stunned the rebels,

the soldiers of the Hill Regiment, travelling behind in a convoy of Pinzgauer section vehicles, would round up and disarm them.

When the lead tank crashed through at 40kph, the General heard the resounding *Whang* as Masela Camp's gates were wrenched out of their stanchions. Sensible rebels sank back into the scrub at the first sound of the tanks' approach, but the dimmer diehards among them thought that if they stood their ground the tanks would be sufficiently impressed by their steadfastness to slow to a stop outside the gates and negotiate. Too late they found themselves joining the kitten carcasses already flattened into the tarmac.

While the first three tanks roared through the camp, the next three crawled over the rubble of the gates and squealed left and right to ride herd on the fleeing rebels, containing them until the infantry arrived.

Hurtling ahead through the camp the first three tanks barely swerved at the roundabouts. Recently painted ornate iron fence palings, shrubs and kerbstones were hurled in their wake as they bore towards a figure in off-white silk shorts and singlet waiting for them on the HQ's main car park. As soon as Ferguson had flashed hand signals to the jubilant tank drivers indicating what should be done, all the rebels' parked vehicles sustained an immediate need for extensive repair.

Four Pinzgauers hummed up to the car park. General Wally jumped out of the first vehicle and switched into gung-ho mode to take the soldiers dashing through the HQ building's main entrance and up the stairs to the Operations Wing. The General himself kicked in the door to Colonel David Marks's office and nearly clubbed the amazed rebel guard's head off his shoulders with one swing of his fist. "Morning David," he cried jovially to his Principal Staff Officer, gagged and bound to his chair. "Can't stop. Moving through. Back in a jiffy. Hang on, will you." The General bounded off down the corridor, but one of the soldiers paused and slit David's bonds with his combat knife and used them to truss the unconscious rebel. David was 'busting', but knew he had to stay in situ until the dust settled. He heard doors banging along the corridors as General Stubbs's hit squad made its way to relieve the Air Force and Naval Ops Rooms.

Outside in the heat the second troop of tanks had encircled the perimeter fence and crashed unopposed through the south western approach gate. They raised choking billows of dust in their wake, enjoying a lap of honour round the inner wire, squashing the remains of the shot vulture at the point where Ferguson had slipped in unobtrusively beneath the fence at dawn. The rebels in the watchtowers maintained a low profile while this armoured gasconade was underway. Fully aware that a burst from one of the tanks' 7.62 machine-guns would stitch them into the brickwork forever all they wanted was to slip quietly down the back stairs and across the fields homeward, but they knew the likelihood of being able to get away was slim.

One of the tanks and two Pinzgauers of infantry had smashed their way through the Ammunition Depot's gates to round up their colleagues in the compound. Dropping their weapons the rebels flung their arms in the air and trundled down the stone steps from the watchtowers to join their comrades. Some of them grinned sheepishly as they were all marched off to join their vanquished brethren herded into the middle of the parade square, shimmering in the noon day sun.

"You did a good job today, Ferguson. I'm proud of you," the General said. "You'd better get those cuts of yours seen to before gangrene sets in," he grinned. "Come on, first we'll drive round the camp and see what's what."

Leaping into the cab of the nearest Pinzgauer he had already started to drive off before Ferguson was able to scramble up beside him. "Come along man, f'Chrissake; we haven't got all day."

Ferguson had never seen the Old Man on such a high before. As a younger officer he must have been unstoppable: easy to understand how his style and ability had driven him through to justifiable Generalship.

"Fucking Pinzgauers: I'll never get used to these gear boxes," he grumbled, slewing the vehicle in a shower of shale round each bend. Ferguson hung on and gazed at the passing landscape as the General lapped the camp's road network where the rest of the rebels were being rounded up by patrolling soldiers. "Right. Seen enough. Everything seems under control. How long have we been away?"

"From where, sir?"

"The Headquarters Building."

"Twenty minutes, sir."

"Right. Plenty of time for them to have sorted themselves out. Let's get back there. I want to see how Air Ops is coping."

Air Ops' Rumour Control Department prided itself on being the fount of all knowledge about everything that ever happened to anyone at any time in Ras-al-Am. Pilots in the air, tank commanders on the ground and ships at sea would contact Air Ops for everything from the latest Test score to what was on the mess menu for dinner that night.

"The Racing Snakes have re-secured the Airport," they were told when they arrived, and General Wally and Ferguson smiled, glancing at each other with raised eyebrows. "The Police have broken out of their Headquarters, and although many of the rebels have been dragged into custody, quite a few have escaped the melée. The Police have laid on coaches to convey the hostages to hotels. The bodies of Captain Danile and the German businessman, Dieter Ritter, have been removed on stretchers to the Police mortuary, along with the American, Chuck Henderson. Ground crews are clearing debris from the airstrip and engineers are standing by to refill the bomb craters. Police launches are ferrying the remains of soldiers and rebels from the fire-fight on Schmidt's Beach yesterday. Apparently they're sloshing about in their body bags like defrosting meat. The body of Captain Bob Davidson has been removed from the FBH casualty wing and taken to the Police morgue, and his wife has telephoned from Heathrow to ask where he is. Apparently he was due home today, at the end of his contract. She's left the contact number of the

234

Information Desk at Terminal Three, and been assured that someone will telephone her as soon as there's news. Nice job for *some*one . . ."

Air Ops quickly resumed its role as an information centre, but Squadron Leader Peter Irwin had imparted the information to them leaning back in his chair smoking a cigarette and sipping a beaker of coffee. Ferguson and General Wally both sensed his controlled annoyance. His delivery was that of a man betrayed. On the other side of the room a group of Ras-al-Ami Air Force officers were manning the communications network.

"Okay, Peter," the General asked him. "What's up?"

"Very well sir, I'll tell you," said Peter, crushing his plastic beaker, tossing it into a bin and standing up to tuck in his shirt. "Just after you and your boys relieved us we received news that the Police fetched up in strength at the Airport and relieved your Hill Regiment's CO of his custody of the rebel leader Suleman al-Bakri, and his principal lieutenant, Majid Zahir."

"WHAT?" the General roared, smashing his fist down onto one of the desks. "I shall have plenty to say about *that*. What else?"

"Well . . . many of the rebels who fled the Police HQ débâcle apparently managed to fight their way back to the Airport, where they've been able to regroup with a lot of the stragglers. The whole pack then mounted up, horses, camels and vehicles, the lot, and set out to return where they'd come from. Their animals haven't been fed or watered and their vehicles are low on juice, so they won't get far, but at this moment upward of two hundred of the blighters are thundering hell-for-leather back along the beach towards Wazin. Then Group Captain Essad entered the scene here and told us that the whole show is now purely Ras-al-Am business and we should stand down because they are taking over."

"What are the implications of that?" the General asked.

"Nothing short of horrific, sir," Peter replied grimly. "As you know, we were fielding Jaguar pilots to support you on Phase Two of the Army manoeuvres tomorrow. They were fuelled up and ready to go, at Raman Airport. Then the Group Captain took it upon himself to have the bloody things armed and bombed-up as well. He's got three of them airborne now, in pursuit of the retreating rebel convoy. They'll be on them in just a couple of minutes. Although I taught him everything he knows, he outranks me and this is his country, so there was very little I could do to restrain him. All he said was that if the Armoured Regiment's tanks can come and smash down the camp gates, then the strike aircraft can go and smash fleeing rebels. On balance, I think I'm rather glad you've turned up, sir."

"Christ, it's never easy, is it," General Wally complained, moving across the Ops Room floor towards the Ras-al-Ami Group Captain. "Essad -," he said, placing one avuncular arm about the officer's shoulder. "I understand you're intending to bomb seven kinds of shit out of your fleeing brethren. Is that the best course of action for a senior officer to take, d'y'think?"

"They are traitors to our country," the distracted Ras-al-Ami Group Captain retorted.

"Of course they are, Essad. But they haven't been arrested, tried or sentenced by due process of law yet, have they? Aren't you taking rather a lot upon yourself? It's one hell of a decision you're making, you know – a senior officer ordering the bombing of two hundred of his countrymen."

"This is our country, and our Sultan against whom they have transgressed. I am the senior Air Force officer here at present, and the seriousness of the situation demands that I assume command and take positive action."

"Yes, that is all very commendable, Essad – but you're jumping the gun a bit, old son."

"I assure you General, I am doing them a favour disposing of them in this way. They would all be sentenced to death and shot in any case."

"I am sure they might be: but bombing and strafing? Essad – you're going to leave half the poor blighters limbless and screaming. You're going to have to live with that the rest of your life."

"I appreciate your concern and guidance, General. But it is my responsibility and I have made my decision. Besides, it is too late for talking. It has commenced."

THIRTY-FOUR

The three exhilarated young Ras-al-Ami Jaguar pilots detailed for the mission were cock-a-hoop with excitement.

Three minutes after take off they had spotted the retreating convoy, moving north-westward along the beach towards Wazin. The incoming tide had smoothed away most of the tracks churned up in their wild advance of yesterday, but the beach bucked the vehicles' passengers about mercilessly. Those whose wrists had been stuck together with Magic Glue had suppurating wounds where they'd ripped themselves free, but despite the rough going they pushed their pace dangerously fast.

The pursuing Jaguar Leader climbed and banked to level off for his bombing run. After years of training he felt euphoric to have been let loose on the real thing at last. Although most of the tribesmen below were from different tribes to his own, he did not feel comfortable about bombing them.

His first drop was ineffectual. The bomb fell wide. It landed 100 metres from the rebels, off the beach in the dunes where the sand absorbed its blast and most of the shrapnel. The Jaguar Leader banked out to sea again in preparation for a re-run.

His Number Two fared better.

He placed two bombs right in the rebels' path, hurling up clouds of sand and hot metal, pile-driving two craters into the beach, which took out a dozen riders and knocked out four vehicles.

The Number Two banked out to sea to follow his leader in a return run.

Number Three pilot entered his run and released the first of four bombs, but when he pressed the release button a sheet of

238

flame shot up his plane's port side, enveloping his cupola. The 1,000lb bomb had pre-detonated 6ft below his port wing.

With the reflexes of a scalded cat he yanked down the blind of his ejection seat. The explosive bolts crashed the seat up the rails which released the canopy into the slip-stream and he was propelled through flames to hurtle 85ft into the sky above.

His parachute drogue snapped open, snatching him away from the seat which fell into the sea, then his parachute deployed. The £6,000,000 Anglo/French SEPECAT Jaguar strike aircraft hit the beach and exploded in a huge fire-ball.

Some of the rebels had seen the pilot eject, saw his parachute open, and watched keenly to see where he landed.

Galloping across the dunes they reined-in their horses while he struggled to release his harness. He stood in the sand in his flying suit while they circled around him. Lathered with sweat the horses pawed the sand and tossed foam flecks from their muzzles.

No words were uttered. The young pilot did not know whether to smile at them or draw his pistol.

With slow motion deliberation one of the riders drew back his arm as if for a polo shot, wielding a cudgel of lead-weighted wood usually employed to beat the life from barracuda hauled aboard his boat.

With a single vicious *craaack* the barnacle-encrusted priest ripped off the top of the pilot's head.

Wheeling their horses the riders galloped off, leaving the dying pilot groping blindly in the sand, oozing brain matter for the crabs and crows to pick at.

Above them, the Jaguar Leader saw the rebels sensibly break into smaller groups, and disperse. Sweeping low along the beach at 800kph he depressed the firing button to send a stream of cannon shells snaking into fetlocks, fenders and fuel tanks.

He banked away to turn at the end of his run and his Number Two swept in beneath him to contribute additional firepower to the carnage below.

The Jaguar Leader was coming in for his second run when he received fresh orders from Air Ops over his headset.

General Wally had finally, too late, convinced Group Captain Essad Saif that enough was enough. Reluctantly he ordered the Jaguars to return to base.

"Jaguar Leader: Jaguar Leader: Acknowledge," the pilot replied grimly.

Both aircraft tore low over the burning wreckage of the downed plane, dipping their wings before peeling off to return to Raman Airport.

General Stubbs had alerted the Naval Base and Police HQ. A flotilla of Patrol Boats put to sea to pick up the pieces and re-establish control.

Shocked and stunned, many of them wounded, the 50 rebels who had survived the horrendous ground-strike regrouped and searched for friends and family amongst the dismembered corpses strewn along the beach or impaled on jagged pieces of their burned-out vehicles.

In the sky above Raman the two young Jaguar pilots climbed into a spiralling victory roll, slid off the top curve of their trajectory and commenced to dive. The sky reverberated with the torn-silk roar of their turbofan engines as they dropped with the menace of a brace of Arthurian daggers plummeting towards the heart of Medieval Earth. When it seemed their only salvation would be for the ground to reveal some 007-like vertiginous subterranean hangar, both planes flattened out of their G-force dives, lowered their landing-gear and released their brake-chutes, which billowed from their tail-cones into 18ft of arresting white mushroom silk behind them and together they streaked along the concrete runway.

Their beaks and talons now blooded, two of Ras-al-Am's young eagles had landed.

THIRTY-FIVE

General Stubbs and Ferguson stood on the concrete at Raman Airport.

They had just watched the two Jaguars land and the pilots jump down and slap each other's backs, but what sickened them was another scene they were witnessing.

Manacled and shackled, Suleman al-Bakri and the jovial bearded Majid Zahir were being led by Police escort across the sweltering asphalt towards the open tail section of a waiting Skyvan aeroplane. They were shoved roughly up its rear ramp, the ramp closed and the Skyvan taxied out to its take-off position. The pilot opened the throttles, let off the brakes and the plane roared down the runway.

"I saw this done in the Congo once, and it's not very funny. 'Vengeance is Mine', sayeth the Lord, and all that stuff. Summary executions like this are barbaric. Isn't there something we can do to intervene, sir?"

"Nothing I can do about it Ferguson, I'm afraid. This is Ras-al-Am. It is still a nation steeped in tribalism, as well as being a Police State. The Police are incensed by what has happened, and tribal feelings have been inflamed as well. The Lord also said 'an eye for an eye, and a tooth for a tooth', remember? You say you saw this happen in the Congo. You've also seen Oxbridge educated Africans roll their eyes and revert to war drums and assegais. At crunch time these fellows aren't too different. Touch the right button to get 'em going and it's back to the days of Saladin again in a flash. This fracas has brought all their medievalism to the fore. It's going to bubble along for a few more weeks, I bet."

"There they go." Ferguson nodded skyward, nudging the

General, drawing on one of his Silk Cuts. Having gained height the Skyvan circled the Airport once, coming in at 500ft as though to land. Then they saw the tail section reopen and what appeared to be two large sacks of flour come hurtling out into the slipstream and plummet earthward.

"Glad there're no women or children here," hissed the General. "How the hell do they do it, Ferguson?"

"Morally, or actually?"

"Actually."

"Their hands are tied behind their backs. The noose is tied round their necks. It's a 500ft drop on a 150ft length of rope secured in the plane. Clunk; click. All over in seconds. Not nice, but effective."

They watched the two ejected bodies dropping through the sky like paralysed parachutists, two loops of hemp straightening out behind them as they fell. Being the heavier of the two they assumed it was Suleman al-Bakri they saw abruptly arrested first. His head popped out from his neck and arced off at a tangent, plummeting earthward to burst like a melon on impact with the ground. The twitching trunk and limbs smacked into the concrete seconds later.

Swaying about in a dangling dance of death overhead, the rope had broken free from the plane and was descending gracefully at its own pace.

Majid Zahir's was a lighter frame. His head did not detach while his feet and nervous reflexes described a parabola in the air. When the Skyvan came in to land, his broken body touched the ground first, like a wasp trailing its sting. Then he was dragged backwards along the concrete by his neck at 100mph.

By the time the Skyvan had taxied to a standstill and cut its engines, there was not much of Majid left at the end of the rope. The rest of him was a smear of shredded flesh along the runway that called to mind the squashed kittens of Masela.

In sombre mood after this spectacle, General Wally and Ferguson drove back to Masela Camp.

Going through its burst main gates they saw regrouped

members of the Baluch Guard Company industriously clearing away rubble. A convoy of blue Police trucks came towards them from the parade square.

"What the hell are *those* buggers doing in my camp?" the General snarled. He wound the car window down and addressed the same terse question to one of the Baluch NCOs nearby.

"Removing rebel prisoners, sir," the corporal told him. "I think no one has the authority to stop them."

"Do the Police control *every* fucking thing in this country? I suppose they could make a case for it. At least it'll get the prisoners out of our hair. Okay, Ferguson – take me home will you? I'm beginning to smell like an uncured boar. I need a bath and clean underwear. Stay and have a brandy."

"I won't if you don't mind, sir. I mean, look at the state of *me*. I've been running around in these silly shorts since four-o'clock this morning. I'll get back to my hotel and clean up. And I need to find Hans. I haven't seen him since I left him parked as back-up down a wadi when I broke into the camp this morning.

"He's alright," said the General. "He reported back to me and then rode in one of the tanks that smashed into camp. You'll find him okay."

After Ferguson dropped him at his residence, the General went to the telephone and dialled Air Ops.

"Air Ops. Can I help you?"

"Hallo, lad. General Stubbs here. Give me that UK telephone number for Captain Davidson's wife, will you . . ."

That evening Raman International Airport resumed normal service, and the former hostages flew back to London, with four coffins stowed in their aircraft's hold.

Next morning at dawn separate burial services were held for the remains of Bas McLaughlin, Lieutenant Dil Murad and the soldiers killed in the Schmidt's Beach fire fight.

Later in the day a Board of Enquiry was convened to ascertain the circumstances whereby one of their Jaguar strike aircraft had crashed.

That afternoon seven coaches with darkened windows drove out of the Police compound and headed for the firing range in the foothills of the jebel. Twenty minutes later several sustained bursts of automatic weapons fire were heard reverberating down the valleys.

The coaches returned empty. An hour later three lorries with securely tied tarpaulins mysteriously left the ranges for an undisclosed destination.

Rumour was rife for a long time, but no one could say for sure where the rebel corpses were taken for their mass burial.

THIRTY-SIX

General Wally Stubbs insisted that Ferguson and Hans move out of the Tasa Hotel and stay with him at his residence until after the National Day celebrations.

"It's a large-scale military parade on the Sultan's birthday, to celebrate another year of national achievements," the General explained to Hans. "It entails exhaustive preparation for weeks in advance. Thank God much of it was already underway before the Army deployed on our manoeuvres. I had an audience this morning with His Majesty who feels it is imperative that this year's parade be the best ever, a display of national solidarity."

Ferguson and Hans rose late each morning and sat around the General's pool doing push-ups, bemoaning the lack of activity and the dearth of women. Ras-al-Am was not Thailand.

"What about that nurse you were sorting out?" Hans enquired.

"Yeah, well . . . I suppose I ought to look her up again," Ferguson remarked pensively. "Truth to tell, I was growing a bit too fond of her for comfort, and what with everything that's happened, I . . . I guess I just thought it best to let sleeping dogs lie."

Masela Camp became a hive of activity. Troops from all over Ras-al-Am converged to participate in the rehearsal programme leading up to the parade, which was to take place in Raman's Sports Stadium. Accommodation at the camp being at a premium, a temporary tented camp was constructed beside the parade square to house them.

Reveille was sounded at 0530 each day.

Out of interest one morning, Ferguson and Hans went along to see what went on. The soldiers were given tea and two slices of bread and jam each before clambering into the backs of lorries and coaches for the 30 kilometre drive to the Stadium.

The Stadium had 40 tiers of seats, a flower-bedecked, red-carpeted Royal Box, a latticed harem enclosure for female spectators, its own copper-domed mosque at one end, and giant banks of floodlight towers standing over 50 metres high, which carried enough power to light the whole of Raman. These lights made the Stadium the largest area in the world lit to international television standards. They would not be used for the parade, however, which was traditionally held at 0730.

"What the hell's *that* thing?" Hans asked, pointing into the Stadium.

Ferguson laughed. "That's Puff the Magic Dragon," he said referring to the Land Rover that could be seen pumping out clouds of insecticide mixed with kerosene from a contraption like a harpoon gun mounted on its trailer. "It's also called Swing Fog. It's a smoke generator to fumigate the Stadium to reduce the effect of flies on the parading troops."

"I see; and what's this lot, turning up here now? Clowns?"

"Those crop-headed guys in blue vests and shorts filing into the stands - ?"

"Ja."

"They're detainees from the prison. They're ferried in for rehearsals to make as much noise as possible. During the march past you'll see them clapping and shouting and jumping up and down, to familiarise the horses with the onslaught of such sounds on the day."

From their vantage point high in the stands Ferguson and Hans continued to watch, while agitated officers with walkie-talkies rushed about countermanding each other's orders, and technicians tinkered with the public address system. Squads of security personnel could be seen scouring the Royal Box for bombs. The massed bands were rehearsing, and the long-suffering soldiery marched around and around becoming hotter and hotter.

"What do you think of all this, Ferguson?"

"Parades like this? I love 'em. Stirs the blood. It's no different to what millions throughout endured under British colonial rule. It must have something going for it, otherwise why would these emerging nations want to copy it, down to the very last detail?"

"Beats me," Hans said. "Presumably they've got enough petro-dollars to finance a space programme, yet they've elected to go for all this Ruritanian stuff: baffling, isn't it?"

At 0930 the rehearsal finished and the troops returned to Masela Camp for a proper breakfast.

That night David Marks invited Ferguson and Hans along to a party in the mess.

"We try to hold one about once a month," he said. "It gives the nurses an excuse to pretty themselves up a bit, and us fellows a chance to hold a woman in our arms, even if only in the pretext of dancing."

"What's the dress?" Ferguson asked.

"Oh, almost anything really," David told him. "On disco nights . . . let it all hang out, man. Not literally, of course. The women have to be a bit subtle. Couple of parties ago some Slack Alice from Casualty fetched up with one tit adrift, stainless steel thigh-boots and a G-string. Went down a treat with us lot of course, but it upset the Muslims a bit."

Arriving at the Garrison Mess at 8-o'clock they found the poolside festooned with fairy lights. Blue jacketed Indian waiters stood attentively behind 6ft tables serving from laden tureens, platters and dishes of curried chicken and lamb, rice, salads and sauces, freshly baked rolls and butter. Glasses of wine flickered seductively in the candlelight. Forty or so casually attired people, mostly British but including half-a-dozen Ras-al-Amis in their dishdashas sat about talking, laughing and drinking beneath gaily-coloured shades and awnings. Tucked in the corner by the open-air film screen a disco was played background music, restraining itself before its impatient operative unleashed heavier decibels as the evening progressed.

The lights in the pool made it resemble a turquoise grotto,

an underwater attraction that later would entice several idiot drunks and tiddly-willing girls to jump into it fully clothed.

Intermittent hissing sounds could be heard as unwary mosquitoes met their nemesis on the ultra-violet insectocutors rigged in the trees.

A shooting star flashed across the clear night sky, seeming to extinguish itself only scant feet above their heads.

The lights of an incoming passenger plane wavered low overhead as it came in to land at the reopened Airport, bringing back some of Ras-al-Am's expatriate employees from leave in Britain, France, Holland – India, Pakistan or Sri Lanka.

The whole scene resembled an artfully lit stage set. Ferguson, Hans and David Marks sat at one of the tables with a chilled Heineken a-piece, watching people arrive.

"Pity Chuck's not with us," Ferguson said. "He'd have liked this."

Hans tipped his beer and raised an eyebrow. "Absent friends?" they said together and toasted his memory.

"*This* pretty little trio should brighten your rotten lives up a bit for you though," David grinned, nodding towards the gate through which three girls had just stepped and strolled onto the concrete poolside together. "Samantha and Jenny," David said, "and . . .?"

"Good God; it's Julie, said Ferguson, slopping his beer. "What do you think – should I go over?" he asked Hans.

"Don't look at me. Since when have *I* controlled your sex life. I don't know how you left it."

"Left what?"

"The situation."

"Pretty open, I think. I can't remember. I was probably meant to call her."

"They're coming this way," David said, pushing his chair back to stand up as they approached. "Ladies – how lovely to see you. Won't you please join us . . .?"

"Thank you – may we? That would be nice. I'm Samantha and this is Jenny," she said to Ferguson and Hans, "and – I believe you already know our Julie, don't you?"

"Yes, we do." Beaming at Julie, Ferguson instantly realised two things – that he really was extremely attracted to this young woman, and also that something was wrong. The lively and carefree creature he had made love to a few days ago, had changed. "Julie – whatever *is* it?" he asked urgently, reaching for her hand. She cowered, lowering her eyes to her lap. The others edged away, pretending to ignore this fraught exchange.

"Julie, we've had a small war on. I'm sorry I didn't call you, but this is ridiculous."

"Hey – c'mon Big Boy," Samanatha cried brightly to Hans. "Come and dance with me."

"You too, David M," Jenny said. Both men allowed themselves to be led unprotesting onto the floor, leaving Julie alone with Ferguson.

"That was a bit obvious wasn't it," said Ferguson. "So what's this all about?"

"Something happened to me," Julie said quietly, still gazing into her lap, unable to meet his eyes.

"Well I can see that, Julie. But you're acting as though you've just received a death sentence. It can't be that bad, surely?"

"It is to me," she retorted, flashing a look at him before lowering her eyes again. "You'll have to decide for yourself."

"Julie, are you going to tell me what's wrong, or not?"

"I've been raped."

"You've been . . . wha -? My God. You're not serious. When? How? Who by? Julie, you haven't."

She started to weep and reached her hand out to take his.

"You *are* serious, aren't you." He encased her hand in both of his.

Julie nodded. "When the camp was occupied some of the rebels overran the hospital, on my first morning there, the day after you and I . . . I was with the Matron in her office when one of them burst in on us. He threw Matron out into the corridor and locked the door. Then he . . . then he . . . "She put her hand up to her mouth and turned her head away with a sob.

"Julie – an Arab *raped* you?" Ferguson asked, willing her to shake her head in denial.

"No," she sobbed quietly. "Not an Arab. Some *vile* European."

"*Whaaat*? A Euro*pean*? I don't believe it. Did you know him?"

"No, of course I didn't. He said he'd seen me showering naked under that standpipe out in the desert, that day we met, when you rescued me. He . . . he was wearing a black eye patch," she sniffed.

Ferguson experienced an immediate rush of blood to the head. His fists clenched and his body shot upright as though electrified.

"Drongo bloody Horne," he snarled. "For this I will *kill* you. I swear it. I *will* KILL you."

"Come in Mister Horne, please won't you sit down," Giles Carrington gushed. "We have lots to talk about, you and I. If you agree, I am going to make you a very wealthy man. The whisky decanter and ice bucket are beside you. Please relax and help yourself. You have been with me three years now, isn't it? Yes – I thought so. And sterling work you've done. You've never let me down. Well – this is the big one . . ."

Drongo Horne took a swig of whisky. He was wearing a T-shirt, slacks and espadrilles. Since the afternoon of the Airport siege he had been keeping a low profile, relaxing in his small bungalow in the grounds of the Carrington estate, running along the beach, swimming, eating and sleeping well, getting himself back into top physical condition in readiness for whatever destiny chose to put his way.

"I want you to kill the Sultan."

Drongo Horne nursed his crystal tumbler and waited for his employer to expand. He raised the glass to his lips and took a sip, replaced it on the small occasional table beside him and crossed his legs.

Giles Carrington continued smoking his Cohiba, as though the two of them were contemplating a topic of no greater import than the result of last Friday's camel race.

The heady aroma of jasmine filled the night air, wafting in from the gardens. A plane flew overhead, and there was a splash as some member of the household dived into the floodlit pool below.

"You heard what I said?"

"Of course. What reaction did you wish to provoke."

"Interest – perhaps?"

"Why do you suppose I should consider killing the Sultan?"

"Because the people who want you to do so are prepared to pay you five million pounds."

"Five million, you say."

"Yes. Five million. Two-and-a-half when you agree to take the contract, and two-and-a-half on completion. I can tell you this Mister Horne, because even should you decline, our nefarious deeds over the years are so intertwined that it would not be in either of our interests to say anything to anyone. Wouldn't you agree?"

Drongo Horne nodded.

"Very well then. There is no need for me to go over the events of the past two weeks – you've been involved with them on the front line. The coup failed. The al-Bakri brothers and Majid Zahir have been executed, as have the majority of the Liberation Army. The Sultan's nephew, Mohammed al-Ajmi has panicked and is sweating, hoping that his part in the uprising will never come to light, which it will not. Neither shall mine. The Sultan believes the threat has passed and that life in Ras-al-Am has returned to normal. Oh – there'll be reprisals and revisions to security, one or two little witch hunts, but apart from these, everyone believes that bar the shouting the whole sorry incident is over."

"It's not?"

"No, Mister Horne. Not by a long chalk. For the good of the country it is imperative that the Sultan should go. America needs to gain a foothold in this country. Ras-al-Am's strategic importance is too great to allow it to continue to conduct its own defence, supported by reassurances and wishy-washy back-up from Britain. If the coup had succeeded – fine. Since it hasn't, we now have to complete the work contracted to us by the CIA."

"The CIA?" Drongo's reaction revealed a glimmer of

251

interest at last.

"Yes, Mister Horne. The CIA. They want Mohammed al-Ajmi, the Sultan's nephew, to take the throne. He has been assured of full American backing, being unaware of course that he will be installed purely as a hireling, a new figurehead on a CIA string. The coup having failed, Mohammed al-Ajmi believes that he has been denied his place in history. He doesn't know that an alternative plan to assassinate the Sultan was devised in case the coup failed. Apart from CIA Headquarters in Langley, Virginia, only I and two other people know what the plan is. Should you agree to execute it for us, and I believe that you will, you will be the fourth."

"Why are you so certain I'll agree?"

"Because you are a sewer rat, Mister Horne," Giles Carrington said – smiling. "Not in any way do I mean this offensively, you understand. Quite the contrary. It enables you to perform your work as effectively as you do. I am so well established that the only way for me to go is down. For you, on the other hand, the only way to go is up. Or sideways – somewhere like Brazil, for example. You see, short of defecating on the altar of St Paul's Cathedral, Mister Horne, there is probably no greater crime than regicide, which is why I believe it will appeal to you. With the added incentive of a five million pound pay-off and a guaranteed escape route afterwards. Now . . .

. . . are you interested?"

"I could possibly be persuaded."

"Good. I was fairly sure you could. Provision is already in train for you to leave Ras-al-Am immediately after the event.

"I see. And what is the plan?"

"It's quite simple, really. You will assassinate the Sultan at the National Day Parade when he is standing in the Royal Box taking the salute during the drive-past."

"That sounds preposterous. Security will be unbreachable."

"Security will *appear* to be unbreachable. But our plan will work. The Commanding Officer of the Sultan's Armoured Regiment is a British officer, but since he has become General Stubbs's Senior Staff Officer lately, Colonel Marks has unwittingly delegated control of the regiment to his Ras-al-Ami second-in-command, Major Mustapha Salim."

"You say 'unwittingly'?"

"Yes, Mister Horne. You see, although his tanks were instrumental in the Army regaining control of Masela Camp, Major Mustapha Salim strongly supports our cause. Three of the Armoured Regiment's Chieftain tanks and three of its American M60s will be taking part in the National Day Parade's final drive past. The last tank in the parade will be armed with live ammunition. You will be in that tank. *You* will fire its 120mm gun to obliterate the Royal Box. And - it goes without saying - all those who are in it."

"Just like that."

"Precisely. The plan cannot fail."

"But then how do I escape from a stadium jam-packed with troops, police and thousands of spectators thirsting for my blood – in a tank?"

"You don't."

"How then?"

"By air. Seconds after the tanks' drive-past there is to be an aerial fly-past of helicopters. The last helicopter will be carrying a giant Ras-al-Ami flag suspended from its undercarriage. The pilot is also one of us. He will release the flag and drop a winch harness above your tank. You will merely have to scramble out of your turret, grab the harness and be whisked away to join a high-speed launch that will be ready waiting off Schmidt's Beach. From there you will be taken up the coast to Dubai and the freedom to fly anywhere in the world. With the mayhem in the Stadium, organised response will be zero. Before anyone rallies you will have been borne safely away."

"Pursued by a stream of tracer up my arse."

"Five million pounds, Mister Horne? There's a remote possibility of course, but I think it unlikely? A miniscule target swinging high in the sky, receding by the second? Not much chance of a hit, would you say?"

"Haven't you cut this whole thing a bit fine? The parade's tomorrow."

"Right, Mister Horne. The parade is tomorrow. At seven-thirty in the morning to be precise. Exactly nine hours time, in fact." Carrington crossed to his desk and opened one of its drawers. He took out an envelope which he handed to Drongo Horne. "Here is proof of the down-payment that has already been made to your Swiss bank account, with a similar amount to be transferred by noon tomorrow."

"How do I know that . . .?"

"Have we ever failed one and other, you and I, Mister Horne?"

"There's always a first time."

"This will not be that time. There is too much at stake. From Dubai I suggest you fly to Singapore and then Australia. From there perhaps you should consider South America, but it is your choice. Don't be tempted to send me a postcard though, will you?" He smiled. "I shall miss you, Mister Horne. You have been an able lieutenant. There is a car outside waiting to take you to the Armoured Regiment barracks. Major Mustapha Salim is expecting you. Collect your passport from your bungalow. Your other possessions you will have to write-off, I'm afraid. It only remains for me to wish you good luck. I know I can rely on you not to fail."

Drongo Horne nodded, and rose from his chair.

A further waft of jasmine floated into the room on the warm night air; the last night he would spend in Ras-al-Am in the service of the only employer with whom he had established any kind of rapport or respect. One last professional duty to perform, and he would retire to luxury for the rest of his life. One more killing – a big one – and he would be free . . . after breakfast tomorrow.

THIRTY-SEVEN

While the party at Masela Camp's Garrison Mess was winding down and Drongo Horne was being driven to join Major Mustapha Salim at the Armoured Regiment's barracks, the Ras-al-Am security forces swung surreptitiously into operation.

A platoon of soldiers was detached to patrol the Stadium throughout the night, with two Land Rover-borne platoons of troops on-call as back-up.

Three Air Force helicopters dropped troops to man outlying piquet positions in the jebel surrounding the Stadium's north-west flank. A section of infantry was dropped on the high ground in reserve, maintaining radio contact with their commander at his concealed control point.

The Racing Snakes positioned snipers at concealed vantage points overlooking the Stadium which offered line-of-sight coverage of the Royal Box below for their high-powered tripod-mounted Mannlicher rifles with their wide-angle telescopic sights.

Raman itself and the roads and roundabouts leading to it were a blaze of light, illuminated decorative arches, flags and bunting.

Posters of Sultan Hamad adorned every street-light and lamp-post.

Raman's International Airport, banks, ministries and public buildings shimmered with multi-coloured light bulbs. It was the eve of their National Day, and Ras-al-Ami pride was running high.

At first light next morning the troops billeted at Masela Camp emerged from their tents and prepared for the parade; the culmination of their gruelling rehearsals at the Stadium.

By 0630 the Stadium began to fill with fidgeting loyal Ras-al-Amis, men with their sons sitting in a sea of white dishdashas, their womenfolk in adjoining stands in glades of fluttering silks.

Although everyone knew that without the British presence and planning neither this parade nor the achievements it celebrated in Ras-al-Am would be a success, the Britons were officially obliged to maintain the lowest of profiles on occasions such as these. They wore slacks, bush jackets, medals, berets and suede boots, while all about them the Ras-al-Ami and Baluch officers strutted like peacocks in full ceremonial uniforms with peaked caps, gold epaulettes, black leather crossbelts, and swords in gleaming scabbards.

"I've got just the answer for you two," Squadron Leader Peter Irwin had told Ferguson and Hans over a drink at the previous night's mess party. "You've seen the dress rehearsal. The parade itself is going to be like a rugger crowd in a heatwave. Why not give it a miss? Come to the Airport instead, and I'll get you in the air as part of the final fly-past. Is that a good idea?"

It was now 0730. In the sandy form-up areas outside the Stadium the troops were ready, nervously waiting to be called on parade.

The Parade Marshal ordered "*Markers* – MARCH ON," and two-dozen ceremonially-clad soldiers marched briskly in through the Stadium gates, heading towards the centre point of the vast arena.

Wheeling left and right, each marker marched to his position, indicated by metal discs hammered into the ground, the Right Guide markers carrying rifles, and the Wheel and Salute markers bearing regimental pennants.

Next into the arena were the Drive-Past troops, marching through the gates in war-like shirtsleeve order. They formed-up and stood-at-ease in front of tanks on the arena's flank. No one noticed that the swarthy gunner beside the last tank, browned-up and dressed as a soldier, was taller and older than the others, and that he wore a black eye-patch.

Sixteen young Ras-al-Ami Ensigns and their Escorts proudly bore their regiments' Colours into the arena, emulating Britain's premier troops on Horse Guards, because this parade had been organised by a Guards colonel with drill instructors flown in from Pirbright.

There was a stirring all round the stands, then the spectators rose and the officers amongst them saluted the passing Colours as the Ensigns marched by to take up their positions.

No sooner had the Ensigns stood at ease than the officers who were to command the troops marched on, drawn swords glinting in the early morning sun.

There was a pause – then a mighty crash of sound.

The troops themselves now came on parade, accompanied by skirling pipes and drums, brass, and shouted orders bouncing off the Stadium walls.

Show Time.

With the Parade now fully formed-up waiting, an expectant hush fell over the Stadium. A lone Ras-al-Ami colonel rode in on horseback with his drawn sword, calf-hugging overalls and a pair of gleaming spurs protruding from the heels of his black leather Wellington boots. He walked his charger to the centre forefront of the parade.

Upward of 1200 men now stood poised, awaiting his first command.

"*Parade* . . . to the Colours . . . PRESENT *ARMS*," he roared in a stentorian Arab voice.

The massed bands played the first six bars of a slow march, the Ensigns dipped their Colours, the troops presented their arms, the spectators in the stands rose and the officers saluted again, the Ensigns re-carried their Colours, the troops shouldered their arms . . . and all waited.

Outside the Stadium a fanfare of trumpets preceded the solemn thud of martial music, and the Royal Palace Guard's mounted band rode into the arena, led by its resplendent Director of Music, diamond-studded cuff links flashing at his wrists, golden spurs at his ankles, riding an ebony stallion.

Wheeling their horses, the 40 Bengal Lancer musicians and

kettle-drummers rode along the front of the parade, heralding the triumphant entry of His Majesty Hamad, Sultan of Ras-al-Am, magnificent in plush red-white-and-gold livery, aiguillettes, epaulettes, sword, sash and enamel orders, mounted on his own white stallion, followed by mounted outriders – his six aides-de-camp, 24 Household troops, 12 Royal Palace Guard troops, and 40 Police troops.

There was another fanfare, a shivering roll of drums and the entire Stadium rose with patriotic fervour as the Colours were dipped and the troops Presented Arms to give the Royal Salute to their King.

No sooner had the national anthem's last strains died away than the Sultan's Artillery, strategically positioned on a jebel plateau behind the Stadium, fired a reverberating 21-gun salute to honour the Sultan's birthday.

With the echoes of this salvo booming through the hills behind them, the Parade Commander rode up to the Sultan, his sword flashing as he nervously paid the courtesies due to their Commander-in-Chief (it's dicey lopping off a king's ear), and intoned: "Your Majesty; Your Armed Forces await Your inspection."

The massed bands struck-up once more, and the Sultan walked his steed along the ranks of his forces. The Inspection completed, his cavalcade of escorts rode off to take up stand-by positions, while he readied himself to take the salute for the March Past.

The 500 musicians stepped-off in slow-time along the front of the parade, wheeled behind the troops and took up position at the rear. The Parade Commander called the troops to attention, they shouldered their arms, the Ensigns brought their Colours to the Carry, and the Parade stepped-off to a renewed blast of martial music.

The spectators rose once more, officers again saluted the passing Colours hanging limp in the humid air, the troops' commanders gave the "*Eyes* – RIGHT," as they drew abreast of their Ruler, and to resounding applause the Parade marched-off out the arena.

The Sultan rode out of the arena and a few minutes later

appeared in the Royal Box to join the other members of the Royal Family gathered there.

Gently stirring the dust, moving forward with fluttering pennants, the mechanised Drive-Past began . . .

. . . eight Royal Palace Guard personnel carriers followed by two light artillery batteries, a medium artillery battery, eight Armoured Regiment Scorpions - then with their 120mm guns traversing to dip in salute, like six senior prefects showing off phallic erections for approval - the heavy Chieftain and M60 main battle tanks . . .

"Time for you two to get airborne," Peter Irwin told Ferguson and Hans.

They loped out across the pan at Raman Airport, to where six stationary helicopters were just switching on their whining motors.

The countdown had begun.

"We'll stick you in the last one." Peter shouted. "Up you jump."

They caught a glimpse of consternation cross the pilot's face, then the helicopter lifted into the air and they were heading towards Raman.

It took 40 seconds to get 18 Jaguar strike aircraft into the air.

While the Mechanised Drive-Past rumbled by the Royal Box in the Stadium, Wing Commander 'Shilelah' O'Leary radioed Peter Irwin at the Airport. Peter's pilots left the crew room, scrambled into their cockpits, streaked down the runway and flew to their aerial gathering point out at sea.

With split-second timing from his place in the Stadium, 'Shilelah' O'Leary gave them their "GO" signal. The Jaguar formation was on its own, knowing that because of the confusion that would ensue, unless it was "ABORT" they should disregard all further directives.

They were committed. They came in over the Stadium at 1200ft in arrow-like formation at 350 knots.

After they had roared impressively past, the helicopters appeared, flying in at 350ft, the last craft in the formation flying a giant Ras-al-Ami flag suspended stiffly beneath its undercarriage.

Concealed in the confined space and heat of the gun turret in the sixth tank, Drongo Horne had to blink away the sweat pouring from his brow.

If he reneged now and scrambled out of the turret to flee across the dusty arena dodging his way between the armoured behemoths, he would be gunned down by the Security Forces' snipers in the hills. If he remained where he was, and did nothing, he would have to account to Giles Carrington afterwards – in addition to forfeiting five million pounds.

He was committed. All he could do now was what he had undertaken to do. He braced himself.

The heavy Chieftain rocked back on its stabilisers as Drongo loosed-off its gun's solitary 120mm shell at point blank range.

From where he stood taking the salute, at the last moment deputising for his uncle who, feeling faint, had withdrawn from the Box and was making his way across to his private ambulance, Mohammed al-Ajmi was blown to smithereens in a turmoil of molten alloy, dust, girders, concrete, shredded palm-fronds and glass.

The entire Stadium erupted in a roar of pandemonium.

Drongo hurled back the turret hatch-cover and leapt out onto the armour plating.

The young Ras-al-Ami tank commander in the turret, stared open-mouthed at him.

The helicopter hovering immediately above released its Ras-al-Ami flag, which floated down to crumple in the dusty arena. The pilot lowered the hawser, confident that the two last-minute passengers inflicted on him would not comprehend what was happening and couldn't do much about it if they did.

Ferguson and Hans looked at each other, said "What the *fuck* . . .?" – and watched while the soldier below placed his foot into the hawser stirrup. The helicopter rose away from the mayhem in the Stadium and chattered off in the direction of Schmidt's Beach.

"Thank GOD," Drongo Horne screamed as the helicopter

whisked him through the air 300ft above the traffic on the main highway and banked out over the salt flats. He felt absurdly like Douglas Fairbanks Jnr performing an aerial ballet in the rigging as he clung on grimly for dear life.

It had worked. He'd nearly made it. What a terrifying risk though. What a gamble. But cold-blooded boldness had been his friend, and it was all going to pay off. Big time.

With one daring deed he had broken out at last, and projected himself into the premier division of world class assassins.

Ahead of them he could see a motor launch riding a kilometre offshore, its propellers churning the water in readiness, two crew members retrieving the anchor. His good eye streaming, he glanced up gratefully at the pilot.

That was when Ferguson saw the eye-patch.

"*Drongo* bloody <u>HORNE</u>," he spat, thumping Hans's shoulder.

Both men's pulses raced. Hans nodded, and clambered over beside the alarmed pilot.

Drongo Horne assumed he was going to be winched down onto the deck of the launch, but instead of the helicopter descending it remained hovering where it was, leaving him spinning in mid-air.

He could see the crew of the launch gazing up anxiously at them. What the hell was happening?

Suddenly he felt himself being winched slowly back up towards the helicopter.

His head drew level with the open door. He glanced up – and then froze.

He was staring straight into the implacable ice blue eyes of that obnoxious blond German body-builder, standing with his legs planted firmly apart, his hands on his hips, staring coldly back out at him.

Squatting beside him on the floor, was that pig-shit Brit.

Drongo cursed himself for not having killed them both when he should have done. But he was confused. What was happening? What had gone wrong? Had Giles Carrington set him up?

261

"Sorry about this, Drongo." The English swine was yelling at him. "Turned out a bit messy for you, hasn't it. There are two ways we can do this. Either you come aboard and fly back with us to face the consequences – or we'll let you do it your way, here. The choice is yours. Which will it be?"

"Can't we talk about this?" Drongo screamed back.

"I don't think so. There's nothing to talk about. You beat up and rape women. It's unfortunate for you that one of them happened to be my lady. You've also just assassinated the Sultan. Either way, you're a dead man hanging, so to speak. All you need talk about now is how you'd like to go. Come back with us to a firing squad – or keep your appointment down there on the launch."

"How the bloody hell can I, for Chrissake, up here three-hundred feet above it?"

"That can be arranged. It's so easy – I'll show you," shouted Hans. Grabbing a strut with one hand he leaned fearlessly out and took a firm grasp of one of Drongo's ankles, yanking it out of the hawser-stirrup so that Drongo released his desperate hold and spun upside down, flailing his arms about frantically in the air. "It's called 'instant decision-making'," Hans shouted.

"I HAD NOTHING TO DO WITH ANY OF THIS," Drongo screamed, his nerve finally snapping. "It was all Giles CARRINGTON."

"Thanks for that," Ferguson yelled. "Now you can go to hell with a clear conscience, can't you."

"Goodbye," called Hans.

In the same way that he had dropped the Thai boxer head first into the bucket at Pattaya, Hans now let go of Drongo's ankle. They heard his receding scream as he plummeted all the way down to land with a squelch on his head on the deck of the launch below.

"Good shot." Ferguson grinned.

"Brought tears to his eyes," said Hans. "I think he might have broken his neck, as well"

Ferguson tapped the subdued pilot's shoulder, and indicated the direction he wanted to fly.

THIRTY-EIGHT

Giles Carrington lay on the lawn by his pool watching the aftermath of the Parade on his portable TV, his three naked Zanzibari women stretched out on towels beside him.

While the Parade was underway and the Sultan inspected his troops, Giles had been more tense than he'd ever been in his 53 years, but once he had seen Drongo Horne's Chieftain buck and rock and the devastation wreaked on the Royal Box by the tank's 120mm shell, he relaxed and cried out with the jubilation of a man whose team has scored the winning goal in the World Cup.

The TV cameras had picked out Drongo clambering from the tank's hull and being whisked away by the helicopter. Soon he would be on the launch heading for Dubai . . . if Iranian or Iraqi gunboats didn't blast him out of the water on the way. The pilot would have ditched his helicopter into the sea by now, and was doubtless also being picked up by the launch as planned.

He saw that Drongo's tank had been surrounded by Police, letting no one near it. Giles chuckled at the thought of the difficult times ahead for Colonel Marks, who would have to face their persistent and usually inept questioning.

He smiled contentedly with the knowledge that the Armoured Regiment's second-in-command, Major Mustapha Salim, was already in the air on his way to a new life in Amsterdam.

The cameras were now playing on the chaos in the Stadium as the terrified crowds created havoc trying to flee the stands. The screen kept flashing back to another camera remaining trained on the carnage that had been the Royal Box, showing the Rescue Services rummaging through the rubble retrieving the broken and bloodied bodies of the rest of the Royal Family.

Giles glanced up, and frowned. He thought he'd heard the unmistakable sound of an approaching helicopter. Helicopters often landed on his lawn, but only by prior arrangement.

With all the activity going on it was hardly surprising there was quite a bit of stuff flying about – but this one was definitely heading for his house though, and coming in to land.

There it was now – just above the trees. A sixth sense told Giles this was not good news. He rose quickly and headed in to the house.

His three Zanzibari women, sensing the alarm, squealed and wrapped their colourful towels around themselves before hurrying after him.

"Stay and guard the pilot," Ferguson instructed Hans as the helicopter settled on the grass.

Jumping down he ran across the lawn and dashed up the steps to the house, drawing his 9mm Browning as he rushed into the hall. Ahead of him was a wide marble staircase. He bounded up this to the landing and sensed intuitively in which room he would find Giles Carrington. He smashed his way through the door, and saw that it was the study.

Giles Carrington was standing on the balcony aiming a rifle at the unsuspecting Hans out by the helicopter. He was just about to squeeze the trigger when Ferguson burst in behind him.

He whipped around and pointed the rifle's barrel directly at Ferguson's chest. Ferguson was already poised like a Police duellist, his Browning aiming straight at Giles Carrington's head.

Stalemate. Both men froze.

"Drongo Horne is dead," Ferguson told him quietly. "You are responsible for the failed assassination attempt on Sultan Hamad."

"Attempt?" Giles Carrington laughed at him. "My dear man, I don't know who you think you are, bursting in to my home like this, although you appear to fit the description of the interfering Englishman Mister Horne told me about. As for the Sultan, he is dead. I saw it with my own eyes, on the television."

"Wrong." Ferguson smiled. "It was Mohammed al-Ajmi, his nephew, you saw blown to pieces. He got his nephew to take the final salute in his place. He felt ill and went to his ambulance to sit down. He is badly shaken, but alive. It was announced just now. Air Ops Control relayed it to us in the helicopter."

The colour drained from Giles Carrington's face, but still he continued to smile. "You're lying, and this intrusion will cost you dearly," he said. "I am not averse to killing anyone at all."

"We know that already. You might blow a hole in my chest, but my pistol is aimed straight at your head, Carrington. I am also not averse to killing either - and I never miss."

"Do you know who I am?"

"Of course. You used to be an influential man in Ras-al-Am, but you got delusions of grandeur. There's not much point in discussing it any more. There is no further place for you here. It is your time to die. Goodbye."

Without compunction Ferguson squeezed his trigger. The Browning bucked in his grip.

Giles Carrington had been good, but maturity and the rich life had slowed and softened his reactions, whereas Ferguson was still up to speed. The bullet smashed into Carrington's skull and hurled him backwards with a wet purple hole in his forehead. The rifle flew from his grasp and crashed onto a glass coffee table.

With an expression of amazement frozen on his face, his body toppled backward over the balcony to crash onto the lawn below.

Ferguson leapt back down the staircase and out across the lawn, hearing the keening of women as he went.

Hans saw him coming. The helicopter rotors started to whir. Ferguson jumped aboard. The craft rose above the trees and set off back to Masela Camp.

Their mission in Ras-al-Am was successfully completed.

EPILOGUE

"The Sultan's delighted, Ferguson. Not too delighted, mind: he's got a broken arm, two cracked ribs and severe concussion after the shelling. Mind you, he contributed mightily, deciding to have that dizzy spell when he did. Fateful slice of luck, that. There's also been a leak in Washington. The CIA's been embarrassed into back-pedalling and agreeing a hands-off policy where Ras-al-Am is concerned. Fancy that, eh? Our own little home-grown back-door effort thwarting the devious might of a Superpower. Quite a feather in our caps. This could become Zeta Group's most notable battle honour. What a sod, that nasty Drongo Horne character. I knew he was in the country. I'd often heard about him and his nastier exploits, but the bugger was always protected by that odious Carrington man and his wretched Intelligence Department. What about him, eh? I've known him for years. Uncrowned prime minister of this place, he was. Fancy blowing it all like this. Now then – down to brass tacks. I am assured that His Majesty is going to transfer some considerable funds to Zeta Group Headquarters in London. When you get back I want you to discuss its equable apportioning with Reuben Dumperley. I was on the phone to him just now and it seems that Chuck does have a sister somewhere. May I charge you with finding her and seeing that she gets his share?"

"Of course, sir."

"Thanks . . . well – I don't know when we'll be seeing each other again next, but take care of yourself, eh cocker?"

"You too, Boss. You're a magic old sod, you know that."

"Waaal, whatever – go on Ferguson – get out of here," the older man said with a catch in his throat, releasing Ferguson's powerful grip.

Ferguson paused at the door, and looked round.

General Wally Stubbs, the Commander of the Sultan's Armed Forces stood with his back to him, carefully studying a wall map of Ras-al-Am, a Silk Cut cigarette smouldering between his fingers.

Aboard Gulf Air's Golden Falcon Tri-Star flight to London, those passengers fastening their seat belts on the port side were able to view Raman Control Tower and observe the usual activity of the Airport's staff and ground crew.

The passengers on the starboard side were thrilled when their side of the cabin suddenly became bathed with bright orange light as the new dawn's sun burst above the eastern horizon.

In one of the aisle seats Ferguson was tugging the quick from one of his nails while thinking what clothes he would need to buy in London to ward off the cold, and what he should do about Julie when she returned there on her first leave. Beside him Hans sat chewing a toothpick and drumming his fingers on the ashtray.

Masela Camp, too, was stirring to meet the new day. Pots and pans were clanking in the cookhouse as the dhal and chappati breakfasts were prepared.

The electric tannoy of the mosque went live with an audible *click*. The muezzin pressed the button of his pre-recorded *Allah-u-Akbar* tape to call the faithful to prayer.

On the taxiing plane, Ferguson glanced at his watch and smiled.

General Wally Stubbs, shaving in his bathroom, cocked his head to listen, nicked his grizzled chin, and swore.

"*Bloody* Ferguson," he cursed, smiling.

The faithful, waiting to pray – looked baffled.

On his way to the Airport, despite Hans's protestations Ferguson had been unable to resist slipping into the mosque and switching the tapes.

Instead of *Allah-u-Akbar* Masela Camp and the surrounding

countryside were being serenaded today by Frank Sinatra singing *I Did It My Way*.

The Gulf Air Golden Falcon Tri-Star flight rose into the air and pointed its gleaming beak towards London.

END